P9-ARG-367

The Marriage Contract

Other Avon Romances by
Cathy Maxwell

BECAUSE OF YOU
FALLING IN LOVE AGAIN
MARRIED IN HASTE
A SCANDALOUS MARRIAGE
WHEN DREAMS COME TRUE
YOU AND NO OTHER

CATHY MAXWELL

The Marriage Contract

AVON BOOKS
An Imprint of HarperCollinsPublishers

This is a work of fiction. Names, characters, places, and incidents are products of the author's imagination or are used fictitiously and are not to be construed as real. Any resemblance to actual events, locales, organizations, or persons, living or dead, is entirely coincidental.

AVON BOOKS
An Imprint of HarperCollins*Publishers*
10 East 53rd Street
New York, New York 10022-5299

Copyright © 2001 by Cathy Maxwell
Excerpts from *All Shook Up* copyright © 2001 by Susan Andersen; *The Marriage Contract* copyright © 2001 by Catherine Maxwell; *Time After Time* copyright © 2001 by Constance O'Day-Flannery; *The Indiscretion* copyright © 2001 by Judith Ivory, Inc.; *The Last Good Man* copyright © 2000 by Kathleen Eagle; *True Confessions* copyright © 2001 by Rachel Gibson
ISBN: 0-7394-1561-1

All rights reserved. No part of this book may be used or reproduced in any manner whatsoever without written permission, except in the case of brief quotations embodied in critical articles and reviews. For information address Avon Books, an Imprint of HarperCollins Publishers.

Avon Trademark Reg. U.S. Pat. Off. and in Other Countries, Marca Registrada, Hecho en U.S.A.
HarperCollins ® is a trademark of HarperCollins Publishers Inc.

Printed in the U.S.A.

To Kevin Maxwell, with love
NLFL   MFML

Prologue

London, 1815

Anne Burnett held her breath as Lady Waldo signed her brother's bold, singular title "Tiebauld" to the proxy marriage contract. The scratch of the sharp quill across parchment resounded in the sudden quiet of the lawyer's office.

Finished, Lady Waldo handed the pen to Sir Rupert, who officiously sanded the signature before turning the document on his desk toward Anne. "Your turn, Miss Burnett." He dipped the pen in ink and offered it to her with a slight flourish.

Anne stared at the writing instrument as if she'd never seen one before. A bead of ink formed on the nub's tip. If she didn't take it quickly, the ink would fall onto the desk and make a splatter. But she couldn't breathe, let alone move.

"It is your turn to sign, Miss Burnett," Sir Rupert prompted again.

"Yes, Anne," Aunt Maeve said, sitting in the hard-back chair beside her niece's. She gave Anne's elbow a little wake-up pinch. "This is no time for missish airs. It's as good as you could ever hope for. Better, in fact."

Anne could only agree, but the minuscule writing of terms and agreements her aunt and uncle had spent hours negotiating leered up at her. No one had asked her opinion. Not once. After all, this marriage was considered the best an orphan with a disgraced past could achieve.

Of course, in fairness, she'd had her chances. Uncle Robert and Aunt Maeve had sponsored her for two Seasons. However, the consensus was her looks, while pleasant—straight brown hair, serious gray eyes, and a mouth too generous for beauty—were not spectacular enough to overcome her lack of fortune or social connections.

No man wanted her save one. Lord Tiebauld, Lady Waldo's brother. The man whose very name made every eligible debutante shudder.

Bitter disappointment replaced fear. Anne had dreamed of marriage, of being loved for herself, and of finally having a place where she was wanted and belonged . . .

Instead, she was to be shipped off to the wilds of Scotland. Dismissed, was more like it. Her relatives couldn't wait to be rid of her.

She reached for the pen and angled the contract on the polished wood desk in front of her. Her fingers tightened on the stylus—and suddenly she couldn't do it.

Not until she asked the question burning in her mind, "How mad is he?"

For a heartbeat, everyone stared as if Anne had spoken in tongues. Politically powerful, socially adept, Lady Waldo appeared most disconcerted of all. Then chaos erupted.

Uncle Robert rose to his feet with a soft oath while Aunt Maeve cried out, "Anne!"

Sir Rupert leaned across the desk, frowning at her uncle. "I thought you said the girl was agreeable to the match?"

"She is," Uncle Robert answered. He placed a warning hand on Anne's shoulder. "She will sign."

"It's nerves," Aunt Maeve assured everyone. "Her father was just as high-strung. She'll calm down."

"Maeve, shut up," Uncle Robert growled, but it was too late. Sir Rupert grasped at the possible implications.

"You told me she was healthy!"

"She is," Aunt Maeve shot back. "Didn't your doctor tell you so? He even verified her virginity."

Hot color flooded Anne's cheeks at the reminder of the invasive and too personal examination the doctor had given her. She started to rise, feeling an urge to run, to hide—but Uncle Robert's hand shoved back down in the chair.

Besides, where would she go?

Sir Rupert turned to Lady Waldo. "I can't let you continue with this endeavor, my lady. Not until we are completely sure of the girl's mental soundness."

Aunt Maeve started a keening protest. The lawyer ignored her and reached for the contract, but Uncle Robert snatched it up. The slip of parchment would make them rich beyond their wildest dreams. They could not let the marriage go, even if it meant coming to blows with London's most prominent solicitor—

"Enough!" Lady Waldo's command cut through the madness.

Their mouths clamped shut.

"Mr. Crisp," she said to Uncle Robert, "place the contract back on the desk." He followed her command with an uncommon docility. "Now leave us. Take your wife. You go with them, Sir Rupert. I don't want Mrs. Crisp listening at the door."

"As your solicitor, I should be present with you," he protested.

"Go," Lady Waldo answered, and to Anne's amazement he did, herding Uncle Robert in front of him.

Following the men, Aunt Maeve paused in the doorway. "Don't do anything to ruin this, Anne. You'll have nowhere to go." She left then, shutting the door firmly behind her.

Her words paralyzed Anne. *Nowhere to go.*

"Miss Burnett, I need your attention." Lady Waldo's curt words brought her back to the present.

It took all her courage to face this formidable woman.

"My brother is not mad." It was an unequivocal statement.

"I only mention rumors," Anne demurred.

"I know. I've heard gossip." The dowager reached into her reticule lying in her lap and pulled out a silver framed miniature. She pushed the portrait across the desk toward Anne. It stopped at the edge of the marriage contract.

"Go ahead, pick it up," Lady Waldo ordered. "It's Aidan, painted during his last year at All Souls. See what you think for yourself."

Aidan. Anne had never heard him referred to as anything other than Lord Tiebauld. In her fears and doubts, she had not asked after his Christian name. She lifted the miniature and caught her breath. The youth in the portrait was not some deformed monster. He had a poet's beauty. Black curly hair, a strong jawline, intelligent blue eyes much like his sister's but without the cold aloofness.

"He's handsome," Anne murmured.

"And no sign of idiocy or deformity," Lady Waldo said dryly.

Anne raised her head. "I didn't mean—"

Lady Waldo cut off any apology. "I know what you thought. Aidan was always considered out of step with his peers. There are those who have too much passion in them, Miss Burnett. Those who refuse to conform. My brother is one of their number. He always felt the world more keenly than the rest of us."

She held out her hand for the picture. Her eyes softened as she traced the image with the tip of her finger. "He's tall. A head taller than most men. His shoulders are broad, but he's thin. Too thin, I think. A wife would be good for him . . ." For a moment, she seemed almost overcome by emotion.

"When did you see him last?" Anne asked softly.

A frown formed between Lady Waldo's eyes. "Six, maybe seven years ago. He's twenty-seven now." She sighed. "A man full grown. There are seventeen years between us, but we were close at one time . . . before my marriage."

"They say you sent him away."

The icy eyes hardened. "He left England by his own choice, Miss Burnett. He is a loner and, yes, eccentric. He did not fit well into Society."

Anne knew exactly how he must have felt.

"Do you know our family history, Miss Burnett?"

"Other than you have Scottish roots? No."

"Then I must tell you." Lady Waldo laid the miniature on the desk. "Our great-grandfather was executed for treason. They say he was the military mind behind the Scottish rebellion in '45. Our family was disgraced, my grandfather brought to England as a hostage. There are those who fear we still hold rebel ideas . . . and those who pray we do."

"Do you?"

"No." The answer was swift, sure.

When Anne said nothing, she commented, "You have no reaction to such an infamous history?"

Anne shook her head, unwilling to volunteer information Lady Waldo might or might not know. "A good number of aristocratic families could make the same claim," she said quietly. "English history is rife with power struggles. But is that a reason to marry a man to a woman he doesn't know?" *Or may not want?*

"It is when the man is the sole heir to a great and respected title. Aidan has a heritage to uphold."

"He is only twenty-seven, my lady. Let him choose his own wife."

"I don't have that kind of time, Miss Burnett."

"Why not?"

"I'm dying."

Her words sucked the air out of the room. Anne drew back in her chair and looked more closely at Lady Waldo. All the signs were there, the tightness around the mouth, the tired lines at the corners of the eyes, the thinness of the pale, delicate skin. Anne had seen mortal illness before. She was surprised she hadn't noticed it earlier. "I'm sorry," she whispered.

"For what?" Lady Waldo said. "Life has been good to me. I have one task left that it is my duty to see completed. With your help, I'll see it done." She lightly touched the miniature. "The title needs an heir, but Aidan is not coming to ground. I have been patient long enough. I want you to marry my brother and breed a healthy child as quickly as possible. In return, I will leave you my fortune. Do you understand what money means, Miss Burnett? It is freedom. No more will you be subject to overbearing fools like your uncle, or to boring, meaningless parties filled with petty people where you must pretend interest because it is expected of you."

Anne straightened, shocked to hear her innermost thoughts spoken aloud. "How did you know?"

"Being a woman isn't easy. Unless we are insipidly stupid—something I don't believe you are—we have all chafed at the restrictions others place on us, or at being paraded like cattle on an auction block. Since Sir Rupert mentioned your name, I've made it my business to know everything about you."

"Even about my father?"

Lady Waldo laughed, the sound rough like a metal wagon wheel over cobbles. "Everything."

"And you still found me suitable?"

"I have run out of *suitable* candidates, Miss Burnett. I am desperate." She leaned forward. "And I sense you are desperate, too."

She was right. Anne hated living with her relatives who begrudged her every morsel of food, every article of clothing. They'd branded her a failure because she couldn't bring a young man up to snuff. It didn't matter to them if the man was a fool or dull or dissolute. Or if Anne felt nothing for him. Passion, love, honor—all the values her parents had taught her to respect and admire—were unimportant to her selfish relatives . . . and to Society.

Her gaze shifted to the poetic, handsome face of the young man in the miniature. His were the features of a scholar. They were sensitive, thoughtful. Yet she'd heard him referred to as the Madman of Scotland. Society wouldn't have made up such a name from thin air if it wasn't true, would they?

Then again, when had Society ever been right about her?

And yes, something inside her thrilled to the thought of at least having a handsome husband, one that would make Aunt Maeve's silly daughters, all successfully married, "ooo" and "ahhh" with admiration.

Plus, she would be a countess. *Countess Tiebauld.*

"Why are you smiling?" Lady Waldo asked.

Anne wasn't about to confess the small-minded direction of her thoughts. Instead, she said, "You give your word of honor that my child would be free of any mental affliction?"

"There is no madness in our family," Lady Waldo said with irritation. "That was rumor, nonsense."

And isn't there a seed of truth in all rumor? But Anne didn't voice the question. Instead, she bargained. "Will I have control of my own fortune?"

"Once you give birth. I will have Sir Rupert draw up papers transferring funds to you immediately."

"I will raise the child?"

"Of course, you are its mother."

Anne wasn't so naïve as to think it would be as simple as that but she accepted Lady Waldo's promise. After all, what choice did she really have?

She reached for the marriage contract. Her hand was steady as she lifted the pen from its inkpot. Her husband's name seemed to jump out at her from the paper. *Aidan Black, Earl Tiebauld.* "What if he doesn't want me?"

"He has no choice," Lady Waldo said serenely. "The document in front of you has the full blessing of the Church and the State."

"But he has not agreed?"

Their eyes met. The corner of Lady Waldo's mouth lifted. "No. It will be your responsibility to inform him."

"Can you marry a man off without his permission?"

"With the grace of the Crown, I can do anything I wish."

Anne stared at the contract in front of her, her mind barraged by a million doubts—and yet she signed.

Sir Rupert, Uncle Robert, and Aunt Maeve were invited in and there was much celebration amongst them, save for Anne. She picked up the miniature and held it in her palm, studying the painted lines for clues to explain the strange circumstances of her marriage.

She overheard Sir Rupert whisper to Lady Waldo, "Did you tell her everything?"

"I told her what she needed to know to reach the right decision," was the reply.

"But did you mention Major Lambert's report—?"

"No."

Anne wanted to hear more, but Lady Waldo sensed she was listening. Their gazes met and then Lady Waldo smiled. "Welcome to the family, my dear."

Chapter 1

It rained almost every day of the trip from London up into Scotland. Side roads were mired with mud up to a man's knees, damp spring weather chilled a person to the bone, a broken coach wheel waylaid them for three days, bad food and uncomfortable beds met them at every stop—and Anne loved it all. This was the great adventure of her life.

She rode in Lady Waldo's well-sprung coach with the Waldo coat of arms on the door and enjoyed the attention she received in passing villages. She'd not had so much freedom since her parents were alive and for the first time felt as if she were coming into her own. Marriage was a good thing.

When the "proper" maid Aunt Maeve had hired quit at the Scottish border because she'd decided she wanted nothing to do with "barbarians," Anne wished the servant a good riddance. She would hire a maid when she arrived in Caithness. Meanwhile, Todd, Lady Waldo's coachman, was more than company enough. With the disapproving maid out of the way, his sense of humor and delight in the ridiculous came to the forefront and in spite of class distinctions he and Anne became co-explorers of the sights along the way.

Scotland's beauty was beyond anything Anne could have imagined. She felt at home in the rugged landscape, the tall mountains, and green valleys. 'Twas was like discovering Paradise. She reveled in the isolation of the wild, untamed highlands.

Yes, the people could be standoffish, especially when they heard her English accent—but she quickly discovered that they could be generous, good-humored, and fair.

But sooner or later, they had to reach their destination. Still, Anne was not prepared when Todd cheerily informed her two days out of Inverness, "We're within two days' drive from Caithness. Mayhap one if I push it. We've got nice weather for travel, too. I like seeing a bit of sun."

In the act of boarding the coach, Anne froze. "What did you say?"

"I said the weather's clearing—"

"No, about arriving in Caithness today."

Todd's proud grin in his wizened face made him look a bit like a happy monkey. "I knew you'd be pleased for the news, Lady Tiebauld."

"But I thought we'd have several days, maybe a week longer."

He shook his head as if confused about where she

could ever have gained such a notion. "No, the road between here and Caithness is good. It follows the coast. You'll enjoy the view, although I'd best keep my mind on the horses."

"Oh. Yes." Anne's stomach twisted with anxiety. Tomorrow . . . maybe today.

She was tempted to turn tail and follow the snooty maid's trail back to London. But she couldn't. She had nowhere to go. Uncle Robert and Aunt Maeve wouldn't want her back and her cousins would all laugh at her.

A moment later, Todd took all choice away when, with a snap of the reins and a happy whistle, he set the horses on the road.

How in the world was she going to break the news to her husband that they were married? How would she introduce herself?

The questions she should have considered earlier chased round and round in her head. She shunned the breathtaking cliff view of the North Sea crashing on rocks by dropping the canvas shade down over the window. She pulled the miniature and her marriage papers out of her embroidered purse. She'd rarely looked at either since leaving London, assuming she would worry about the matter tomorrow. Now, tomorrow was here.

With the avid attention of a legal clerk, she pored over each word of the contract—and found no answers as to how to smooth the initial introductions. She studied the miniature, trying to decipher the mysteries of her husband's personality. Was he kind? Gentle? Understanding?

The tiny painting gave away no secrets.

And what of the carnal side of marriage? Would he expect her in his bed the first night? She knew she must consummate the marriage. It was her bargain with Lady Waldo. But what if he took one look at her and sent her packing?

The possibility made Anne's blood turn cold . . . especially since her knowledge of the intimacies between men and women was sketchy at best. What *really* did go on behind closed doors?

Worse, she'd been lazy this morning and worn her hair down with a simple ribbon. And she would have donned something other than her comfortable blue cambric if she'd thought she was to meet her husband.

Anne pulled the ribbon from her hair and shook hair pins out of her reticule. She'd put it up and then make Todd stop the coach so she could change clothes—

The coach came to an abrupt halt. It started to back up and shake. Todd shouted. Anne lifted the canvas covering the window. On one side of the road, they hovered on a cliff, high above the rocky coastline of the powerful North Sea. To their other side were rough terrain, grouse, and ravines. This didn't seem to be a safe place to fuss with the horses.

At that moment, she heard what sounded like a woman's shriek, and yet it wasn't. She didn't have time to consider the problem before the horses reared, screaming. Todd called them "bastards." He struggled to control them. Anne stuffed her marriage papers back into the purse and leaned against the velvet seats, clutching the miniature in one hand. If Todd didn't get a handle on the horses, they could plunge the coach over the edge of the cliffs.

Todd swore long and colorfully. Anne could imagine him practically standing in the box, pulling on the reins. The coach tilted, almost rolling over. She threw her weight to the other side. She didn't want to die. Not this way.

There was a bump and she knew one of the wheels had gone over the edge of the road. *Dear God!*

"Yah!" Todd shouted just as the hair-raising shriek cut through the air again. *What was it?*

The coach heaved and she felt all four wheels bounce back on the road. She gulped for breath, but then the horses bolted, dragging the coach across the hilly country on the other side of the road.

It all happened in the wink of an eye. One second, they were at a standstill; the next, Anne could imagine herself flying. Up, down, the coach rocked this way and that. She was thrown from the seat, her legs tangled in her skirts, her arms doing everything they could to protect her from injury, which was silly, because she and Todd were going to die; she knew it. These were her last moments on earth.

And she'd never gotten to meet her husband.

Perhaps it was wise she hadn't bothered preparing an introduction.

Todd cursed, unable to bring the horses under control. He yelled, "I'm cutting them loose. Hold on! Hold on!" Before she could grab a handhold of anything, a great cracking and splintering reverberated through the coach. The horses thundered off in one direction. The coach went rolling over and over itself in another before coming to a shattering halt.

Anne opened her eyes. It took several minutes before she could place her surroundings. She lay in a jumbled heap on the coach floor. No, it wasn't the floor. The heavy coach lay on its side and one door had been ripped off. That was why she could see the sky.

She was still alive . . . although she sensed she'd been unconscious.

Gingerly, she took an inventory of her person. Other than a few bumps and scrapes, she seemed to be all right.

But why was the world so silent?

"Todd?"

Nothing.

She made herself sit up. Every bone in her body had been rattled from its sockets. Her hair was a tangled mess and the sleeve of her blue cambric was torn. Carefully, she came to her feet. The coach rocked a bit. She took a moment to shake her skirts down and then stuck her head up through the open door. "Todd?"

Still no answer.

The coach had landed in a gully surrounded by shrubs and a few spiny junipers and gorse. The wheels were split and broken. Her trunk, which had been tied to the top of the coach, had vanished, but her scarves, dresses, and other possessions were strewn all over the hillside. Her lacy formal petticoat, caught on the black gorse, flapped like a pennant in the breeze at the top of the hill. If she didn't hurry it would soon be gone.

Todd was nowhere to be seen. The eeriness of such quiet sent a chill up her spine and she warned her fanciful imagination to remain practical.

Perhaps Todd had left to search for help. Yes, that was it. He wouldn't leave her alone for any other reason.

She levered herself up and out of the coach, pausing a moment to sit and pull the lopsided ribbon from her thick, heavy hair. It fell to her waist and she absently braided it with her fingers and tied it off. Then she decided to collect her clothes and wait for Todd.

Anne jumped to the ground, wincing as pain shot up her ankle, but she wasn't going to stop and rest. Her goal was to rescue her petticoat. It was a way of establishing normalcy in a world turned upside down. She hoped Todd would not be gone long.

The ground was rough. She stumbled as she climbed to reach that bit of white muslin and lace. With her luck, it was probably torn. She was a few feet from the petticoat when she almost stepped on Todd. The ground dipped to a hollow place and there he was, his head tilted at an odd angle, his eyes staring at the sky without seeing.

He was dead.

Anne gave a small cry and stumbled back, losing her footing, and almost tumbling down on her rump. At that moment, a shriek rent the air, the same one that had spooked the horses.

She scrambled toward the petticoat, her thought being that whatever it was wanted the coach. Not her. It didn't want her—and for good measure, she told herself so twice.

Almost convinced, she reached the top of the hill, put her hand on the petticoat, and found herself eyeball-to-eyeball with a wildcat.

Anne didn't think she'd ever seen anything so ferociously dangerous in her life. The creature had the general form of a yellow tabby, but was three times the size, with teeth that looked as if they could tear open a bull. The cat's yellow eyes took her measure and then it licked its chops.

She knew she was about to be dinner. She cowered just as the cat's gaze shifted to a point past her shoulder. It hissed and crouched with an angry growl.

From behind her, a voice as deep as Mephistopheles' said, "Don't move."

Anne's heart stopped. She'd thought herself alone . . .

So: who stood behind?

She turned and found herself looking—not at

Todd's ghost, but at something more startling. Less than an arm's length behind her stood a mythic Celtic warrior, over six feet tall and with shoulders so broad they blocked the sun.

He wore a kilt of forest green cloth, rough suede boots, and nothing else. Muscles banded his chest. His legs appeared carved of solid oak. Bits of leaves and twigs clung to his dark shaggy hair, which hung down to his shoulders. But most frightening of all was the vivid blue paint covering his face and the sharp, wicked knife in his hand.

Anne screamed at the same moment the cat attacked.

"Bloody hell," the warrior said, and unceremoniously pushed Anne's head to the ground.

The wildcat leaped past her and sank its claws into the Celt's shoulder. Real blood appeared. She could smell it. He was no ghost but flesh and bone.

For a second, man and animal struggled over her head and then his hand holding the knife lifted and he buried it in the animal's back. The wildcat jerked spasmodically, but continued to fight. They fell to the ground, mere feet from her, and battled to the death.

Terrified, she watched, not knowing which she wanted to win. The scene reminded her of a picture she'd once seen of the mighty Hercules fighting a lion. The very earth seemed to shake from their struggle.

Again the knife blade appeared and the warrior stabbed the writhing cat over and over until at last the animal went still.

Anne released the breath she'd been holding. She was crying. Silly. She never cried. And yet she'd been doing it without realizing it. She swiped at her eyes.

The warrior moved. He turned his head and looked right at her. In the evening light, his eyes burned brightly. They assessed her critically, and Anne had one clear thought: now might be a good time to leave.

Carefully, awkwardly, she got to her feet. He rose with her, his movements easy, almost graceful for such a large man. He lifted the knife.

Anne froze, expecting him to plunge it into her heart. Instead, he bent to wipe the blood off his blade against the cat's fur.

Her gaze on his bowed back, Anne edged one step away and then the other. He turned to her and she stopped, her feet suddenly glued to the ground.

"Are you all right?"

She took a full minute to comprehend that he'd spoken to her, and she couldn't reply. Her mouth refused to form words. Even if he was human, such a man could be capable of *anything*. She took another step in the direction of the coach.

"I've been hunting this animal for hours," he explained as if she'd asked the question. "A sheep killer. A cat like this is too dangerous to leave free."

He spoke the King's English with a trace of a brogue but she wasn't going to chitchat with him about it. Instead, she hiked her skirts and took off running for the shelter and safety of the coach.

"Wait!" he shouted.

From the shadows surrounding the overturned vehicle stepped two men dressed in the same half-naked, blue-faced fashion of the warrior. They weren't as huge or powerful, but they appeared just as disreputable.

She skidded to a halt. Were they men? Or devils?

Anne didn't think; she reacted, swerving away from them. Her foot almost tripped over a hefty piece of wood broken off from the coach's crash. She scooped it up, hefting its weight in her hand.

"What is the matter with you, lass?" the shorter of the two warriors asked. His was the strong lilting brogue she'd come to expect from the highlanders.

"Don't come any closer," she warned, holding her stick like a club.

"And who are you, lass, to be threatening us?" the older one demanded belligerently. The carrot-red of his hair and sparse beard were a comical contrast to the blue paint. His clean-shaven, blue-faced companion was much younger, with brown curling hair covering not only his head but his chest and back. It was all very unnerving.

Before Anne could answer, she heard a step behind her. *The warrior.* He'd moved with such stealth she hadn't been aware of his approach.

"Here now." He reached for her makeshift weapon.

Anne whirled to defend herself, swinging her club with all her might and whacked him hard right across the midsection.

Unfortunately, he moved at the same time and she hit him a bit lower than she'd planned.

His response was immediate. The air left his body with a "whoosh." He doubled over, falling to his knees right in front of her.

Anne took a step back. She hadn't known she was so strong.

The brown-haired man winced in sympathy. "*Och*, right in the bloody bollocks. Did you see that, Deacon? The lass neutered Tiebauld."

Neutered? Tiebauld?

Anne dropped the club, her mind numb with horror. "You are Lord Tiebauld?"

The warrior couldn't speak. He wheezed something which the man called Deacon interpreted: "He says he is." Deacon's voice was laced with lazy humor.

"He may never be the same," his companion predicted.

"Aye," Deacon agreed. " 'Tis a pity. The lasses will have to turn to us for comfort, Hugh."

"We'll be forced to work twice as hard to please them," Hugh answered.

Anne didn't care about their problems. She had to make amends with her husband . . . before she could tell him he *was* her husband. "I'm so sorry," she whispered, reaching to help him rise.

He pulled back, his arm staving her off. "It will be fine. Shortly." His voice was hoarse from pain.

"Please, I—" She fell silent, seeing what she should have seen from the very beginning. Sharp blue eyes identical to Lady Waldo's. The eyes in the miniature . . . although the rest of him was now a far cry from Anne's image of an idealistic scholar. Lord Tiebauld had filled out as a man. More than filled out—he seemed to have doubled in size. The effect was intimidating, even when he was on his knees.

And then he stood up.

It hadn't been her imagination—he was tall. And strong. Anne wiped her nervous palms against her skirts and stepped back. For the second time since she'd been in his company, words stuck in her throat.

A strand of hair had come loose from her braid. It blew across her face. He surprised her by pushing it back, a gentle gesture, a thoughtful one. Certainly not a threatening one from a man called the Madman of Scotland—

"Is the man on the hill your husband?"

Anne blinked, disoriented by the word *husband*. Then she understood he wasn't speaking about himself. "Todd? No, he was my coachman."

Now was the time to tell him.

She hesitated. Then, "How did you know I was married?"

Straight, even teeth flashed in the blue paint of his face. "That is a wedding ring on your finger, isn't it?"

Anne had an unreasonable desire to hide her hand in the folds of her skirts. She clenched her fist. She wasn't ready for the confession, not ready at all.

He misinterpreted her fears, his gaze softened.

"Your husband will be happy to know you are safe after such a bad accident."

"I hope he will," she managed to say. *Tell him*, her inner voice urged. *Now.*

But Deacon had joined them. "Our faces probably frightened the wits out of her, Tiebauld."

Her husband looked down at the way he was dressed and laughed in agreement. He had a melodic, carefree laugh, for such a large man. Anne knew he would have a fine singing voice, too. And he didn't sound maniacal at all.

"It's a ritual Hugh, Deacon, and I have," he explained, with a touch of sheepishness over his peculiar dress. "Based on Celt customs. Well, actually, they are customs of our own. They make the sport more enjoyable. Adds to the game of the chase."

"Game?"

"Aye, a little danger is a healthy thing." He shrugged with a rueful grin, like an overgrown boy who couldn't help himself from pulling a prank.

Relief teetered inside her. Her husband didn't sound *raving* mad—just unconventional. He had a reason for being blue. Of course, she didn't know what to make of a man who considered it a game to fight a wildcat with his bare hands, a man who *enjoyed* danger—but then, this was Scotland.

And as long as he wasn't howling at the moon, her marriage might work.

The notion made her feel wifely. She should nurse the scratches left by the cat's claws. Simultaneously, she was relieved his chest didn't have as much hair as his companions. Also, his chest could have been two of theirs.

The directions of her thoughts must have shown on her face because he crossed his arms, making his muscles flex and tighten.

Heat rose in her own cheeks. She attempted to make her interest a purely medical one. "Perhaps someone should put a salve on those scratches."

"They can wait." He changed the subject. I'm sorry, I don't know your name."

Here it was, the perfect opportunity to introduce herself as "wife." She had to tell him before courage deserted her. She opened her mouth just as Hugh cried out, "You are not going to believe what I've found!"

They all turned to where his head poked out of the coach door. He had wandered off to explore and now waved the silver framed miniature in his hand.

"Is it money or a woman?" Deacon asked baldly.

"Neither."

"Then it can't be of value," Deacon replied dismissively.

Equally dismissive, her husband prodded her for an introduction, "I'm sorry. You were saying?"

"It's a picture of Tiebauld," Hugh announced grandly, "when he was nothing more than a beard-less youth. Remember when he first came here, Deacon, what a sad, sorry sight he was?"

Now he had her husband's full attention. "A picture of me?"

Hugh climbed out of the coach and jumped to the ground. Her husband's long legs ate up the distance between them. He grabbed the miniature from his friend.

"I know that picture. My sister had it." He looked at Anne with new eyes. "Did you come from Alpina? Have you seen her?" A pause. "Is she well?"

His voice held genuine concern. She answered honestly, "She is not."

"Tell me." He walked back to her. No, he stomped back. A man of his size didn't move quietly when angered.

"I don't know much about her illness." Anne lifted her chin, pretending a courage she didn't feel. "She sent me to you."

"For what purpose?"

Here it was. Anne could avoid the confrontation no longer. She held out her ring finger. Even in the fading light, the family heraldic badge could be seen etched in the gold. She was surprised he hadn't noticed it before. "She chose me for you. My name is Anne. I am your wife."

Chapter 2

Hugh and Deacon gathered around for a look. Hugh made a low whistle. Deacon scowled.

Aidan's response was more direct. "You lie."

Pride flashed in the Englishwoman-named-Anne's eyes. "I never lie."

"And I've never married," Aidan shot back.

She didn't like his answer. "We were married by proxy. Your sister arranged it."

"Ah, the things you can do in England," Hugh observed drolly. "A man can be shackled to a bride sight unseen." He grinned with the sly knowledge of an inside joke. "And they call *us* barbaric."

"It isn't," Deacon answered sourly. "It's the way of the moneyed classes."

Aidan shook his head. He was in no mood for Hugh's humor or Deacon's democratic cant. "I suppose you have documents to prove your claim?"

"Yes, of course," she answered crisply. "They are in my reticule in the coach. Perhaps your friend will fetch them for us?"

"Hugh isn't a lackey," he replied, more to be perverse than for any other reason. The trouble was, now that he'd had a moment to digest the woman's claim, he realized it wasn't beyond Alpina to arrange a marriage.

He should have anticipated such an outrageous action. His sister had been nagging him since his university days to breed an heir for the title. In her last letter, she'd warned him he was growing long of tooth and if he wasn't careful, his seed wouldn't be potent.

Aidan hadn't responded. The thought of discussing his "seed" with his sister made his stomach curdle. However, Alpina did mention in the letter that her health was not what she'd expected it to be and she wanted to see the matter of an heir settled. Aidan should have been forewarned. Alpina had proven in the past she would do anything to gain her way. She could easily justify marrying him off to a chit sight unseen—and she had the political influence to accomplish it.

"Then *I* will fetch them," his unwanted bride snapped, obviously irritated by his lack of so-called gallantry.

Aidan watched her walk toward the coach. Her back was ramrod straight in the fashion of all good finishing schools. He wondered if her pride would be lowered to realize her huffiness added a delightfully indignant, but decidedly feminine, sway to her hips. Her braid bounced with her rhythm.

Anne. Her straightforward name suited her.

"What do you think this is about?" Deacon asked.

"No more than what it appears," Aidan answered.

"It could be an English trick."

He pulled his gaze away from where Anne contemplated the best way to climb back into the coach while preserving her dignity. Her first small jump had been woefully unsuccessful, especially since she'd kept one hand on her skirts to hold them down. "You wouldn't think so if you knew my sister," he told Deacon and added with a reassuring smile, "Don't worry. All will be fine. This bit of a muslin is not some English spy."

"And Delilah wasn't a barber, either," Hugh interjected.

His jab hit home. Hugh might be a clown but his keen eyes saw everything. He'd caught Aidan admiring the lass. "She's not for me," Aidan said.

Hugh's smile turned skeptical while Deacon snorted his opinion.

Aidan's temper rose. He tucked the miniature in the waist of his kilt. "The two of you fetch the horses. We need to take the coachman's body back with us to Kelwin and see to a decent burial."

"What of her?" Deacon asked.

Anne had managed to pull herself up onto the coach, exposing quite a bit of leg in the process. She had trim, lovely ankles. And long legs. Aidan liked long legs. He forced his gaze away from the sight. "What do you mean?"

"Do we take her with us?" Deacon asked.

"Of course. We can't leave her here."

"Yes we could," Deacon replied. "If we were wise, we would. Your sister has built a trap and baited it well. She knows your weakness."

"Which is women?"

"An *English* woman, Tiebauld. She reminds you of your *English* past, of where your sister believes you belong. Where it is safe." He took a step closer, lowering his voice. "Your sister has powerful connections. You don't think she suspects . . . ?" He let his voice trail off.

"There is nothing to suspect," Aidan said calmly, but he knew what Deacon meant. He trod a fine line, one complicated not only by the British military commander Lambert's undisguised hate for him but also Deacon's firebrand brother Robbie, who was the zealot leader of a brewing rebellion amongst the highlanders.

"I've agreed to help Robbie smuggle in the Danish gunpowder, but I'll do no more, Deacon."

"Not yet," Deacon assured him. He glanced at Hugh, who dropped his gaze, not wanting to be a part of a deadly decision, before saying, "Be careful, Tiebauld. The time is coming when all men must choose sides. You will have to decide if your loyalty lies with England or with Scotland."

Aidan replied tightly, "My decision will rest on what is best for my clan."

Deacon smiled. "Then you've made your choice.

'Tis a king of our own and self-rule that will make Scotland strong."

"And if we are caught with the gunpowder, we will all be hanged."

At that moment, Anne tumbled through the coach door. She let out a shout as she fell, followed by a thump Aidan could hear from where he stood.

Dismissing the men with a wave of his hand, he jogged toward the coach. "Miss Anne?" he called, as he drew closer.

She groaned.

With a bound, he leaped up onto the coach side, stretched out on his belly, and looked down through the door. She sat in a heap of skirts, rubbing a spot on her head. "Are you all right?" he asked.

She frowned. "I didn't mean to do that."

Aidan laughed. He couldn't help it. She appeared comical . . . and it was a sign of her temperament that she didn't lash out at him as any number of people would. Instead, she held up a sheaf of folded papers she'd removed from the brown silk bag in her lap.

He took them. "Do you need help up?"

"Help would be nice," she admitted dryly.

Reaching down, he grabbed her offered hand by the wrist and easily lifted her to sit beside him. She was a mite of a thing. Average height, slender build, but with nice breasts. He'd noticed those almost immediately, although he hadn't wanted to admit it, since it fell in line with Deacon's suspicions.

Deacon was overreacting. Aidan admired all

women's breasts . . . of course, he'd also noticed Anne's fine gray eyes framed by long black lashes. Honest eyes. Intelligent ones. She was so refined, so sophisticated—so *bloody English*.

Sitting cross-legged, he opened the documents. The first was a letter from Alpina. "Dear brother," he read aloud, but then stopped and scanned his sister's words silently. She was ill, she wanted *his* affairs in order before she died, she had chosen a young woman who was everything *he* could hope for in a countess . . . "Fondly, Alpina."

He glanced through the marriage contract. A proxy marriage. Who would have thought such things existed in this day and age? He would have assumed both parties would be required to approve or at least *know* of the alliance before the marriage could take place, but since the contract was signed by both the Archbishop of Canterbury and the Archbishop of York—with the High Lord Chamberlain's official seal for additional measure—he inferred his opinion had not mattered.

He had to admire Alpina. She was thorough.

Rolling the documents into a tube, he announced to the proud woman waiting anxiously beside him, "This is absolute nonsense."

"Your sister is very sincere."

"My sister is always sincere. It doesn't mean she is right."

He expected her to fire back justification of some sort, but instead she asked, "Is it really true you were a scholar at All Souls College?"

The change of subject caught him off guard. Then, he understood. "You have trouble believing it?" Grinning, he rubbed the blue paint on his face to emphasize the point.

She lifted a critical brow. "Your scholar status would be more believable if you wore a touch more clothing."

Aidan enjoyed her discomfort. "You sound like a wife already."

His barb brought the blood rushing to her face. "That was not my intent. I was merely . . . curious." She averted her eyes, suddenly interested in a piece of splintered wood beside her. "However, I believe I should tell you now that in spite of the unusual circumstances of our marriage—"

"Marriage?" Aidan laughed. "Anne, my darling lass, you must forgive me if I don't feel wed."

She stiffened, her gaze still intent on the splinter. "The clergy performing the rite in London suggested we have another ceremony here in Scotland after our marriage has been, well, you know," she finished, suddenly shy.

He leaned toward her shell-shaped ear. "No, I don't know. Explain."

Her head snapped round. Her nose almost touched his, her fine gray eyes opened in surprise. Then they narrowed in suspicion. "You know *exactly* what I am trying to tell you."

"Do I?" Aidan stretched out on the coach, propping himself up on one elbow and smiled at her.

"I'm not certain. You aren't being exactly clear. Do you care to enlighten me?"

Her lips twitched as she bit back a sharp retort. She knew he was toying with her. A lesser woman would have pouted or thrown a tantrum, but Anne apparently had determination and spirit. Two qualities he admired. It was almost a shame he would be sending her back to London on the morrow.

Bravely, in spite of blushing furiously, she said, "I am talking about the consummation of our union. I have agreed to be a wife to you in every way. I will do whatever you ask of me—" She paused, as if abruptly realizing her own boldness. "Whatever you ask," she forced herself to repeat, lowering her head, the gesture feminine and submissive.

Suddenly, Aidan wasn't so cocky. In fact, he was intrigued. Sexually intrigued.

Dear Lord, she was obviously a virgin. Alpina wouldn't have sent him anything else, and Aidan had to sit upright lest Anne noticed he was fully aroused.

Darkness was close. Twilight shadows stretched around them. He didn't know where Hugh and Deacon had gone off to, and he didn't care. For a moment, he could imagine the two of them alone in the world.

Aidan Black and a London debutante—and not even one who was cream of the crop. Aidan had spent his time in the drawing rooms and ballrooms of the *ton*.

He knew someone like Anne must have been desperate for a husband, else she wouldn't have accepted such a bargain as Alpina had offered. There had to be something wrong with her, although he'd be hard pressed to see what it was.

Still, it pricked his male pride.

Years ago, he'd been a tongue-tied, awkward scholar pushed into Society by Alpina to search for a bride. Fresh from school and a life lost in books, he'd no idea of how to go about wooing a woman, especially the lovely young debutantes paraded before him, dewy and fresh, and well aware of their own self-worth.

They'd made fun of his awkwardness. He'd overheard a group of them mocking him at a garden party when he'd become lost in a maze.

He'd actually been searching for Louise Tarleton, one of the group. He'd been infatuated with her almost to the point of madness. Hearing her disdain over what a love-sick fool he was had been one of the most humiliating experiences of his life. Worse, he'd been expected to dance with her that very evening. He'd tripped over his own feet. Made a complete ass of himself.

It was the last Society function he'd ever attended. A week later, he'd kicked the dust of London from his heels and left for the Highlands to discover his heritage and to become a man.

No one laughed at him now. Hard work and age

had filled him out. He'd never looked back or even had a desire to . . . until this moment.

Deacon had been right. Alpina had known what she was doing. This innocent young debutante was more of a threat to Aidan's senses than the whole English army.

"I'm not ready to marry," he said bluntly.

She blinked. "But you must. You are. It is your responsibility. You owe it to your title."

Aidan frowned. "How cold you are. And here I thought women were the ones given to the finer emotions."

She shook her head in confusion. "I don't know what you are talking about."

"Love, Anne." He said her name deliberately. It felt good on his tongue. Too good. "You've heard of love, haven't you? The singing of birds, the cry of angels, the lament of poets."

"I understand what love is," she informed him tartly. "I've just never heard a man speak of it."

"Well, we are poets at heart here in the Highlands." He paused before adding, "And lovers."

She did not mistake his meaning. Her face glowed, it turned so bright red, but she did not back down. "I repeat. I have agreed to the terms of the marriage."

"Yes, yes, yes, and you will be dutiful. Well, I don't need a dutiful wife—especially in bed. I am a passionate man," he said almost brutally. "I have plenty of lovers who please me well enough."

That set her back. She groped for words and then blurted out, "You can still have them. I understand men must have their distractions."

"Distractions?" He couldn't imagine Bonnie Mowat or Kathleen Keith or any number of the happily married wives in his clan telling their husbands they could keep "distractions." But he could see them angrily chasing their spouses with butcher knives.

Her acceptance of such a sham marriage made him angry. Unreasonably so. He embraced the anger as a barrier between himself and the disturbing memories her presence evoked.

Deacon and Hugh had returned with the horses and were busy at the top of the hill preparing the cat's carcass and the coachman's body for the return to Kelwin.

Aidan jumped to the ground. "It's time to leave, Anne. Come." He held up his hands to assist her.

She didn't move. "You're angry."

Was there a woman in the world more obstinate than this slight Englishwoman?

"When I marry," he announced proudly, "I will not keep 'distractions,' as you so tactfully put it."

"Because you will marry for love?" Her brows rose in surprise.

"Yes," he declared—although he'd not really considered the matter before. The devil with it. She might have charmed him momentarily, but she could just as easily prove annoying. "Now, are you ready to leave, *your highness*, or do you wish to spend the night here? Of course, I can't guarantee there won't be another wildcat in the area."

Her nose went up in the air. "Has anyone informed you sarcasm is the lowest form of wit?"

"My sister, but I never listen to her either. Good night, *Miss* Anne." He turned and started up the hill.

"No, wait!"

Aidan stopped. "Yes?"

She balanced on top of the coach, holding her precious documents to her chest. The braid in her hair had fallen completely out and she appeared very young and very defenseless. She compounded the impression by admitting, "I need help getting down."

He allowed himself one smirk and then returned to the coach. Placing his hands around her waist, he lowered her to the ground. She weighed less than goose down, although underneath her high-waisted dress were some intriguing curves.

"Thank you," she murmured.

"Come along." He started walking again, but stopped when he realized she didn't follow. "What now?"

"I need to gather my things," she explained.

"What things?"

"My clothes." Her gesture took in the surrounding area. "My dresses and things that fell out of my trunk when it crashed."

Aidan really hadn't paid much attention to the bits of material littering the hillside. He didn't waste time thinking about trivial matters. "I'll send some-one for them tomorrow."

"By tomorrow the wind may have blown every-thing away."

Women. They were stubborn, although he had a suspicion Anne might be more stubborn than most. Another excellent reason to ship her back to Alpina.

"Well, do it, but be quick," he said with little grace. He reached for an article of clothing caught in the gorse and discovered he was holding a silky un-dergarment. For a second, he could only stare at it. After countless days of cotton and homespun, he'd forgotten the cool smoothness of silk.

"We have the horses loaded, Tiebauld," Deacon called. "Are we ready to go?"

Aidan shifted his gaze to the top of the hill, where the two men waited with stamping horses. They'd already removed the paint from their faces. He'd forgotten about it on his, and the idea struck him she probably thought he appeared ridiculous. Well, to the devil with her!

"*My lady*," Aidan used the title flippantly, "needs to gather her belongings."

Deacon rolled his eyes with ill-disguised impa-tience, but Hugh said, "I'll help." He dismounted and started combing the hillside, finding a thing or two here and there.

Aidan approached the horses. His animal Beau-mains nickered a greeting. The huge gray gelding was his pride and joy.

"What are you holding in your hands?" Deacon asked.

It embarrassed Aidan to be caught rubbing a slip of silk between his fingers. They'd seen him; he had no doubt of it. The three of them never missed an opportunity to goad each other. "It's Anne's."

But there was no humor in Deacon's voice as he repeated, "Ah, Anne's."

"Yes, Anne's," Aidan snapped. "And she is leaving on the morrow."

"So was I right?"

Aidan frowned. "There are times, Deacon Gunn, you are a pushy bastard." He was tempted to wipe the blue paint from his face with the silk, but he couldn't do it. Instead, with studied casualness, he tossed the garment over his saddle and removed his rolled shirt and a scrap of homespun he'd brought for the purpose.

"And?" Deacon prompted, indicating with curve of his finger there was more Aidan needed to say.

"And you were right." Aidan pulled his shirt on before adding, "But not in the way you think. She has stirred old memories. Things I'd thought I'd long put behind me."

"We never escape our past, Laird Tiebauld, *you* should know *that*."

Hugh and Anne approached, their arms full of personal belongings. "You can use my hunting sack for your clothes," Hugh offered.

"Thank you," Anne said. "I didn't find as much as I'd hoped—" Her voice broke off. She stared at Aidan.

"Is something the matter?" he asked.

"Your face," she said. "You look—"

She hesitated and Aidan caught himself waiting for her answer. Most woman found him handsome in a rugged sort of way. Her dumbfounded reaction was not completely uncommon. After all, he was the laird.

"—-Almost normal," she finished.

So. The kitten had claws. Worse, Aidan—who usually had a good sense of humor—didn't like her answer. He was tempted to fire a salvo back, but she'd begun stuffing her clothes in the hunting sack, her attention turned completely away from him.

Unfortunately, Hugh didn't know when to leave well enough alone. "Is it a good or bad thing, my lady?"

Anne appeared a bit befuddled, as if she'd forgotten what they were discussing. Then she swung an assessing glance toward Aidan. "I haven't made up my mind. Although he needs a haircut. Desperately. Long hair is not in fashion."

Aidan almost snarled at her off-hand comment. An unusual reaction from him. He wasn't a vain man. Or at least, he tried not to be. But then, he hated debutantes. He gave a proud toss of his hair. He didn't have time for frivolities like haircuts.

Deacon came to his defense. "You realize," he

said to Anne, "Hugh uses his bag for dead birds while he's hunting. They are usually covered with dirt and lice and all sorts of vermin."

She paused in her packing, then continued, pointedly ignoring him.

Aidan's gaze met Deacon's. *She leaves tomorrow,* he silently promised his friend.

Deacon grunted skepticism and put his heels to his horse. The cat's carcass was tied to the back of his saddle. He took off ahead of the others.

Aidan said to Anne, "You'll ride with me."

He started toward Beaumains, expecting Anne to follow. However, Hugh's animal sidled forward, and before she'd taken a step, she was confronted with the grim face of the dead coachman draped over the horse's rump. Rigor mortis had not yet set in.

Anne paled. Aidan waited, anticipating a bout of hysterics and a plea to return to London . . . but it was not meant to be.

She released a shaky breath, and then, to his surprise, raised her hand and lightly touched the coachman's grizzled jaw. "He was such a kind man. A good man."

"We'll bury him at Kelwin," he said. "Did he have family? They should be notified."

Anne gave a small, sad laugh. "He had a multitude of wives. He claimed one in every county. I'm certain your sister will know who to contact."

"You can talk to her about it when you reach London," Aidan answered decisively.

Her gray eyes—yes, the fine ones—darkened. He read mutiny in their expressive depths. Apparently, so did Hugh, because he decided he'd best follow Deacon and urged his horse on.

Aidan waited until they were alone. "You are leaving tomorrow," he assured her.

"And what of our marriage?"

"We have no marriage." Was she daft? "It hasn't been consummated—and it *won't* be. You will return to my sister and she can see to an annulment plus give you a fat settlement, since this is all her doing. It is the best I can offer."

Anne bowed her head. Suspicious, Aidan waited for her next sally, but when it didn't come, he realized how tired she was. He tempered his tone. "Come along. You'll feel differently after a good night's rest." Dear Lord, he sounded like a nursemaid! He mounted Beaumains. The horse stamped, impatient to follow the others.

Her gaze followed the line of the horse from the tip of one mammoth hoof, past his broad chest, up to his alert ears. "How am I going to climb up on that great beast?" she demanded.

He waved the hand he held out impatiently in front of her face. "The same way I lifted you out of the coach."

"But where will I sit?"

Aidan felt his temper sizzle dangerously. "Miss Anne, you can walk, if you'd rather."

She placed her hand in his. Her fingers were long

and feminine and her skin felt like the silk of her garments. He heaved her up to sit in front of him.

He had no doubt he was making the right decision to send her back. She was obviously unaccustomed to hard riding. Her hands didn't have calluses. Her clothing was too thin for Highland weather. She would never survive country life.

She was also sitting right in his lap, her rounded bottom pressed against his hardening staff.

Well, at least she hadn't neutered him.

She shifted. Aidan bit back a retort for her to hold still and the sound came out as a half groan. Her cheeks turned bright pink. "I'd forgotten about your injury," she hurried to apologize. "I could sit behind you."

Ah, yes, and wrap her long legs around him lest she fall off, her breasts pressed against his back. "Stay where you are." He was damned either way. "We've a ways to go and it is growing late. I don't want to worry about you falling off the horse."

And it was a good thing she was leaving tomorrow. Tomorrow, tomorrow, *tomorrow.*

Chapter 3

Anne couldn't relax. Her husband's body surrounded hers. The horse he rode was no tame hack, but big and powerful, much like its master.

She wasn't certain what to do. She'd never met anyone like Aidan. He wasn't gallant or scholarly or weak, but overwhelmingly masculine. He was nothing like the figure in the miniature. The nose that had appeared straight and noble now had a slight bump. Evidently it had been broken at one time or another. Character and maturity lined his face as did the shadow of a heavy beard. Remaining bits of blue paint clung to the stubble.

Try as she might, she couldn't picture him in London. This man would never crimp his hair to make it curl or wear a starched collar. He played by rules she'd not been taught. Bold, brash, and wildly eccentric: those were the words she'd use to describe him.

And that nonsense about marrying for love—

"what rubbish!" Did he really believe she was that green?

"Did you say something?" his deep voice asked.

"What?"

He scowled down at her. "You said something. Were you speaking to me?"

"No," Anne averred, embarrassed to be caught talking to herself. She sank down.

He appeared ready to say something else, then changed his mind.

They rode on in silence. The rhythm of the horse's hooves threatened to lull her to sleep. Now she understood why he'd wanted her to sit in front of him—and she was becoming accustomed to being this close to him. Actually, his body warmth was quite nice.

The days were long this far north, but the hour grew late and at last a silvery half moon dominated the sky. They caught up with Deacon and Hugh on the coast road, the same one Anne and Todd had been taking when the horses had smelled the wildcat. All seemed so peaceful now.

Anne kept awake by considering her options.

Leaving him might be a very good decision. Todd's death made her wonder if her marriage hadn't been doomed from the beginning. She speculated on what Aidan meant by a "handsome settlement." She didn't need much—just enough to buy a home of her own.

When she was a child, and too restless to sleep,

her mother would settle her for the night by playing a game where they would pretend to design their very own castle. Her mother had a fanciful imagination. She'd encourage Anne to fill it with grand things like stone walls, colorful pennants, a well-filled moat, and enough bedrooms for her mother, father, and herself. Oh, yes, and plenty of food on the table for everyone.

The two of them would lie side-by-side on Anne's narrow cot, dreaming and wishing until Anne grew drowsy and finally fell fast asleep. Those nights were some of the happiest memories of her childhood.

Later, after her parents' deaths, she had continued the game out of loneliness.

But it was never the same. She could build the castle in her mind, it would help her sleep, but the game could no longer bring her close to her mother and father. They would never be there to live in the rooms she created for them. She wished that just once she could feel her parents' presence, sense that they were with her.

Anne stared at the moon, and added to her wishes that her husband had been someone different. If he couldn't be a kind, sensitive scholar, she regretted he wasn't someone more exciting and romantic. More like a Moorish prince than a half-savage Pict— albeit a tall one. As a Moor, she could imagine him in flowing robes with a huge palace and a fortune in gold so she could do whatever she pleased. Everyone would admire her, including married cousins, because people valued money over human emotions. Yes, they would respect her—

"Wake up," her Moorish prince said in a blunt, rumbling voice. "We're almost to Kelwin."

Anne blinked a moment, and then came to her senses. She had fallen asleep. Her head rested against his chest, the material of his shirt rough against her cheek. She could even hear the beating of his heart.

She sat up, alarmed to have confused her husband with a quixotic Moor. He would think her silly if he could read her mind . . . and use her silliness as another reason to ship her back.

"What's Kelwin?" she asked.

"Home."

Home. The warmth he infused in the single word sent a surge of anticipation through her. He said it exactly how she would have said it if she'd had a place to call home.

"Do you ever miss London?" she asked suddenly.

"No."

Anne nodded. She wouldn't grieve either if she never saw the sooty city again.

Anxious for her first glimpse of Kelwin, she leaned forward, his strong arm keeping her safely in place. They rode over the crest of a hill and the scene before them stole her breath.

The moon's light sparkled off the North Sea's

white-capped waves like a pathway to the stars. The coast was dark in comparison and there, by the edge of the sea, was the silhouette of a *castle.*

"It can't be," she whispered. It was perfect, complete with turrets, towers, and blazing torches. She grabbed his arm. "Stop. Please!"

He reined in the horse. Hugh and Deacon did likewise. "What is the matter?" her husband demanded.

"That castle. Is it Kelwin?"

"Aye."

"Your home?"

A touch of impatience entered his voice. "Of course."

"It's like a fairy palace," she said with awe.

He and the others laughed. Hugh said, "But no fairies live there."

Anne shook her head. They didn't understand her meaning, but it didn't matter. Her mother would have loved Kelwin. This was the dream castle they'd plotted and planned.

He'd not send her away now.

She'd never let him.

"I can't wait to see it," she urged. "Hurry."

If the contrariness of her actions confused him, he didn't say. Instead, he did as ordered.

Kelwin Castle. She even liked the sound of its name. Kelwin Castle of Caithness. How noble!

Wide-eyed and alert, she watched as they rode closer and closer. She never wanted to forget this moment, every sight, every smell. Even the night air had taken on a different, more velvet texture as they'd approached the gates.

When the horses' hooves thudded hollowly over the wooden bridge above a dry moat, Anne could have laughed with joy. She craned her neck to see everything about the stone entrance, even in the dark.

The courtyard was well lit with burning torches and alive with activity. People milled about. Men, women, children. And dogs. Anne didn't think she'd ever seen so many different canine shapes and sizes all in one place.

As her husband charged into the courtyard on his mighty steed, the people started cheering. Exactly as anyone should if they lived in a castle.

"Did you kill the wildcat?" a short, grizzled-hair man demanded.

"Aye, Fang, did you think I would not?" her husband answered.

Fang laughed. "I knew you would never live it down if you came back empty-handed."

Deacon held up the wildcat's body and the crowd roared. It was a hero's welcome. Anne glanced at her husband, seeing him with new eyes. These people adored him. They must be his clansmen—*her* clansmen, now.

"He did it with his bare hands," Deacon told them. "And saved this lass's life as well." He gestured toward Anne and everyone turned to gape at her.

His actions surprised Anne. She been too caught up in the moment to prepare for introductions. Self-consciously, she raised her hand to her hair, expecting to be introduced as Lord Tiebauld's countess.

Instead, Deacon was done. Her marriage was not announced and her husband didn't seem to feel a need to correct the oversight.

In fact, the clanspeople appeared more interested in Todd's body and the story of the coach wreck. They didn't even want her to tell it. Deacon, Hugh, and her husband told the tale—and they hadn't even been there!

"Oh, the poor girl," several whispered to the others, casting Anne in the role of tragic heroine—and promptly lost even that little interest once the ale keg was rolled out.

Aidan swung off his horse. Anne straightened, expecting him to help her down, but he didn't. Instead, he strode off for the keg, throwing orders over his shoulder for several of the lads to see to Todd's body, without so much as a backward glance at Anne. Fang handed him a foaming tankard of ale. He drained it in one gulp and called for another.

Even the thoughtful Hugh had deserted her, losing himself to the charms of three young women who threw their arms around him and showered his face with kisses.

Anne looked away, embarrassed by such blatant behavior . . . although she did sneak another peek. She could almost hear her Aunt Maeve hissing that decent women shouldn't act that way—yet Hugh appeared happy.

What was worse, Anne didn't know how to gracefully slide off this mountain of a horse.

So she sat there, feeling awkward and alone. Several of the women sent puzzled, surreptitious glances in her direction, but no one approached. She could imagine them whispering amongst themselves, talking about her.

Anne acted as if she did not notice. This first reception at Kelwin was very much like the balls and routs of the *ton*—she was the wallflower. Again.

The trick was to behave as if she belonged there. She affected an air of disinterest, pretending her husband's desertion was understandable and she had some *true* purpose for sitting on this beast of an animal. She shifted her focus away from the people with their prying eyes and focused instead on the castle surroundings.

Torchlight danced along the crumbling line of the ancient stone walls, and for the first time she realized a good portion of her castle was in ruins. At one time, this had been a formidable keep, but that had to have been ages ago. Someone had already worked hard to rebuild a portion of the walls, but there was still much to be done.

"Those Whiskey Girls are the disgrace of Caithness," a woman's voice whispered to another.

Anne tilted her ear in the direction of the speaker. Two older women huddled together in conference. They were quickly joined by others, many younger than themselves.

"Men need to have that kind of woman around," one of them whispered. "A bachelor like the laird has needs."

Anne wondered if by "needs" the woman meant the same as "distractions." She listened harder.

"A bachelor like the laird needs to find a wife," the first speaker declared crisply—winning a place in Anne's heart! "Then we'd have a wee bit of organization and common sense around Kelwin."

"Men don't think of such things," another observed.

"It's still disgraceful." And they all agreed. "Someone should run those Whiskey Girls off."

"You can't run off the distiller's daughters," another told her with a laugh.

There was a sharp reply, but Anne didn't hear it, for at that moment a red-headed boy took her horse's bridle and said, "Do ye need help, Miss? I'm goin' to be takin' Beaumains to his stall. He's ready for a nice rubdown."

The horse beneath her shifted his weight as if letting her know he had been patient long enough. He swished his sweeping tail in her direction.

Anne confessed, "I can't get down."

"Oh." The lad looked around and hurried off into the crowd to return in a second with a thick log, three feet high, which served as a mounting block. Anne was relieved for the opportunity to dismount with some dignity. Still, Beaumains was a tall horse, and she glanced around to see if anyone had noticed her less than graceful scramble down.

People were more involved with themselves than the antics of a stranger. The crowd was beginning to disperse. The hunters had returned victorious and there was no longer a reason to linger, save for one last tankard of ale. The people shifted and moved around her, making their goodnights to one another or plans for the morrow.

With the expediency of the young, the stable lad had walked off with the horse leaving Anne still standing on the mounting block. She felt very alone and out of place. Again she looked to Aidan and what she saw made her eyes pop open.

He was no longer drinking with Fang. Instead, he was now surrounded by the same women who had welcomed Hugh. The Whiskey Girls. They'd abandoned Hugh without a backward glance.

One of the Whiskey Girls laughingly messed Aidan's hair with a bold familiarity that made Anne's blood sizzle. They were definitely sisters with the same coal black hair and ample, jiggling bosoms which they thrust up at her husband in a decidedly provocative manner.

Then, the hussy who'd pulled Aidan's hair took his hand holding the tankard and rubbed it, tankard and all, back and forth across her overflowing breasts, the nipples already tight and hard against the tight material of her skimpy bodice.

And Aidan let her.

Reason fled; shyness evaporated, as did her promises made earlier during her pretty speech about allowing him his "distractions."

Anne would be damned to be so publicly humiliated. And she didn't care about his "needs." Something possessive rose inside her. In a voice as sharp as a governess's, she said, "Take your hands off my husband."

Her words cut through the air. Everyone froze in surprise, including the erring Whiskey Girl and Aidan.

"Husband?" the Whiskey Girl repeated dumbly.

"Husband?" the good women of the clan echoed.

Chapter 4

In the ensuing dead silence, Anne reflected that perhaps her announcement had been a bit brash.

There was naught she could do now. She met
Aidan's gaze with her head high. This was not how
she'd wanted to be first presented to his people. But
if she didn't stake her claim, he would send her
away without anyone being the wiser.

She wasn't being replaced by a tart. And she
wasn't leaving her castle—even if the look her husband sent her way could sear meat.

Reading her mind, he insolently put his arm
around the shoulder of youngest and prettiest
Whiskey Girl, who to Anne's surprise stepped back.
"I'll not be going with a married man, even if he is a
laird. My mother didn't raise me that way."

"Don't worry," Aidan assured her. "My *wife* will
not be with us long." He raised his voice to reach
every corner of the courtyard. "This is Miss Anne—"
He paused. "What is your last name?"

"Black," she said defiantly, giving his surname.

"It is not *Black*."

"It is." Anne hated arguing this point in front of everyone but she had no choice. "I have my marriage papers to prove it." She held up Hugh's hunting sack where she'd stuffed the documents in with her clothing.

Aidan pleaded his case to his clan. "It's a proxy marriage," he explained. "I've never set eyes on this woman before in my life until today. Hugh and Deacon can tell you it's true."

"It's true," Deacon agreed readily, helping himself to the keg of ale.

Anne frowned. Deacon had been set against her from the beginning. But if Aidan could present his story to the people, so could she. She turned in the direction of the woman who had complained earlier about the Whiskey Girls. "Lord Tiebauld's sister Lady Waldo chose me. He has a responsibility to his title. She felt it was time your laird took a wife."

"Especially one who looks like she's been rolled around in a dustbin," Deacon said slyly.

The mean-spirited comment stunned Anne, but to her surprise, her husband championed her. "I've warned you once, Deacon. Leave the lass alone." He then said to her, "But don't think I've changed my mind. You leave tomorrow."

Not if I consummate the marriage tonight, her wily inner voice said. Fatigue vanished, to be replaced with a sense of purpose. "My documents are legal. I could present them to your clergyman and he would support me."

"There are no clergy at Kelwin," Aidan told her. "I am the laird. I am the law. Give it up, Anne. Your claim won't stand."

She glanced at the faces of those who watched their exchange with avid interest and realized he was right. However, she would not leave, not without a fight. She changed the subject. "I am tired. I wish to go to bed."

The interpreted meaning of her words didn't sink in until several people raised eyebrows and more than a few whispered and guffawed.

"Hush, now, she's an innocent," Aidan announced, clearly irritated by their speculation. In a curt tone, he told Anne, "Come along." He started for the castle's front door but stopped to look at the Whiskey Girl who he had flung his arm around. "I'll be seeing you later, Cora."

A chorus of "oooo's" went up around Anne. It took all her courage to follow her disgraceful husband into the castle. If he thought she was going to ignore such a slight, he was wrong. Of course, right now, she had no choice but to trail in his wake, along with what seemed to be an army of dogs in many different sizes and varied dubious heritage. The smallest one almost tripped her when it crossed her path. She had barely noticed it in the shadows.

Fortunately, she didn't fall. She couldn't have stood the humiliation. Not right now, when everything was so raw.

The main door was tall and narrow. She'd remodel to widen it if she had her preference, especially since she had to wait for the pack of dogs to trot happily after their master. It led though a narrow alcove designed to keep cold air out of the main room, although it smelled of wet dog.

Deacon held the door open for her. "Countess," he murmured as she passed. She snubbed him.

Hugh followed at a safer distance.

Again, Anne waited for doggie feet to precede hers before she entered the main room. But once she did, she was wonderfully surprised.

It was a true medieval great hall with an arched ceiling supported by oak trusses blackened by age. Torches in wall sconces lit the room with flickering golden light. A fire burned in a fireplace of carved stone, the opening almost as tall as a man.

But what captured her attention were the windows lining the back wall. They were shaped like those in cathedrals, their curved shape mimicking the line of the ceiling. Stone scrolls decorated each window pane. One would have expected stained glass. Instead, their panes were clear, and the view of the moonlight on the North Sea was a scene more breathtaking than anything devised by man.

"You like them, don't you?" Aidan's words were

more of a statement than a question. Apparently he'd set aside the gauntlet to indulge his obvious pride.

"They are incredible," she answered, before surveying the rest of the room. Her pleasure turned to open-mouthed shock.

The place was filthy—and colorless. Everything was gray or brown. There wasn't even a hint of color in the utilitarian furnishings.

The dogs deserted Aidan to settle themselves in front of the fire. She knew it was their usual place because of the litter of bones scattered all over the floor. A keg of ale with a dripping tap resided proudly beside the hearth. Someone had set a bowl on the floor to catch the drips which a dog used as a water bowl.

In front of the bank of windows was a raised dais with a long table and several chairs turned out as if whoever had been sitting there had just gotten up and left. Stacked pewter plates, tankards, and a platter of what looked like a half-eaten leg of lamb waited to be cleaned up. Anne wondered if anyone had cleared dishes in days.

Hugh wandered over to sit on the table, pushing over tableware to make space. The little dog that had almost tripped Anne jumped up in his lap.

Worst of all, the room smelled. The scent of wet dog extended beyond the alcove. It permeated the air. Anne wrinkled her nose. The smell came from the floor, which was covered by a drab mat of dried stems and grasses. Huge stains and oil spots marred the surface. It was almost too vile to stand on—even with shoes.

She gagged. "What is on the floor?"

To her surprise, her husband said in a scholarly tone, "They are called rushes. It is a medieval practice. A layer of dried grasses, reeds, flower petals, and some sweet-scented herbs are mixed and then spread across the floor."

"Whatever for?" And if there were sweet-smelling herbs in this matty mess, she'd walk back to London!

"To insulate," he said matter-of-factly. He added with a touch of pride, "I'm a medievalist. It was my line of studies at University. I followed a technique completely realistic to what was done six hundred years ago."

"What is the matter with rugs?" Anne asked.

Hugh winced and Deacon guffawed, both already anticipating her husband's reaction.

"*Rugs* don't fit the character of Kelwin," her husband said definitively.

And I suppose dirt and flies do? Anne almost flashed back, but caught herself in time. She was growing too tired and too overwhelmed. "Do you have servants?" she asked to change the subject. She assumed from the condition of the room the answer was no.

"There's Norval and the cook," Aidan said. "They are enough to meet my needs. Besides, we don't stand on ceremony here. I left London to remove myself from the claptrap of so-called refined society. Here I'm free to pursue my interests without answering to anyone."

As he spoke, the dog left Hugh's lap. Its toenails scratched the table as it crossed to the lamb leg and started to gnaw.

Anne thought she would swoon. In two shakes, she was up on the dais, shooing the dog off the table. Her actions didn't bother him. He just crawled under the table and hopped back up again. And Hugh let him!

She could hold her tongue no longer. "This place is little better than some, some *hunting lodge!*"

"What is wrong with hunting?" Hugh asked, honestly perplexed.

"Yes," Deacon agreed easily. "We like hunting."

"Enough to paint yourselves blue and dress in skirts," Anne snapped. "It's almost like a child's game."

From behind her, Aidan's deep voice said, "These are not skirts."

She turned, recognizing her error. "I meant no offense—"

"You thought we were silly," he corrected. "We wore hunting kilts completely authentic to the times of this castle. I agree the blue paint may have been a . . . silly touch, but it's a ritual Deacon, Hugh, and

I have. Rituals are important to medieval societies."
He could have been lecturing at Oxford.

Deacon enjoyed her discomfort and obviously felt
the urge to twist the knife further. "Besides, since
the Crown has allowed it, many proud Scotsmen
wear kilts. If you are going to stay here, lass, you
must become used to a man's legs."

"She is not staying," Aidan said firmly.

For a moment, Anne *almost* declared herself ready
to leave immediately—but then she reminded herself of the emotions she'd had when she'd first laid
eyes on Kelwin.

She reined in her temper. "I have much to learn.
Perhaps it is best if we discuss the matter in the
morning."

"There is nothing to discuss, Anne."

"There's always something to discuss," she
averred, using a tactic her Aunt Maeve often used
on Uncle Robert.

But it didn't work on Aidan. He exploded. "After
four hours of marriage to you, I would never, *never*
agree to continue this charade!"

Anne didn't know how to respond. She was all
too aware of Deacon's grinning countenance and
Hugh's empathetic presence. "Actually, we've been
married a little more than a week and a half."

"Pardon?" Aidan said, his tone almost dangerous.

She cleared her throat. "I pointed out we have
been married over a week . . . counting from the day
of the ceremony."

"*I don't want to be married.*" He raised his eyes heavenward. "God, what have I done to deserve this?"

Anne backed up. She'd never had anyone pray to God about her before. "I really would like to go to my room."

"By all means," Aidan practically growled. He walked over to a staircase and started shouting for Norval.

An old man shuffled in from a side room. "Yes, laird?"

"Show Princess Anne to her room. The *guest* room," he emphasized.

Anne could have protested but didn't. Now was the time to practice discretion—something she should have done when she'd first walked into the room.

Her best course was to be docile. Years of being the poor relation had taught her to be cannier than she'd just been with Aidan. Now she would have to make up for lost ground.

At the foot of the stairs, Norval picked up a candle from the bits and pieces lying on a rude table and lit it off a wall torch. She slid a glance at her husband. Aidan stared into the fire, frowning. "Goodnight," she said softly.

He stiffened but didn't answer.

Following Norval up the stairs, Anne learned why the great hall had not been cleaned. The man was too old to be doing any chores.

"Are there maids that can be hired for service around here?" she asked.

"Hmmm?" Norval stopped on the stairs and made a full turn to face her. "I beg pardon, lass? Did you say something?" He cupped his ear, his accent so thick she could barely understand it.

She raised her voice. "Maids! Are there maids who could work here?"

"Mates? Do you mean breeding?"

While she tried to decipher what he'd said, he answered, "We breed sheep and horses. The laird has a fine hand at breeding." Or so she thought that was what he'd said.

Nor was she ready to discuss Aidan's breeding capabilities.

Fortunately, they had come to the top of the stairs where a long, narrow hall led off of the main building. There were a number of doors on either side. Following him, Anne overheard him mutter, "Guest room . . . guest room," as if he wasn't sure which one it was.

In fact, he almost walked by the room before recognizing it. "Och, this be the guest room . . . I believe?" Confused, he looked to her for confirmation.

Anne nodded. What else could she do? But she also seized opportunity and asked, "Which room is the laird's?"

Norval knew which room it was. "The one at the end of the hall. It's the biggest in the whole castle and a fine room it is," he confided, as he reached for the door handle. Unfortunately, he missed and almost toppled to the ground.

She caught him and received a good whiff of his breath for her trouble. He was drunk.

But of course.

He fit the ambiance of Kelwin to perfection.

She shook her head. Aidan needed a wife for no other reason than to organize his household. "Have you been in the laird's service long?"

"All my life," Norval allowed. "I was born in the castle and have never been anywhere else." She had to turn her head, unable to stand his breath this close.

She reached for the handle. "I'll open the door."

"Thank you, Princess Anne."

She frowned at his use of Aidan's sarcastic title. He stared at her, the picture of innocence. She took the candle stub from his hand before he burned himself as well. It was made of tallow and not of good quality. Her father had been a country doctor, a satisfying but not monetarily rewarding life. She remembered a happy childhood that included hours helping her mother make candles and soap. It appeared as if she would be doing quite a bit of both at Kelwin.

The room was dark. The slits of windows barely let in enough moonlight to matter. Anne held the candle high, Hugh's sack tucked under her arm. The thin light highlighted the foot rail of a bed and reflected in the dusty mirror hanging over a wash basin on the opposite wall. She set her bag down beside the basin.

"Norval, please set a fire in the hearth," she shouted, to ensure he heard correctly.

"Och, the night is too mild for a fire."

"But you have one downstairs."

"I don't need to scratch my ears."

Anne stood nose-to-nose with him. Her patience was at an end. She didn't even bother to shout, but spoke slowly through clenched teeth so the words would permeate his ale-soaked brain. "You hear better than you pretend. I know what tricks servants play."

He suddenly heard very well. "The hour is too late to go fetch peat, my lady, and I'm an old man who needs his sleep," he wheedled.

"Or to *sleep it off*," she countered. "Do you treat Lord Tiebauld this way?"

The servant almost lost his teeth over the audacity of such a question. "I serve the laird well."

"Does he have a fire in his grate?"

"Every night. There's a bath waiting, too." He lowered his voice, "The laird's a bit queer that way. He likes to bathe every day, even on the coldest."

Anne made a face to give the impression she shared Norval's concerns, but inside, she was deeply reassured about her husband.

Games aside, she said calmly, "I want a fire *and* hot water. Please see to it."

Norval made some sort of ducking bow. "I will return, my lady." He shuffled out of the room.

She thought about adding a request for more candles, since this one was sputtering, but decided not to press her luck. A fire would do much to cheer the room. Then maybe she could think. She dearly needed to pause and reflect.

A snore sounded from the direction of the bed.

Anne froze.

The circle of candlelight did not extend beyond the footboard—but someone was in the bed. Or some*thing*, her active imagination warned her. What human sounded like a bear being baited?

Then "it" snored again.

Anne's already frayed nerves overreacted. She screamed, dropping the candle to the floor. It extinguished immediately and she was trapped in the dark with "it." She ran straight for the door, found the handle, and charged into the hall, where she couldn't see where she was going or feel her way in unfamiliar surroundings.

Fortunately, Aidan bounded up the stairs, holding a torch to light the darkness. Deacon and Hugh and a horde of dogs were in step behind him.

Blessed, blessed light, Anne thought, as she rushed toward her husband. "There's something in there," she warned them.

"In where?" Aidan asked.

"My room. Something or someone is in the bed."

Aidan frowned. "There shouldn't be anyone here.

Take the torch, Hugh," he ordered as he reached down and pulled out a knife hidden inside his boot. He stepped into the bedroom.

Anne hurried after him, her heart pounding. She hadn't imagined bloodshed. Before she could say anything, her husband approached the bed, where there was obviously someone under the sheet. The knife poised in one hand, he ripped off the sheet with the other.

The man in the bed shouted in alarm.

Aidan shouted back, "Roy!"

"Yes, Laird?" He scrambled upright, sleepy eyes blinking in surprise. He had broad, hairy shoulders, an overflowing stomach, and short arms and legs. Anne could see why she had mistaken him for a bear. "What are you doing with a knife, Laird?"

"He was about to gut you," Deacon answered.

"By all that's holy?" Roy asked, starting to tremble.

Aidan frowned. "We thought you were a brigand."

"What's a brigand?" Roy asked dumbly.

Without answering, Aidan replaced the knife in his boot. "Anne, this my cook, Roy. Roy, this is Miss Anne who-won't-tell-me-her-last-name."

"Black," she said.

"Yes, Black," he replied absently, before going straight to the point. "What are you doing here, Roy?"

"I had a wee bit too much to drink. Elma shouts at

me when I'm drunk coming home." He shrugged. "Ye wouldn't understand, laird, since you're not a married man."

"I'm beginning to have some feeling for your dilemma," Aidan muttered. "But you can't sleep here tonight, Roy. We have a guest. This is her bed so you'll have to be up and out of it. You can sleep in the kitchen or in front of the hearth with the dogs."

"Yes, Laird." Roy practically fell out of the bed. Thankfully, he wore breeches but no socks or shoes. He padded barefoot past without another word. The dogs followed him out, probably hoping for a bite of the lamb leg on the downstairs table.

"There," Aidan said to Anne. "You can sleep now. Good night." He started to leave but she stepped in his path.

She nodded to the tangled, wrinkled bedclothes, and announced, "I will not sleep in sheets someone else has slept in." She was certain they hadn't been changed in years, at least, not if Norval had been expected to do it.

Aidan loomed over her. "I'll make you the same offer I did Roy. You can sleep in the kitchen or with the dogs."

He was serious.

"Well, then I will sleep here."

"Good. Sleep well." He stomped out of the room. Deacon followed, laughing.

Hugh lingered to put the torch in the wall sconce by the door. "You will want the light."

"Thank you," she murmured but then he, too, hurried to catch up with her husband.

Anne stood alone a moment. She could barely look at the unmade bed. There could be lice in the sheets or all manner of untold beasties. Suddenly, in a fit of temper, she crossed the room and slammed the door.

"He's rude, coarse, obnoxious—!" She doubled her fists and silently screamed out her frustration. No wonder people thought he was mad. Who walked around with a knife in his boot? "It's probably some medieval thing," she said to her reflection in the grimy mirror. "No wonder people question his sanity."

He was the hermit in the castle, free to parade around in kilts and wield knives and pretend he lived in another time.

Well, not completely. "He still bathes," she reminded herself . . . and right now, she'd give her soul for a hot bath. She didn't doubt Norval had completely forgotten her. *He* only took care of the laird—

Anne cut off her ranting.

There was a bath waiting a few steps down the hall . . . in her husband's room . . . where she was *supposed* to be. And suddenly she realized what she had to do.

This was her wedding night and she was wise enough to know she couldn't consummate her marriage in a separate bed.

She'd also wager *he* had fresh sheets.

Anne turned to her reflection in the mirror. "It's a war of wills," she reminded herself. "One that I'm going to win, just to prove to him I can." Money no longer mattered. She was going to make this marriage work, or be damned trying.

So, he didn't want to be married to her. Well, he wouldn't have been her first choice either, although he was somewhat handsome. "When his face isn't blue," she reminded herself.

After picking up her sack of clothing, she relit the candle off the torch, and left the room. No one lingered in the hallway and his door was unlocked.

Anne turned the handle and pushed the door open, almost afraid of what she'd find.

To her delight, her husband's room was beautiful. It had arched windows, smaller versions of the ones in the great hall and with the same view of the powerful moonlit sea. A fire burned brightly in the hearth, warding off the chill of early spring.

Extra light came from two wall torches on either side of the largest bed Anne had ever seen. It was massive, with a carved mahogany headboard that almost reached the high ceiling.

The sheets hadn't been turned down, but one didn't notice immediately because of the layer after luxurious layer of beautiful furs spread out across the bed. She recognized some, like the fox pelts and the sable, but there were many she'd never seen before.

A medieval diary was open and turned upside as if Aidan had been reading it in bed and wanted to save his place. She picked it up and carefully closed it. Such treatment was bad for the book's spine. There were also books on the floor beside the bed, books under the bed, and books by the tub in front of the fire.

She approached the tub. It was huge, but then, it had to be for a man Aidan's size. She tested the water. It was still hot. Lazy Norval probably boiled it so that it would still be warm whenever Aidan decided to use it.

Attached to the edge of the tub was a small tray holding a bar of soap. She sniffed it experimentally. The scent was pleasing. Sandalwood and oil of orange. Two of her favorite fragrances.

Anne began undressing.

Chapter 5

Aidan marched downstairs, followed by Deacon, straight for the ale keg. His blood still churned from the alarm her scream had sparked.

Women! They were ridiculous creatures. Imagine anyone being afraid of Roy.

But as he filled his mug, he glanced around the room and had to admit she was right. It was a pig sty. His stables were cleaner than his great hall.

He was surprised. He spent his days rebuilding the estate and coming in at night so tired he could barely stand. The maintenance of his household had been Norval and Roy's responsibility, but obviously they hadn't been doing a good job.

"When did it get this bad?" he asked the room in general.

One of the dogs sat up to scratch viciously at his ear. Fleas. Aidan scratched his collar bone in sympathy.

"When did *what* get this bad?" Deacon asked. He was cleaning his nails with a table knife.

"The hall." Aidan walked to the center of the room. His rushes idea was completely accurate to the time period . . . but the ancients changed their rushes several times a year. He couldn't remember when he and Norval had laid a fresh layer down.

Hugh came downstairs. "I think I'll go to my mother's for the night." He cast a guilty glance at Aidan. "We have gotten a bit out of hand, haven't we?" He left.

But Aidan called him back. "Take the dogs with you. Put them in the stables." He'd seen another one scratch ferociously.

Hugh raised a surprised eyebrow but did as he asked. Not all of the dogs went willingly. York, the smallest, tried to hide, but Hugh picked him up and carried him out.

Deacon surveyed the room as the dogs crowded out. "So, things need to be picked up around here." He shrugged. "Have Norval do it in the morning."

Aidan didn't answer. Anne's reaction to Kelwin had unsettled him. The place did look like a hunting lodge after a raucous night of bachelor carousing. If he wasn't careful, he would turn into an old roué.

For the first time in his life, he sensed time was passing.

"What are you thinking, Tiebauld?"

Aidan shook his head. "Nothing."

"She must be gone before the Danes deliver the

gunpowder," Deacon said quietly. "Which could be any day."

"Who?" Aidan looked up.

"Don't pretend ignorance with me." Deacon stepped down from the dais. "I know you are thinking about the Englishwoman."

"She'll be gone in the morning."

"If she doesn't manage a way around you."

Aidan tossed the untouched contents of his glass into the huge fire, where it hissed in retaliation. He faced his friend. "Either way, it is not your concern."

Deacon pulled back. "Is it not? Tiebauld, I had thought you'd have joined us by now, and yet you hesitate to commit fully to our cause."

"I'm smuggling in the gunpowder. What more do you want?"

"We want you to lead us."

Aidan turned away from the argument, but Deacon followed. He lowered his voice. "I've heard word from Robbie." He referred to his brother, Fiery Robbie Gunn.

The Gunns had been a poor clan, loyal to their Jacobite heritage, and victims of a practice termed the "Clearances." Wealthy landlords with strong political ties to England were allowed to turn tenants, farmers, and weavers out of their homes, burning the cottages if need be, to clear the land for the more profitable endeavor of sheep grazing. The Gunns wanted to strike back, not only for their land, but for their birthright as proud Scotsmen. They wanted to throw the English out of Scotland for good and would settle for nothing less.

"We need you, Tiebauld. All the clans would join the uprising if you were with us."

"I have no fight. My clan is safe, my relationship good with the neighboring landlords."

"But mine was destroyed. Robbie and I lost everything. Mark my words, the English will not stop until no highlander is left! They'll come after your land rights. Especially that dog Lambert. His entire life is spent to see you forfeit your title. He'll do it, too. See if he won't."

Aidan lost his temper. "Save your rhetoric for the pamphlets. What is between Lambert and me is personal. Nor is war the answer. Have you and your brother thought about what will happen if you start a war and do win?"

"We'll stop the Clearances. We will return people to their rightful homes."

"But what of the future? Are you ready to put a government in place? To deal with the loss of industry and markets severing our ties with England will mean? And what if you lose—*which you will*? The English will crush you, just as they did my grandfather under Charles Stuart. He lost his life. I lost my country, my identity. However, this time the English will be even more brutal than before. Let us say you do escape and find a safe haven in Denmark or Holland. Can you live with the deaths and destruction of those you've left behind on your conscience? I can't."

Deacon clenched his hand into a fist. "I burn with righteous anger, Tiebauld. Robbie and I won't rest until we're avenged. And there are many who follow us. Many more, if you will help."

"I can't."

Deacon knocked over a chair. "I know it is not because you are a coward," he said bitterly.

Aidan sometimes wondered. How did a man know if he was brave? He'd been testing himself these past seven years, and still didn't have an answer.

For a moment, the two men studied each other and then their friendship, a bond almost as strong as brothers, rose between them. Deacon apologized, "I know you are braver than most." He set the chair upright. "My temper gets the best of me." He paused. "And so far you have managed to see your clan prosper. But Tiebauld, you cannot serve two masters. The time will come when you must choose sides."

"When the time comes, I will," Aidan said soberly. And it was coming soon. He sensed it. Deacon was right. He'd restored his family's estate, but it could be destroyed again with one wrong decision.

Suddenly, the weight of it all was too much for him. He started toward the stairs. "I'm to bed. I'll see you in the morning." He didn't wait for an answer. Deacon would sleep in the great hall, as was his preference. He lived in fear the English would come hunting for him because of his and his brother's rebel activities and wanted to be ready to run. He'd confided once his greatest fear was being trapped by the English in his bed. He'd considered it humiliating.

If Aidan wasn't careful, he'd be living with the same fears, although there had been a time when he'd been full of fire, like Deacon. He'd proved his mettle though building, hunting, and wenching.

Now, although he still enjoyed the three activities, he often found more solace in his bath with a good book. He was changing, he realized, climbing the stairs. The anxious young buck was fading and in his place was a more mature man questioning the meaning of life and his own place in the world.

Thoughtfully, he proceeded down the hall, slowing his step outside the guest room door. Anne was probably fast asleep.

For a moment, he shook his head. He loved his sister, but she'd attempted to bully him too many times. Granted, this trick was the most outrageous one yet. He'd ensure Anne didn't suffer for it with a nice financial nest egg, one large enough to assuage his conscience.

He couldn't help admiring Alpina's choice of debutantes, though. Anne had spirit. She'd make a man a good wife—as long as *he* wasn't the man.

On that thought, he went to his room. Opening

the door, he found his bath waiting for him in front of a cozy fire. The water would be tepid by now, but it didn't bother Aidan.

He undressed quickly and climbed in. He had sacrificed a good part of his fortune on repairs to Kelwin and rejuvenating the livelihood of his clan . . . but baths and French-milled soap were guilty pleasures from his London days he could not give up. He loved the sensual feeling of rich lather against his skin. No matter how hard he tried to economize, the homemade soaps were not the same.

He was puzzled to find his soap already soppy wet. He hoarded it carefully and didn't like the idea he might be sharing it with Norval. It would be another item to discuss with the servant in the morning.

He washed the blue paint completely from his person and reached for the linen towel always kept on the chair beside the tub. It was gone.

Aidan swore softly. What had come over Norval? He never forgot the details of Aidan's bath. No matter how drunk he was.

Rising from the tub, Aidan snatched up the shirt he'd discarded and dried himself off. He hung it on the chair to dry.

He'd hang Norval by his thumbs in the morning. Right now, he wanted sleep. In two steps, he fell face down on the rumpled furs. Ready to drift off to sleep, the thought crossed his mind he'd like his sheets changed more often and the bed made up every day, too.

He reached for the bed covers to pull around him—and discovered he was not alone. *Someone was in bed with him.*

For one paralyzing moment, he feared it was Roy.

He rolled over and found himself staring into a pair of sea gray eyes. "Anne?"

She swallowed and nodded.

Aidan jumped out of the bed, pulling a red fox skin off to wrap around his waist for modesty. "What the bloody hell?"

Anne scrambled to sit up. Dressed from neck to toe in a heavy white cotton nightgown, she was the very image of how he'd imagine a young gentle-woman, no *virgin*, would dress for bed. Her soft, straight hair had been brushed until it shone and then pulled back into a neat braid. Her eyes were so wide with apprehension, they tugged at his heart. The impact of her presence was more erotic than if she'd been naked.

"I didn't mean to alarm you," she said, her voice slightly breathless.

"What are you doing here?" he demanded, tuck-ing the end of the fur in around his waist and hop-ing she didn't notice his obvious arousal.

But then she was an innocent, innocent, innocent, he reminded himself. Naïve, even.

Seductive.

And it was getting damned painful to be around her.

"It's our wedding night," she said in her throaty, sweet voice.

The sudden surge of hot blood her words conjured within Aidan almost sent him howling. He struggled with the urge to take her down on the bed and not let her up from under him until Sunday next.

"You don't have any idea what you are doing," he ground out arrogantly. It was a stupid thing to say. His body would love to demonstrate, but he had willpower, damn it all!

She came up on her knees, the very image of a supplicant. "I've been told to do whatever you wish of me."

Such a harem statement almost shattered his self-control.

What was it about Anne that attracted him so?

He'd known women lovelier and certainly more experienced. If he bedded her, she'd be a noose around his neck for the rest of his life. And he hadn't been deliberately teasing her when he'd said he hoped to fall in love some day. He hadn't been touched by such an emotion yet, but it appealed to his romantic nature.

Besides, he was his own man. He didn't need his sister procuring a wife! Especially such a contrary and argumentative one, with eyes that melted all his resistance. In spite of her obstinacy, there was something fragile about Anne. It brought out the protector in him.

His best defense was retreat and Aidan retreated all the way back to the tub. If the bathwater had been colder, he might have jumped in. As it was, when the back of his leg hit the tub edge, his precious soap plopped into the water.

Aidan welcomed the distraction. But as he reached in the water to retrieve it, he thought, "Soap." He straightened, his temper soaring and obliterating desire. "You used my soap!"

She skewed her face as if she'd pictured many vivid possibilities when she'd committed the brazen act of placing herself in his bed. But being accused of using his soap hadn't been one of them.

"I used it to bathe," she admitted. "I didn't think you would mind."

"You used *my bathwater*? And *my towel*? You are the one who took my towel?"

"Well, yes, I did. I mean, you couldn't expect me to walk around wet."

The image her words evoked almost brought Aidan to his knees. He sat down in the chair, clasping his hands. Did she think he was a eunuch?

Or was she wiser and more experienced than he had first imagined?

"I laid the towel in front of the hearth to dry," she was saying. "Otherwise it would have been too wet for when you bathed."

He whipped his head around to look and sure enough there was his towel within arm's reach of the tub. He just hadn't noticed it.

"And I didn't peek while you were bathing," she assured him. Her face grew beet red and he knew she was chaste. No female wiles could fake such a glowing blush other than modesty. He hated the word.

Aidan released his breath on a defeated sigh. "Anne, I have known many a rattle-pated person in my time, but you are a prize. You could wear me down—if I let you. Which I will not," he added decisively. He rose to his feet, his body back under some semblance of control.

"I want to consummate the marriage," she insisted. "I want to honor our agreement."

"Your agreement is with Alpina. Consummate the marriage with her."

She frowned. "I can't do that." But before he could shoot back some biting bit of sarcasm, she stretched out on the bed, lying on her back, her gown covering her to her ankles, her bare toes pointing upward. "I'll close my eyes. I won't make a sound. Please, do it quickly."

The sight of her limp and waiting with closed eyes on the furs restored Aidan's equilibrium. He walked over to her side. She didn't open her eyes but her body tensed, waiting for him to pounce.

For a moment, Aidan stood in silence. Then, he couldn't resist. He leaned over and tickled her feet.

It wasn't what she'd expected. And she was very ticklish. She practically stood up in the bed.

"What are you doing?" she demanded.

"Counting your toes," he answered. "You know, 'how many little pigs go to market?' "

"Are you mad?"

"There's a rumor to that effect," he answered, and started laughing. She did too, and it was almost his undoing. Anne had a tinkling, merry laugh.

It was more arousing than anything she'd done yet.

Aidan took charge, fearing he really would go mad if this continued. He grabbed her by the knees, tossed her over his shoulder, and started out of the room.

"Wait! What are you doing?" she said.

"Taking you to *your* room. In answer to any questions you may have, the answer is no. No, we are not consummating the marriage. No, you are not staying. No, I'm not putting up with any more nonsense from you or anyone else." He kicked open the door to her room and dropped her on the bed.

"Goodnight, Anne."

But as he turned away, she grabbed his fox skin. "No, please, you can't leave."

It was not a good move. He'd been all too aware she'd worn nothing beneath her night dress, and while his mind said no, other parts of him had not been so submissive. And he hesitated to parade in all his glory before her. If she knew her impact on him, he'd be clay in her hands.

He grabbed the fur. "Let go, Anne."

"Please, you can't send me back." She tugged.

He pulled. "I promise you will be handsomely compensated."

She released the fur. "You don't understand! I can't go back. There's nothing to go back to! Nothing!" Tears welled in her eyes—and he was undone.

Aidan hated to see a woman cry. It tore into him. He never knew what to do when one cried. "Here now, Anne, don't go all upset."

"I'm not!" she denied. A lone tear escaped and ran down her cheek. She took an angry swipe at it. "I don't cry. *I don't.*" But three more tears in quick succession branded her a liar.

She turned away from him to face the back wall.

Aidan should have walked out the door. He should have ignored her. But he didn't. He couldn't. He sat on the edge of the bed and offered a corner of the sheet to her. "Here."

She shook her head, refusing his help.

"Anne . . . It's not so bad. In England, you'll find someone who will make you happy. With the money I'm going to give you, your parents will be pleased—"

"My parents are dead."

Her words lingered in the air. She looked over her shoulder, her eyes dry now. "I'm an orphan," she said almost defiantly. "I lived with my aunt and uncle. They don't want me back."

Aidan felt terrible and it must have shown on his

face because she said, "Don't pity me. I've spent a
good portion of my life being 'Poor little Anne.' The
last thing I want from you is more pity." She
swiveled around to face him. "Aidan, I will be a
good wife to you. Maybe I'm not your choice, but
you aren't mine, either."

"What's wrong with me?" he asked, his pride
piqued.

"Nothing . . . except, well, you are a bit of a character. I don't think I've ever met anyone as eccentric." She paused. "What's wrong with me?"

"Nothing . . . except I don't want a wife. Especially one who ramrods her way into my life and
turns the world upside down."

"I didn't want to," she conceded. "If I was someone beautiful or came from a well-connected family,
I wouldn't be here. I've had two Seasons. No one offered for me. No dowry, no connections. Nice personality, well bred, but most men can do better. If I
didn't marry you, my uncle was going to hire me
out as a companion. I couldn't live at the whims of
some old woman. It would be better to be buried
alive."

"Anne . . . " He didn't know what to say. Plati-
tudes died in his throat.

She looked up at him. "I want a husband and children and a home. Tonight, when you said we were
going home, I felt such longing it frightened me.
Then we came to Kelwin and I didn't think I'd ever
seen anyplace so lovely."

"That's not what you said in the great hall."

His flat statement surprised a laugh out of her. "Well, it is a mess."

"It is," he agreed, and couldn't help but smile with her.

Her smile died. "Don't make me go back. Even with your money, I would be considered a failure by my relatives. I'll do whatever you want. I'll even sleep in the bed with the lice. I have nothing to return to. You can't imagine what that is like."

Aidan stared into her beseeching eyes and wanted to tell her, he did know. Growing up in England, he'd always felt an intruder. It wasn't until he'd come to Kelwin that he'd realized he'd been searching for this place all his life.

He came to his feet. She rose with him. "Are you going to send me back?"

"I don't know," he replied honestly. Deacon had been right: he couldn't have an Englishwoman lingering around as he smuggled Danish gunpowder to fuel an insurrection.

Nor did he have the heart any longer to pack her off to Alpina.

He waved toward the door. "Here, sleep in my bed. I don't want you itching like one of the hounds."

"Then I'm going to stay?" she asked hopefully.

He wouldn't make that commitment. "We'll talk in the morning."

She spontaneously reached up and kissed him on

the cheek. It was probably the most unloverlike one he'd ever had from a woman within ten years of his age on either side. But her eyes had grown shiny again and both he and she were embarrassed.

"Don't cry," he warned her. "I don't like women who cry."

"I never cry," she promised, and meekly followed him out the door. He led her into the bedroom, where he picked up the sable throw.

She held back shyly. "Did you hunt for all of those furs?"

He shook his head. "Some are gifts from the Danes and other traders. Some homage. I only hunt for food."

"I thought you said you hunted for sport earlier."

"There is sport in it."

"The sport is painting your face?" she teased softly. Then, "Are you really going to let me stay if I wish?"

"We'll discuss it." He moved toward the door. "For tonight, the room is yours."

Her shyness evaporated. "Yes, goodnight," she answered happily.

Her obvious relief to be out of his presence irked his male vanity. Minutes ago, she'd been begging him, and now she seemed cheerful to have the bed to herself.

"The room is all yours *for tonight*, Anne," he re-phrased pointedly.

She smiled serenely. "Goodnight, Aidan."

At the doorway, he paused for one last look. She waited by his bed, sweet, uncompromised, vastly relieved to escape his clutches. Women!

He threw the sable blanket over his shoulders and left the room, shutting the door behind him.

Downstairs, Deacon was enjoying a pipe in front of the fire. He'd stretched out in two chairs to sleep, as was his custom.

Deacon eyed Aidan's fox fur loincloth and said, "Tiebauld, I've gone along with your medieval schemes in the past, but whatever it is you are planning, this is one outfit you're going to have wear alone."

Aidan lay down by the fire and rolled himself in the sable. "It isn't a costume. She's in my bed."

"Hmmmm, I had imagined that was her intent all along." Deacon tapped his pipe. The ashes fell on the floor, close to Aidan's head. He thought about complaining, but didn't.

"So, she is leaving in the morning," Deacon reiterated, as if fearful something had happened to change Aidan's plans.

And something had. "We'll see."

Deacon sat up. "Tiebauld—"

"It's not for discussion, Deacon. I said we'll see and so we shall."

His friend wanted to say more but Aidan rolled toward the fire and shut him out. His rushes smelled doggie. It was cold on the floor, too. Rugs would be better. But he didn't need a managing female to help him come to those conclusions.

Aidan closed his eyes, certain he'd sleep well. Anne had practically run him to the ground.

Suddenly, he was hit with an idea. He might not be made of the sort of stuff to force Anne to leave, but what if she *chose* to leave? What if she found highland life was so arduous and so difficult, she couldn't wait to return to London?

Taking a sniff of his rush mat, he had an idea of how to make that happen.

He went to sleep with a smile on his face.

Anne snuggled down in the rich, warm furs, happily dreaming of riding a flying horse.

So it was a complete surprise when suddenly, her horse overturned her—

—And she found herself landing on her bum in a cascade of bedclothes and furs.

Dazed, she looked around and realized she wasn't dreaming. Someone had tossed her out of bed.

"Good morning, wife." Her husband grinned at her from over the edge of the cotton stuffed mattress. He let the mattress fall back in place.

"Why did you wake me?" she murmured.

"I can't have you sleeping until noon, can I?" he asked pleasantly. He walked around the bed to help her up. "You can't run a household from bed."

"What do you want me to do?" She had trouble

keeping her eyes open and was conscious he was completely dressed and not in a kilt. He wore thigh-hugging breeches and a white cotton shirt, but without a stock. He'd also shaved already and pulled his hair back in a neat queue.

He looked handsome. Devilishly handsome, as her cousins would have said.

"You know everyone wears his hair short in London nowadays," she said inanely.

"I am aware that I am not a tulip of fashion. But I'm also hungry. You'd best get down to the kitchen and give Roy direction."

"Doesn't he know what to do?"

Aidan feigned surprise. "But *you* are the lady of the castle. He needs your guidance. And then afterward, you can see about cleaning up the mess you complained about last night. I've got laundry. It backs up and Norval doesn't always deliver it to the wash woman in a timely fashion. There are a few rips I'd like you to mend and some darning. You'll understand what to do when you see it."

"You want me to darn?" she repeated, still sleepy.

"You do know how to use a needle and thread, don't you?"

Anne nodded.

"Then yes, I do." He walked toward the door. He stopped. "Oh yes, I invited Fang Mowat to go with me to the other side of Wick to look at some sheep. He's bringing his sons and they'll all be here for breakfast in"—he shrugged—"say ten minutes."

With that, he was out the door.

"Ten minutes?" Anne squeaked.

Aidan popped his head back in. "Fang has nine sons. They'll all be here. They like their mutton well done." He left again.

Anne thought she would swoon. "Thirteen for breakfast?" She started searching for her clothes sack in the mess of sheets, covers, and furs.

Chapter 6

Anne searched for what few hair pins she'd owned but they had been lost in the coach accident. It was disappointing. She would have liked to pin her hair high on her head and sweep regally down the stairs like a countess.

She compensated by tying her hair up with the blue ribbon, throwing a dress of sea foam green muslin trimmed in lace over her head, and hurrying downstairs to the kitchen, where she discovered Aidan hadn't been jesting. The room was full of men. Hungry men. They milled about in the way men do when it is time to be fed and they are waiting.

She recognized Fang Mowat. The gray-haired man stood out in the midst of what seemed an army of tall, strapping, handsome young men. His sons ranged in ages from the early twenties down to eleven, and each had a head of red hair of varying shades.

The dogs were there, too, weaving in and out of people's legs, looking for a scrap of food or a friendly pat. The smallest charged up to Anne, wagging his tail so hard it shook his whole body.

Aidan shouted for their attention. "Everyone, this is Anne, my countess. She will see to breakfast. Won't you, darling?"

Darling? Anne looked at his handsome, smiling countenance and knew he was up to something; she just didn't know what. "I'll check with the cook."

"Good, because Fang and his boys are starving."

Fang himself stepped forward. "Good morning, Lady Tiebauld," he said respectfully, his hat in his hand. "I thank you for inviting me and my boys for breakfast, especially on such short notice. Gives my Bonnie a bit of a break. Takes her a good long time to feed this horde, meal after meal."

Anne smiled her response. She was on to Aidan's trick. Did he think she would swoon or throw a fit? Or demand to return to London?

She'd show him. She'd serve the best breakfast Fang Mowat had ever had in his life. But first, "Aidan?" She motioned him closer to whisper in his ear. "Where is the kitchen?"

Oh, he loved that. His eyes danced with anticipation. "Let me show you." He took her arm and guided her across the room to a side hallway. They went out a door onto a small landing leading to a cook house.

Aidan banged on the door once and pushed his

way in. "Roy, look lively, now. The mistress has arrived."

Anne gagged at the condition of the kitchen. If she'd thought the great hall was bad, the state of the kitchen exceeded it a hundred times over.

The air smelled of cooking onions along with a dozen other different odors, some pleasant, some decidedly not. She covered her nose and looked around in horror. Dirty dishes were piled everywhere. A haunch of venison had been leaned against the table like a walking stick set aside. The meat dripped into a pool around it on the floor.

But the cook appeared the worst of all. Roy wore a dirty shirt over the breeches from the night before. In the daylight, stains of dried blood and whatever else could be seen clearly. His feet were still bare, but his hair was greasier, if such a thing were possible. He glared from his place behind a chopping block table.

"Why'd you bring her here, laird?" Roy asked rudely.

"Roy, she is my wife," Aidan said patiently. "She is here to direct you."

"I don't need no directing," he said, his burr rolling r's.

"But she is the lady of the manor. The kitchen is her responsibility."

"I've been running this kitchen, laird, since before the days you came. I've never needed direction before."

"I realize that," Aidan said soothingly. "But now we have a fine lady with us. *From London.* She will want to make improvements."

Roy lifted the heavy knife in his hand and brought it down with a resounding whack on the hare he'd been dressing. He cut the leg off clean. "We don't need no English opinions."

"Oh, it is not opinions she'll be giving, Roy," her husband hurried to assure him, "but guidance."

The cook's eyes narrowed. "Guidance on what?"

Aidan turned to Anne as if soliciting her opinion, but answered for both of them. "Whatever she desires," he replied easily. "Enjoy your morning, wifey. But don't dally. Fang's sons are hungry." He was out the door before she could respond.

Roy slid his beady eyes in her direction. "I've been running my own kitchen since I was tall enough to stand at this chopping block." He whacked off another rabbit leg for emphasis. "There's naught you can teach me."

Anne tried to appease the angry cook. "I don't want to teach you." She did want the kitchen clean, but thought it best not to broach that subject at this moment. "You continue what you are doing and I will watch."

"Why?"

She stumbled for words and then quickly gasped, "I hope to learn something."

He didn't believe her but with a grunt let her know she could do as she pleased, provided she didn't interfere with him. He proceeded to chop the rabbit meat into pieces, which he tossed into the bubbling stew pot.

Anne grew anxious. They were going to need help serving to so many guests. "Is Norval available?"

Roy had laid down his butcher knife and now wielded a wooden spoon like a scepter. He used it to point to a corner.

Anne followed his direction and discovered Norval asleep on some meal sacks. The old man was passed out cold. She tried to wake him with a hard shake, but to no avail. She slapped his cheeks. No response. She even pulled open an eyelid. He didn't wake.

"Is he dead?" she asked Roy.

In answer, Roy picked up a bowl containing water and tossed it on Norval, splashing some onto Anne at the same time.

"What? What? What?" the old servant sputtered.

Deciding to turn the other cheek and handle Roy's insolence with tolerance, she said quietly but firmly to Norval, "We have guests, and you are needed to serve them."

The old man had to crawl to a stool for help rising. His knees cracked loudly, and Anne worried for him. "What do you need done?" he asked, his eyes still half closed. He was obviously under the weather from overimbibing the night before.

"We need to wash bowls and spoons," she said. "You must fetch water."

"You don't need to wash those," Roy counter-manded her, nodding to the stack of dirty dishes. "There's a sand box over there. The food on them is dry. Rub a little sand on the plates and they'll be clean enough."

Anne had never heard of such a thing, but Norval had. This was obviously the standard practice. He shuffled over and began preparing bowls for stew. She decided she didn't think much of Roy's method as she watched Norval clean bowl after bowl with the same sand.

Her appetite for breakfast vanished, especially as Roy used his spoon to take a slurping taste of the soup.

She directed her attention away from Roy and poked around a bit. She knew what a kitchen needed. Before her Uncle Robert and Aunt Maeve, she'd lived with a distant cousin who had considered her little more than a servant. What little cooking skills her mother had taught her were refined in Cousin Gen's kitchen. She knew how to bake bread and that the loaves should be started in the morning . . . although she didn't see any.

"Are you baking bread today?" she asked Roy.

He ignored her. Norval began setting bowls out on a huge wooden tray.

Roy's insolence miffed Anne. She also knew she couldn't continue to let it go unchallenged, espe-cially in front of another servant. She walked over to the chopping block where he was cutting off turnip heads.

"I asked if you were baking bread today?"

The cook's lip curled in derision. "No need. The laird won't be here."

"But I will be. Furthermore, he'll be back this evening and expect something to eat."

"He won't want bread," Roy answered. "He drinks his dinner. Ale gives him everything he needs." He turned his back on her.

Anne stared at him, wishing she could make him vanish with a blink of her eyes. But that wasn't going to happen. She came around to his side of the chopping block. "Roy, I want you to bake bread."

Norval had stopped his chore to watch the exchange. Both Anne and Roy were conscious of their audience. A well-trained servant would have acquiesced to her request.

Roy was not well trained.

His pig eyes traveled the length of her person with such insolence that Anne felt the color rise to her cheeks.

And then, he made a gargling sound in his throat and spat into the stew.

Anne stared in shock. She pulled her gaze from the distasteful spittle congealing in the middle of the stew to the cook's face. He was grinning at her. "Would you like for me to do it again?" he said almost pleasantly.

A red haze descended over Anne's mind. "You

are the most disgusting person I have ever met," she announced.

Her words didn't have any impact on Roy until she picked up the butcher knife. What? Did he think he was the only one who knew how to handle a cleaver?

"Get out of my kitchen," she said, in a voice she could barely recognize as her own.

Roy wasn't laughing now. "Come along, my lady. You'd best put the knife down."

She sliced the air with it, inches from his belly. "Not until you leave." She brought the cleaver down with a resounding "thwack" on the chopping block, neatly splitting a turnip in half.

By the time she turned to threaten him again, Roy was off and heading toward the door. Anne followed. "And don't come back until you have a little respect," she told him, slamming the door in his wake for emphasis.

She'd seen him run in the direction of the great hall. She knew his type. He was probably going to whine to Aidan and weasel himself into looking like the abused party.

She faced Norval. "Dish up that stew."

The old man was practically shaking. She had to lay down the cleaver before he could take a step, but she'd never seen him move so fast or efficiently. He had thirteen bowls of piping hot stew ladled out in a wink. He picked up the tray with more strength than she would have credited him.

"Come along," Anne said, and led the way to the great hall.

Everything was as she'd expected. The men were sitting, impatiently waiting for breakfast while Roy held center stage accusing her of being out of her wits. His knees still shook.

It pleased her to make an entrance looking like the very soul of civility. "Are you ready for your breakfast?" she asked sweetly. Without waiting for an answer, she nodded to Norval to start serving.

"Roy has been telling us a fascinating story, my lady," Aidan said.

Anne glanced at the cook, who blanched. She smiled at her husband. "Oh, really? Is it believable?" Out of the corner of her eye, she noticed Deacon had already dug into his stew with gusto.

Nothing could have pleased her more.

Aidan leaned forward, his eyes bright with curiosity. "He said you threatened his life with his own meat cleaver."

"I did." Fang and his sons were now gobbling the stew. Everyone had touched it but Aidan. Drat. She could postpone the coup de grâce no longer. "Did he tell you why?"

"He said you were a madwoman."

"I *was* absolutely furious," she admitted. "Especially after he spat into the soup you are all eating."

She looked right at Deacon when she said those words, and the satisfaction of seeing his jaw drop with a spoonful of soup in his mouth made her want to do a jig!

Spoons hit the table. Fang's sons spat the contents of their mouths back into their bowls. The dogs, who were begging under the table, went wild with the commotion.

Fang stood. "Is that true?" he demanded of Roy.

Roy appeared ready to collapse. He shot a pleading glance to Norval, who quickly side-stepped away, lest he also be accused.

"I meant nothing by it," Roy said, a tremor in his voice. "All cooks do it."

The men at the table stared in dumbfounded silence a minute, a few a bit green in the gills. Then Fang's oldest son stood and yelled, "I don't think we should let him off easy, lads. I say, he deserves a dunk in the privy!"

His words were met by a roar of approval, and before Anne realized what was happening, the Mowat boys jumped over the table to descend upon Roy, who took off running. He headed for the kitchen door, but Deacon tackled him and the hapless cook was hoisted high and carried out the front door.

Anne watched the mob of boys, men, and barking, excited dogs in a state of shock. It had all happened so quickly.

She turned to the dais. The table had been knocked over. Bowls and stew were everywhere. Several of the dogs had stayed behind to lap up the bounty on the floor.

And there was Aidan. He sat in his chair exactly as he had before chaos had over taken his great hall. He was watching her.

"Happy?"

"I didn't expect such a reaction," she allowed.

He rose and stepped down from the dais. With a catlike grace, he approached. "Well done, lady wife," he said in a voice as smooth as silk. "You flipped the tables neatly, no pun intended."

She didn't answer. She was wary of him now, waiting for the next game he wanted to play.

He stopped, so close she could make out the weave in his shirt. She caught a whiff of sandalwood and orange oil and intimately knew from where it had come.

She was also becoming familiar in a way only a wife could with other things—like the muscles of his chest, or the size and breadth of his hands.

He tilted her chin up to look at him. He had a lovely mouth. She had not noticed it before. Now, she couldn't take her eyes off it.

He spoke. "*Touché*, Anne. You've been very clever."

"Do you think Roy will be back?"

"I doubt it. And you have dinner to prepare . . ."

He said the last with mock sadness. She knew he was certain the task would overwhelm her.

It almost did. She hid behind her pride, refusing to be intimidated. "Are you having guests for supper tonight?"

He pretended to consider a moment. "No. Just Hugh, Deacon, and me."

"Deacon should be more careful whenever he sits at my table."

Aidan's eyes sparkled and he laughed with genuine amusement. "I think he learned a lesson this morning."

She nodded mutely. When he smiled and looked at her with admiration and a hint of something else, something she couldn't quite define, it was difficult for her to breathe, let alone think.

"Have a good day, wife," he said, and left to join the others. As he opened the front door in the alcove, Anne heard Fang's sons yelling outside. ". . . three . . . four—!" The door closed behind Aidan.

She started to have a little sympathy for Roy.

Looking around, she searched for Norval. They had a lot of work to do, but the servant had disappeared. Frowning, she hunted for him in the kitchen. He wasn't there.

He was either taking a nap . . . or could he have bolted?

Anne stood in the center of the filthy kitchen and realized she was defeated. She couldn't clean this room in a week, let alone in a day. And then there were the great hall, the bedrooms, the laundry, the candles, and those ridiculous rushes.

It was enough to make her want to return to London.

And that was what he wanted, wasn't it?

The door opened. "Excuse me, my lady?" a woman's soft voice said.

Anne turned. A group of women crowded in holding buckets, mops, and brooms. She pushed a stray lock of her hair back. "May I help you?"

A rosy-cheeked woman stepped forward. Her eyes were the blue of the sky on a sunny day, her hair the red of a rusty nail. She bobbed a curtsey. "My lady, we don't mean to intrude, but we've come to welcome you to Kelwin. I'm Bonnie Mowat. I'm the mother of that brood of boys you fed this morning."

Anne was surprised such a tiny woman could birth such strapping sons. In her bitter frustration she couldn't help saying, "Welcome me? Do you mean you don't mind that I am English?"

Mrs. Mowat laughed. "We despaired of the laird ever getting married. There isn't a lad in the parish, including mine, who feels his obligation to settle down and raise a family, because they all want to ape the ways of the bold and heroic Laird Tiebauld. Oh, don't mistake my meaning. The laird is a great, generous man. There's none like him . . . but he's been needing a wife. You've done us a favor, my lady. A great favor."

It was on the tip of Anne's tongue to tell them she'd be sent back to London posthaste after today, but she didn't. She wasn't ready to admit defeat— yet. "Thank you, Mrs. Mowat. I appreciate your welcome."

A tall, silver-haired woman pushed forward. "I'm Kathleen Keith. You know my son, Hugh?"

"Yes, I've met him," Anne said.

Kathleen smiled with a mother's pride. "I'd like to see him married too. He's a fine lad, but the time has come he made me a grandmother." She turned to the women close to her. "This is Mary MacEwan and her daughter Fenella." Mary looked almost as young as her daughter, who was a lovely strawberry blonde.

Suddenly, Kathleen changed the subject. "I understand Roy is gone."

Anne didn't know how to answer. Were they his friends? Would they blame her for his fate? "Well . . . he—"

"You don't need to explain," Kathleen said in her forthright manner. "It's good riddance to him and to his lazy wife, too. I hope they run all the way to Edinburgh. But you'll be needing a cook, and Mary and Fenella are the best in the village."

Anne hesitated. Aidan hadn't said anything about household accounts or hiring servants.

Bonnie read her mind. "If Laird Tiebauld can spend what he does on sheep, then he can spare a few coins for a good meal every night at his table."

She lowered her voice to confide, "Mary's husband died last month. The laird slipped her a bit then. I know he has been worrying about her. He'll be pleased if you hire her."

Anne gestured to encompass the kitchen. "I don't know if it is a position you would want," she told Mary. "The place is—" She broke off with a shake of her head. There were no words adequate enough to describe the mess.

"It will be fine," Mary assured her. "Nothing is wrong here that good hard work and soap won't clean."

"Oh, yes," Anne agreed. "But I don't know if there is enough soap to meet all the needs of Kelwin."

"That's why we're here," Mrs. Keith said proudly. "We've come to welcome you, and to offer our help. I've been itching to get my fingers on that mush of stems and leaves the laird takes such pride in on the floor of his hall."

"I'd like to see it gone, too," Anne agreed.

A sly smile lifted the corners of Mrs. Keith's mouth. "Then let's see it gone together . . . before he comes home."

"I can't expect you to help—" Anne started to protest but Mrs. Mowat shushed her.

"It's a housewarming we are giving you, my lady. If we'd known you were coming, we would have forced our way in before your arrival."

"Yes," Mrs. Keith agreed. "We would have barricaded those bachelors—and their dogs, too!—out of the castle, and scoured the place with boiling water."

"It needs it," Anne said. "But it is almost too big a job, even for us."

"Och," Mrs. Mowat said, taking Anne's arm and leading her forward. "It's not just us. Come along, my lady, and meet the rest of the women in the village. They are outside waiting."

Mrs. Keith swooped in to take her other arm. "And they are armed with buckets, brooms, and mops."

"And enough soap to scrub every brick in this drafty place," Mrs. Mowat added.

As Anne stepped outside, the sun came out from behind a bank of clouds and she caught her breath. What they'd said was true. There were close to fifteen women and their children of all ages waiting to pay their respects. Their names ran together during those initial introductions in her mind, but she would never forget their welcoming smiles. Each of them was unique and special.

"I can't believe you are all so generous," Anne told them. "This isn't going to be easy."

Mrs. Mowat gave her arm a squeeze. "We don't mind. We do this because you are one of us now. You are the laird's wife. The Lady of Kelwin."

For a moment, Anne couldn't speak. Their open-armed acceptance swept her away. Nothing like this had ever happened to her before.

She was one of them.

Mrs. Keith took charge. "Let's clean," she cried out like a commander leading the troops into battle, and the women sallied forth.

Chapter 7

The trip to McKenzie's to buy sheep was a hard one for Aidan. He usually took pleasure in the company of Fang's sons, although this time only the eldest four rode along. Their good-natured rivalry and bantering tended to make him laugh. Plus it was a good day for traveling. He should have enjoyed himself.

But he didn't.

In the past, the eldest boys, Thomas and Douglas, rode with him. Now, they stayed close to Deacon—and the others followed their brothers. There was a new sense of manliness about the lads, a determined set to their jaws, an unspoken purpose that Aidan hadn't seen before, and he feared the source.

Deacon had recruited them. When the time came, they would march against the English.

On the return trip, he nudged Beaumains closer to Fang's horse. Ahead of them, Hugh, Deacon and the boys were making outrageous wagers and laughing whenever someone lost.

"Are you really going to let your sons go with Robbie and Deacon Gunn?" he asked Fang.

The old man's eyes hardened and then softened on a weary sigh. "Do I have a choice? Thomas and Douglas are men full grown. William and Andrew are old enough to make their own decisions, too."

Aidan rode in silence for a moment, then said, "I have known your sons since the youngest was a toddler. I don't want to see them go to war."

"Strange words from the descendant of Fighting Donner Black. Especially since Deacon told me you were in."

"He did?" Aidan frowned. "He goes too far. I have yet to commit myself."

"But you are smuggling in the gunpowder."

A trap seemed to close in around Aidan. "Aye."

"Then you are in, Laird."

Aidan rubbed the polished leather of Beaumains, reins between his gloved fingers. "I hope to avoid it. My family knows first-hand war is never a solution. My grandfather taught me the lesson."

Fang shook his head in sad agreement. "Aye, but sometimes, Laird, a man must make his own decisions—even if it has dangerous consequences. I canna stop my sons from being the men they must be. They are young and full of spirit. If there is a war, they will go."

"Would you join them?"

There was a heartbeat of silence. "Do I have a choice? I must protect them. I canna let them go without me. They are my heart."

The trip lost all of its luster for Aidan after Fang's words. The Mowats were an important part of Aidan's clan. He couldn't imagine not having them around Kelwin . . . if there still would be a Kelwin.

Deacon had been right. Too soon the time would come when he could no longer hover between the two factions but must choose a side. Either way, his clan stood to lose.

The sun was setting when they rode into the courtyard where Fang's youngest sons and their friends waited to take in the horses. They loved to act as Aidan's groomsmen.

Handing Beaumains' reins to Davey, he paused, listening. "Why are the dogs barking?"

"Because you are here, Laird. They've been happy up till now," Davey said.

"Where are they?"

"In the stables."

The stables? Aidan had always given them the run of his estate.

Sure enough, when one of the boys opened the stable doors, the whole group of hounds charged Aidan, who rubbed their heads with true affection.

"What are you doing out here?" he asked them.

Davey answered. "Our lady said they'd be happier here with the other animals and so they have been."

Aidan frowned. Anne had ordered the dogs to the stables? He turned to Fang. "Will you come in?"

"No, Bonnie will be waiting." He bade Aidan farewell and left with his sons.

Aidan nodded. Hugh and Deacon had already gone in. He followed and then stopped abruptly when he discovered them standing in the doorway leading to the great hall, expressions of stupefied wonder on their faces.

He pushed his way through, and then it was his turn to gape. The room was more than clean; it sparkled. The rushes were gone, but he didn't notice their absence until he'd been favorably impressed by all the other changes.

Two chairs sat in front of the hearth with a small footstool for comfort and a colorful rag rug for warmth. The table had been set with covers over delicious smelling food. Hot food.

Hugh's stomach grumbled. When the other two looked at him, he whispered, "I can't help it. I'm hungry." He entered first, heading for the table. Halfway across the room, he made a small circle and said happily, "Can you believe it? It's a miracle."

"It's not a bloody miracle. It's housekeeping," Deacon muttered as he marched in a straight line for the ale keg by the fireplace.

The dogs followed him in, but they too acted out of place. Some moved toward the fire, York charged after Hugh, but they all ended sitting on the floor, their brown eyes searching the room as if asking where the bones and smells had gone. They were obviously ill-at-ease without them.

"Tiebauld, you should come eat." Hugh pulled his chair out at the table. "It's fantastic! There's a feast here fit for a king." He lifted a slice of meat, the juice dripping from it, and plopped it in his mouth.

Since he'd had no breakfast, Aidan quickly joined him. It was an amazing meal. He couldn't remember the last time his table had been set correctly. Under the dish covers were slices of tender mutton, peas, and boiled potatoes. But what had really excited Hugh was the fresh bread.

He bit into it and pretended to faint. " 'Tis better than my mother's."

"You had better not let her hear you say that," Deacon responded. He'd been hanging back, a victim of his own suspicious nature, but now he wandered closer. He lifted the covers on his own plate—and sat down.

The three men made a good meal. But there wasn't any sign of Anne.

Norval crept in when they were about finished. "May I remove the dishes, my lord?" At Aidan's assent, he docilely went around the table, clearing dishes. His hair was even combed.

Aidan stared, dumbfounded.

"How did she do it?" Hugh asked the question Aidan wanted answered.

"She's new," Deacon replied impatiently, his mouth

full. "He wants to please a new mistress. Servants behave in that manner."

"But a clean Norval is something I'd never thought to see before I died," Hugh countered.

"I think I will find out the truth," Aidan answered, rising from his chair.

"Are you going to go ask Norval?" Deacon said.

"No, I'm going to go find Anne."

Deacon muttered something unintelligible, but Aidan didn't care to listen. Anne's success had piqued his curiosity. Since when did London debutantes know the intricacies of house cleaning?

He bounded up the stairs taking them two at a time. A torch lit the hallway. He went to the guest room. She wasn't there, but he did notice the bed had been made with clean sheets. Cobwebs, dust, and grime had disappeared as if they had never existed.

Not bothering with the other rooms, Aidan walked straight to his. He opened the door.

His room had never been kept as poorly as the rest of the house, but there were obvious signs of cleaning here too. Dust had been swept away and wood polished with oil.

Two candles gave the room a soft light and there was the smell of cloves in the air. His bath waited, warming in front of the fire in the hearth. His soap was dry and his towel hung exactly where he liked it. But there was no sign of Anne.

Until he turned to the bed.

She lay there, fully dressed and fast asleep, her braid a silky band across the sable spread. Dark circles marred the tender skin beneath her eyes. Her hands were roughened red from hard work.

Guilt pricked his conscience. He walked over to her. "Anne?"

She didn't move.

He understood how hard she slept. There had been days at Kelwin when he'd dragged himself up the stairs and fallen on his bed, unable to have taken another step even to undress himself.

Funny, but he'd never noticed the graceful line of her neck before . . . and the faint birthmark located right under the curve of her jaw. He'd found her attractive from the beginning. Her stormy eyes were her most spectacular feature and she did have long legs . . . but now he saw other things, refinements, the details one perceived only after having lived with another for a while.

He removed her shoes from her feet. She'd ruined the heel of her stockings. There was a huge hole there. He wondered what she'd done. He was also going to have to get her sturdier shoes. Kid slippers were fine for tapping toes to a musical beat at some ball or spending a day in idle shopping, but not suitable for highland life.

Stunned by the direction of his thoughts, Aidan dropped the shoes. They landed on the floor, one thud followed by another. He backed away. He was not going to buy shoes for Anne. Buying good sturdy shoes for a woman was a more personal act than purchasing perfume or jewelry or even a closet of silky small clothes.

When you bought practical shoes for a woman, she was your wife!

He headed for the door, needing to put distance between himself and Anne. Good food and cleanliness had sparked these thoughts, he assured himself. He would never have had them otherwise. Besides, every bachelor had weak moments when his belly was full.

Deacon met him in the hall. "I discovered what happened, Tiebauld," he announced pompously. "The English lass didn't do this all herself. She hired Mrs. MacEwan and her daughter Fenella to cook. The village women came in to clean. Norval said there was an army of them."

Aidan stared at him, barely comprehending his words, and when meaning did sink in, he frowned. "Of course she didn't do this all herself."

"You knew it?"

"She couldn't have. Think, Deacon, my stables were cleaner than this house. She couldn't have done it all in one day."

His brows came together. "You aren't angry to find out she cheated?"

Aidan silently begged for patience. "It wasn't a game, Deacon. There was no cheating."

"I thought you were hoping she'd grow so frustrated with the task, she'd leave."

"I was."

"But?"

Aidan sliced the air with his hand. "But nothing. I set up the task. She performed it."

"She hired a cook! Did she ask you? What sort of wife hires servants without permission from her husband?"

"A sensible one," he snapped, and then growled in frustration at his defense of Anne. "I don't consider her my wife," he said more for himself than Deacon. He drew a deep breath. "I am not displeased she hired Mrs. MacEwan to cook. I've been meaning to do something about Roy for ages. Anne has taken a load off my mind—"

"But the Danes—"

"I know," he said, cutting Deacon off. He shot a warning glance toward his bedroom door. They must be careful of every word. Deacon, like his brother Robbie, often let his temper overrule his good sense.

Deacon lowered his voice. "Their signal could come at any time." Shepherds and village men kept watch nightly in Kelwin's left tower for the Danes' signal, a green and red light raised and lowered at the same time.

Aidan didn't know Anne well enough to trust her. "I will have to be harder on her tomorrow," he said. "She'll leave . . . eventually."

"What if the Danes come tonight?"

"If they send the signal tonight, she'll not know a thing. She's so tired she might as well be dead."

"Now that could be a solution."

"Deacon!"

"I was joking," his friend said.

Aidan wasn't so certain. "I'll have no harm coming to her. If it does, you answer to me."

"A joke, a wee joke," Deacon reiterated.

"Yes, like your talk of a rebellion. That's the way it started, you and Robbie playing 'what if.' Now Fang's sons are among those involved."

"And all your neighbors."

"Not all. I can't imagine Argyll and Sutherland anxious for such a thing."

"They are some of those we are revolting against." But he understood Aidan's point and changed the subject. "So what are you going to have her do tomorrow? Build chicken coops? Patch the cracks in the walls? The keep itself is immaculate right now."

Aidan smiled thinly. "Coops aren't a bad idea, but I'm ready for my bed."

"Your bed? Where she is?" Deacon asked cynically.

"Relax. I'm sleeping in the guest room. She *will* leave. A plan will come to me before morning. By the way, when you go back downstairs, tell Norval to put the dogs back in the stables."

Deacon shifted uncomfortably before admitting,

"You said they'd cleaned all the rooms up here. I thought perhaps I'd claim one for myself."

"It's nice to have clean sheets, hmmm?"

Deacon shrugged, then confided, "Norval says they smell of fresh air."

"You are welcome to a room, Deacon. Pleasant dreams." He went to the guest room.

Tomorrow, a plan to scare her off would come to him before tomorrow . . . but his last thought before drifting to sleep was that the sheets did smell of the sweet highland air they'd dried in.

Anne sat up and stretched. Every muscle in her body ached. Outside, the sun was just rising over the North Sea. For a moment, the beauty of the brightening sky captured her attention and then she glanced around the room. The tub and towel were where she'd had Norval place them last night.

Had Aidan not come home?

She'd assumed he would wake her. For no other reason than to tell her to get out of his bed, she mused. But she had wanted to see the expression on his face when he first walked into the great hall.

She put her legs over the edge of the bed and frowned at the wrinkles in her dress. Why did she fall asleep in it?

She had plans for this day, finishing touches she wanted to add. There was no time for pressing a dress. She knew better than to ask Norval to do it.

The man should be pensioned off and given a cottage of his own. He was too old to work so hard, and yet yesterday he had gamely kept up with the women. She'd talk to Aidan about the issue later.

But first, she had to dress. She chose a periwinkle sprigged muslin that made her feel like spring had arrived. It was her best dress of those left from the wreck. Wisely, she threw on a yellow Kashmir shawl because the air was damp, especially this time of year.

Her hair was another problem. She grew tired of the braid and so tied it with a scarf. She was too old for such a style, but without pins there was nothing she could do.

Slipping on her shoes, she left the room.

In the hallway, she noticed the door to the guest room she'd been using was slightly ajar. Curiosity urged her to tiptoe quietly and take a peek to see if Aidan was home.

He was. The misty dawn light through the narrow window highlighted his body; he lay sprawled out on his back. His large frame took up the whole bed.

He was naked—or at least, she thought he was. His chest was bare and his long legs hung out beneath sheets that covered him enough across the middle to keep him decent.

She couldn't help but admire him. Her husband was a handsome man, but it was the strength and grace in his hands and feet that captured her attention. She'd always been attracted to men with strong hands . . . but the feet. A shiver went through her. Bare feet were intimate. No one save your lover saw your feet.

The word "lover" sent a wave of heat down to the pit of her stomach.

Anne hoped they would consummate the marriage soon. What she had once considered with grave reservations, she now daydreamed about with a combined sense of curiosity and anticipation.

She was about to close the door and let him sleep when some imp of mischief caught hold of her mind. The idea was so vivid, she couldn't shake it, even knowing there would be repercussions.

But he deserved it.

Anne eased into the room. Aidan didn't even move.

On silent cat feet, she walked to the bed, grabbed hold of the mattress, and yanked it up with the intention of toppling him over onto the floor as he'd done to her the day before.

But her plan didn't work as she'd expected. For one reason, he was heavy and her muscles were sore. She could barely get the mattress to budge.

For the second, once roused, he could move with lightning speed. His hand grabbed her by the bodice of her dress and threw her down on the bed. He pinned her in place with his body, his forearm pressing her chest, his hands around her throat.

Anne couldn't breathe. She stared up at her husband, fearing the madman he'd become.

Slowly, he focused on who she was. "Anne?"

She nodded, unable to speak. Frowning, he lifted his arm. "What are you doing here?"

Her lungs filled with fresh air. She went to rise, but his hand came down on the other side of her, barring an escape.

"You were going to dump me out of the bed," he accused, answering his own question.

"What if I was? I owe you a dump," she said sulkily, all too aware of his legs alongside hers and the warmth of his body heat. The man was a furnace. A woman would never be chilled sleeping by his side.

He chuckled at the thought of a dump on the floor, before pronouncing her a "little minx." She started to retort, but he was climbing out of bed, and giving her a very good view of a well-formed male bum. She'd been right: he had been sleeping naked.

Words died in Anne's throat.

He reached for his breeches and with an economy of movement pulled them on before facing her. "I didn't hurt you, did I?" he asked, fastening the buttons. "You should know better than to sneak up on a man in his sleep."

She rubbed her throat, sitting up. "Don't you think you are carrying your medieval fascination a bit too far?"

He laughed. "It isn't my medievalism that made me respond. Man is a natural protector. Any man would have reacted as I did."

"No, not any man. Most would be sleeping soundly."

"And end up dumped on the floor." He squatted in front of her. "Here, let me have a look at you."

His hair was sleep mussed. An overnight growth of beard shadowed his jaw. The effect on her senses was a bit overwhelming . . . especially when he tilted her chin so he could see better. He ran his fingers lightly ran over the pulse point of her throat.

She wondered if he noticed how rapidly her heart was beating.

"You are going to have a bruise. It's red right now, but the redness will fade." He dropped his hands and sat back. "What will they think in London when they see it?"

She didn't say anything. What could she say— that she was not returning to London? She tired of repeating herself. That she wondered why he wasn't as affected by her nearness as she was by his? She didn't know if she wanted to hear the answer.

"This is yours, isn't it?" He picked up her yellow Kashmir shawl and offered it to her.

Anne took it, so disappointed in his insistence she leave, she couldn't look at him. She rose from the bed. He stood with her, but took a step back. "I didn't really hurt you, did I?" he asked, misinterpreting her silence.

Wrapping the shawl around her shoulders, she said, "I'm fine."

Her words came out sharper than she'd intended. He drew back, then reached for his shirt draped over the footboard, giving her his back. In a casual but studied tone, he said, "You have impressed me, Anne. What you have done to Kelwin is beyond belief."

You have impressed me, Anne. So stiff, so impersonal. But then, what had she expected?

Something more, her imagination whispered.

"Thank you," she replied, her voice as carefully neutral as his. "I'd best check on the kitchen." She would have run out of the room but then remembered a detail she'd better tell him before he found out from Deacon. "I hired Mrs. MacEwan as a cook."

"Fine. Do whatever you need to do." Polite, distant, proper.

"Yes, thank you." She escaped and didn't draw a full, easy breath until she was down the stairs and into the great hall.

For a second, she leaned against the stone wall.

Anne was not so naïve she didn't realize what was happening to her. She'd been attracted to many, but none had ever made the impact on her senses as Aidan had. Her heart still raced from being on the mattress beneath him ... and she was light-headed—giddy, even ... and furiously angry at his stubbornness, his coldness. She was not a stranger. She was his wife.

And, she was falling in love.

Love. It was not what she'd imagined it. No bells sounded. No birds sang. The heavens didn't open.

Instead, love slipped quietly past one's defenses. It stole your heart before you even realized it was in danger.

She stared at the wedding band on her finger. She hadn't removed it since the bishop had placed it there. She would never take it off.

In this single moment of insight, her life changed in a way she'd not expected . . . in a way she could not yet fathom. Dazed, she made her way to the kitchen.

Mrs. MacEwan and her daughter were busy cooking. The smell of fresh bread permeated the air. Sausages sizzled in a pan over the fire.

"Good morning, my lady," Mrs. MacEwan greeted her happily. "Would you like a cup of tea before breakfast? I've been brewing a pot."

"Yes, please," Anne said, pleased with the atmosphere of the busy kitchen and surprised to see Hugh was there. He'd stepped back into the shadows of the pantry but now came forward.

"Good morning, my lady," he said almost sheepishly.

"Good morning," she returned with uncertainty until she noticed a blush on Fenella's cheeks. So that was the way the wind blew.

She hid her smile while accepting a cup of tea

from Mrs. MacEwan. There was a small pitcher of milk on the table. She was reaching for it when Mrs. MacEwan exclaimed, "What happened to your neck? It's all red."

Anne had almost forgotten about the bruises. She rubbed her neck lightly. "It's nothing. I barely notice it."

"Nothing?" Mrs. MacEwan said. Her eyes flashed. "There are finger marks. Who did that to you?"

"I woke my husband—"

She didn't get a chance to say another word. "The laird did such a thing? Heaven's mercy!"

"Tiebauld would never hurt a woman," Hugh said loyally.

"He's right," Anne stressed. "It was an accident."

"You mean he really *choked* you?" Hugh demanded.

"Not on purpose. I woke him. He was surprised." Anne could see her words of explanation fell on deaf ears. She decided to retreat. "Is breakfast almost ready to be served?"

"In a moment," Mrs. MacEwan replied briskly, obviously upset.

Anne went into the great hall. Aidan already sat at the table, talking in earnest with Deacon, who frowned when she entered the room . . . but was it her imagination, or did he seem less set against her than he had previously?

She hoped it was so.

Stepping up on the dais, she could have taken a seat next to her husband, but she suddenly turned shy. It was almost hard to look at him. Like yesterday, he wore leather breeches, well-worn boots, and a white shirt. He'd slicked his wet hair back from his face, and she could smell the scent of his shaving soap. It had become a heady fragrance for her.

She took a seat down the table from him.

He didn't seem to notice where she sat. He and Deacon were discussing the sheep they had purchased the day before. Much of their talk was of little interest to her. She spent her time almost slavishly, but covertly, staring dreamy-eyed at her husband.

Mrs. MacEwan served breakfast while Fenella followed with the additional plates. Mrs. MacEwan made a great show of placing a board of piping hot bread in the center of the table. Then she set a plate of sausages in front of Anne. She served Deacon next.

Aidan smiled. "Sausages are my favorite breakfast." His eyes almost twinkled with expectancy.

Mrs. MacEwan slid his plate in front of him and Aidan's smile fell. His sausages were blacker than two pieces of coal. He looked to Deacon's plate, then Anne's, and finally raised his gaze to Mrs. MacEwan.

"Aren't my sausages a bit overdone?"

"Burned to a crisp," Mrs. MacEwan said proudly. "Which is what I'll do to you if you ever harm our precious countess again."

Embarrassed, Fenella tried to divert her mother and pull her back to the kitchen, but Mrs. MacEwan was on a mission.

"Your wife," she said, "is a fine, fine lady."

"She's English," Deacon said, his mouth full of sausage.

Mrs. MacEwan whirled on him. "She's the laird's wife and one of us now. You should have seen her yesterday. She worked harder than anyone!"

Deacon shot Aidan a glance that said clearly, *I told you so.*

But Aidan ignored him. Instead, he said, "Thank you, Mrs. MacEwan."

She made a hasty curtsey. "I dinna mean any disrespect, Laird."

"I understand, Mrs. MacEwan."

"Enjoy your breakfast, Laird."

"I will."

She turned and left the room, her expression satisfied. Fenella hurried behind, her expression mortified.

Anne was almost afraid to look at her husband. When she did, she found he was eating the burned sausages.

He met her gaze. "My clansmen are an independent lot," he said, explaining Mrs. MacEwan's behavior to her unspoken question.

Deacon burst out laughing. "They're Scottish!" Aidan started laughing with him. The two were laughing so hard, they had trouble finishing their breakfasts and even Anne was caught up in their mood.

But if she thought Aidan was done with her, she was wrong. No sooner had they finished their meal than he said, "Come with me, Anne." He started out the front door. She had to skip to catch up.

"Where are we going?" she asked.

"You'll see."

She followed quietly a moment and then, "Have you, Deacon, and Hugh always been friends?"

"We're actually cousins. All related in distant ways, the way many of we highlanders are. They came to me when I first arrived and told me I wasn't fit to be laird until I could best them."

"So did you?"

"Not on the first go round."

"Go round? What did you do?"

"I wrestled them."

Her nose scrunched in distaste at such an activity. "You wrestled? Isn't that considered common?"

"Yes, it is a very common sport, and we had a bloody good time at it, too." He continued across the courtyard and up a path to the stables, which was a stone barn not quite as old as the main house. A gull flying on the currents overhead called mockingly to her.

"Why are we here?" she asked.

"You'll know in a moment." He walked in.

One of Fang's youngest sons and his friend were waiting for him. "We turned them out, Laird."

"Good job, Davey," Aidan said to the Mowat boy.

Anne looked around, impressed. There were thirty boxes. "Do you have this many animals?" A fat yellow-orange tabby who appeared to be an outstanding mouser greeted her by rubbing against her skirt.

"I have seven, including Beaumains. It's enough for my needs."

"Indubitably," Anne murmured.

He shot her a glance as if he wasn't certain she didn't tease him. Remembering her conversation with Norval the first night, she asked, "Do you breed horses?"

"I'm thinking about it, but sheep have always been king here. You should see the sheep sheds. They are four times this size."

"Where are they?"

"About a half mile toward Wick and further inland. The earls of Tiebauld learned long ago it wasn't wise to keep livestock too near the coast, where raiders could easily steal them." He lifted a manure fork. "Davey, you and your friend run along now."

"Don't you want us to muck out the boxes?" Davey asked.

"No," Aidan said.

"Aye, but they be needing it, Laird. If we don't do it, who will?"

Aidan smiled. "My wife."

Chapter 8

Anne stood in her yellow Kashmir shawl and fine periwinkle morning dress and couldn't believe her ears. "You're joking."

Aidan shook his head, as the two boys ran off. Holding the manure fork high, he asked, "Have you been around horses, Anne?"

"I had a pony as a child." She still didn't want to believe.

"Good. Then I won't have to explain it all to you. I like new bedding laid daily. It is better for their hooves."

"Mucking a stall is simple enough." She frowned. "But you can't expect me to do it dressed like this?"

He acted as if he'd just noticed her fine clothes. "Do you have anything else to wear?"

"Hardly. You know I lost most of my clothes when the trunk broke. They were blown every which way. You were going to send someone to see about fetching what had to be left behind. Did you?"

He snapped his fingers. "I forgot. I'm sorry, Anne. I'll send someone to do it now. Also, I had word this morning from the Reverend Oliphant in Thurso. He will arrive this afternoon to bury your coachman."

Anne nodded, suddenly solemn. It was a relief to know Todd would be given a decent ceremony. "I need to write your sister and tell her. I was so busy yesterday . . ." Her voice trailed off. She was usually very good about details. She rarely put off even unpleasant tasks, but Todd had died and she'd yet to inform anyone. Worse, she hadn't given him a moment's thought the day before. "Poor man."

"Yes," Aidan agreed soberly, then brightened. "All right. As I said, not all the boxes are in use. Muck the ones that need it and see fresh hay is laid."

"You really are going to make me do it?" Anne felt her temper begin to sizzle.

He was all innocence. "Anne, I thought you wanted to be my countess."

Incoherent words of anger twisted her tongue. She swallowed them back, tasting bitter bile. To think she'd almost imagined herself in love with this, this, this—she searched her mind for the worst word she could think of—*bounder!*

In a voice shaking with her effort for control, she said, "I'll do what you want because I won't give you the satisfaction of making me run. I won't return to London."

She grabbed the manure fork out of his hands. Her cheerful yellow shawl fell down over one shoulder. She shook it off and shoved it right into his stomach. "Here, take this to the house." In spite of his abdomen being hard as the stone walls around them, she caught him off guard. His grunt of pain gave her great pleasure.

Anne marched into the first stall and picked her way gingerly through the straw to a pile of manure. Her hair flopped forward into her face. With an irritated shake of her head, she rested the fork handle against her chest and quickly braided it. "I wish I had pins," she muttered.

"What did you say?" Aidan asked.

"Nothing to you," she snapped. "Why are you lingering around here? Or don't you think I can muck without supervision?"

He laughed at her display of temper. "I rolled the wheelbarrow out for the muck. When you're done, take it out back and there is a place to dump it. You'll know where immediately."

"I'm sure I will," she echoed, images of overturning the load on his boots making the situation more palatable.

"Well," he hedged with a sly, wicked, ungrateful smile—how had she ever thought his smile charming?—"I've other matters to attend to. Enjoy."

She grimaced through clenched teeth. She wouldn't give him the satisfaction of defeat. Picking up the fork, she scooped manure and carried it to the wheelbarrow.

This was not a task one did in a skirt one wanted to keep unsoiled.

Anne efficiently cleaned the stall and moved on to the next, planning to lay fresh straw in all the stalls when she'd finished. Already she itched from the chaff stirred up into the air. A blister started to form on her right hand which had been tender from the work the day before.

The whole situation was deeply humiliating!

Halfway through cleaning the second stall, she'd almost convinced herself to find Aidan and tell him she wanted to leave for London this very day. He could go to the devil. She'd take the life of a lady's companion over being his wife and personal drudge. She doubted any woman would wish to marry such an egotistical, self-satisfied, irritating—

The sound of a footstep by the wheelbarrow broke off her thoughts in mid-tirade. She looked up over the box wall, hoping it was Aidan. If it was, she wouldn't hold back. She would give him a good piece of her mind.

But it wasn't her husband.

It was one of the Whiskey Girls—the young dark-haired one whom Aidan had asked to bed the night Anne had arrived. She stood by the wheelbarrow, her doelike eyes apprehensive.

Anne lifted her chin in disdain. For a long moment, the two women took each other's measure. The Whiskey Girl dropped her gaze first.

"May I help you?" Anne asked, her tone imperious. She hated being caught performing such a debasing job as mucking out stalls by the likes of a Whiskey Girl.

The girl rubbed her palms on her skirt. Her voice shook slightly when she said in a soft, lilting accent, "Please, my lady. I've come to ask for a job."

Anne was incredulous. "You want a position in *my* employ?"

The girl's eyes appeared ready to swallow her face. Her feet took one step back from Anne but she answered, "Yes, my lady."

Leaning the fork against the wall, Anne walked out of the stall and took a good hard look at the doxy. She was a lovely thing, younger than Anne herself. But it almost seemed as if youth itself had passed her by. The difference was in her eyes. They had seen too much to be innocent.

The Whiskey Girl shifted her weight from one foot to another, ill-at-ease under such scrutiny.

Anne frowned. The girl's request was preposterous. It was an affront to Anne that she'd even made the appeal.

Crossing her arms against her chest, Anne said, "What is your name?" Aidan had used it the other night, but Anne had forgotten.

"Cora, my lady."

Yes, Cora. She forced herself to look at the girl as she asked the question burning in her mind. "Are you my husband's mistress?"

* * *

Aidan's conscience had started to bothered him.

He'd left to go to the sheep shed, but couldn't rid himself of the image of his strong, stubborn Anne swallowing her self-respect and mucking out the barn. He understood that kind of pride. Her dignity touched him.

He turned around and headed back. He'd tell her she didn't have to do the chore and round up Davey to finish it. He didn't know how he was going to convince her to leave, but he couldn't do it this way.

He'd been about to enter the barn from a side door when he realized Anne wasn't alone. She was talking to Cora. What the devil was distiller Nachton McKay's youngest daughter doing here?

Then Anne rocked him backward by asking, "Are you my husband's mistress?"

He immediately ducked back into the shadows, holding his breath, waiting for Cora's answer.

The color drained from the Whiskey Girl's face . . . and Anne thought she knew the answer. Part of her, the practical side, wondered inanely why she had asked the question—but her woman's sensibility understood she could not live at Kelwin and have everyone know what she didn't.

"Not his mistress, my lady," Cora whispered.

"Then what?" Anne asked, still fearing the answer.

"I've slept in his bed a time or two." She swallowed. "But not since I was told he was married. Neither my sisters or me will lie with a married man."

Her honest confession went straight to Anne's heart. Of course, Aidan would choose this girl as bed partner and not herself. Cora was lovely and round and soft—and sensual. She knew the mysteries of what happened between men and women. Anne did not.

Worse, in the presence of this sensual younger woman, Anne felt like a child. "I'm sorry," she heard herself say, as if from a great distance. "We have no position open." She backed toward the door and then turned, ready to run, not knowing where she was going or why.

Cora stopped her. "Please, my lady. I overheard them talking amongst themselves in the village that you were going to hire help. Please let me have a chance. I can work hard."

The catch in the girl's voice caught Anne's attention. She hesitated, and then forced herself to face her rival. She drew a steadying breath. "Why should I give you a chance? I need a maid to help in the house where you would be close to my husband at all times."

There, she'd admitted it. She was jealous and feared she could not compete.

"I have no designs on the laird," Cora said. "He's your husband."

Anne couldn't speak. She would not acknowledge Aidan didn't want her, not to a woman he did want.

"Please, my lady, I know I'm not a good choice for a maid. I don't even know how to be one," Cora confessed. "But I'm willing to learn. Everyone says I'm bright—"

"Then why don't you ask them for a position?"

Cora swallowed and lifted her chin defensively. "Because no one will hire me." Her hands clenched into fists. The lines of her face deepened and Anne realized she was struggling with pride and shame. "You wouldn't understand, my lady. You don't know what it is like."

The girl's proud posture struck a chord of recognition in Anne. "Tell me. Tell me what it is like to be you."

The Whiskey Girl smirked. "If you were my kind, you'd have to become accustomed to people always whispering and talking about you whenever you pass them on the path. They might smile and say hello to your face, but you know they'll be gossiping about you later."

Anne understood all too well what she meant. "What else?"

"People think you are stupid . . . or maybe they are deliberately trying to hurt your feelings."

"Maybe they don't believe you have feelings at all," Anne agreed softly.

"That is true. The women don't want to spend time knowing you to find out any different, and the men only want you on your back."

"How will being my maid change that?"

"It will be a chance, you ken?" Realizing Anne didn't understand the Scottish word, she corrected herself, "You understand? I want to be something else. A want to be *one of them*. My oldest sister, Meg, is twenty-eight, but she looks fifty. She has a child, my lady, a lovely little girl named Marie who will grow up and be like the lot of us. Pa doesn't mind. We're good for his whiskey business. But when I look at Marie and see how precious she is and know someday she will be like me—"

Cora broke off. She stared hard into space a moment, her eyes suspiciously shiny, but she didn't cry. She wouldn't either.

Anne understood. You couldn't cry about the way people treated you. If you did, it would hurt worse.

"I want to raise Marie," Cora said. "Meg will let me. Marie is in her way as it is now. But I need money to feed and clothe a child. You are my last hope. There is no one else who will hire me."

For a second, Anne couldn't speak. Cora was so pretty, of course Aidan would choose her over Anne.

Still . . . their marriage was in name only. She had no right to be jealous. What did it matter what her husband did, as long as she could stay at Kelwin?

Cora misinterpreted her silence. She retreated a step. "Yes, my lady, I understand. I wouldn't hire me either." Before Anne could blink, she turned and started hurrying toward the door.

Anne went after her. "Wait!" She had to say it again before Cora stopped in the doorway, her head bowed.

"I will hire you to be my maid."

The girl turned. "Why?"

Anne answered honestly. "Because I know how it feels to be the outcast . . . to be the one not chosen."

"Yes," Cora said quietly.

"Back in London, someone wrote something about me in the newspaper once." Anne had to pause. The pain of the public embarrassment still had the power to hurt. "The person who wrote it was an odious man. He made his living selling gossip. He was completely despicable, although he thought himself clever and witty. He called me a toad eater. Do you know what that is?"

"No."

"It's a female relation with no money, who is dependent upon the members of her family. It is not a flattering description and certainly not anything a single, marriageable lady wants printed publicly about her, because no gentleman wants a poor wife."

"It was cruel of him to print such a thing."

His column had all but destroyed her socially. She

put the pain behind her. "Disagreeable people are often cruel. But we don't have to abide by their opinions and I've managed to survive being refused a voucher to Almack's. It all seems silly now, when one is this far from London, but at the time it was very serious. I had a friend who was lovely and wealthy. She championed me. She couldn't obtain entrance to Almack's exclusive rooms for me, but she did insist that hostesses who wished her to attend their functions must invite me, too. She gave me a chance."

"What is Almack's, my lady?" Cora asked, confused.

Anne shook her head. "It's . . . nothing." She gave the woman a hard look from toe to head. Her clothing was worn and too tight, but she was clean and presentable. "Don't disappoint me, Cora. I do not want to regret making the decision to employ you."

The girl fell back against the barn door as if her legs could no longer support her weight. "You'll never be disappointed in me." This time when tears came, she made no attempt to hold them back.

"No, I don't think I will," Anne said, praying she wasn't making a heartbreaking mistake. "But I warn you, I expect you to work hard and learn well."

"I will, my lady." Cora even bobbed an awkward curtsey, as if to prove her words.

"You'll live in the servants' quarters."

"I didn't even dare to wish that much. A room of my own?"

"Yes, unless we hire more servants," Anne said, but added sternly, "And I expect your conduct to be beyond reproach."

"It will be, my lady."

"If Norval or any other man—" She didn't know how to finish, but that was all right, because Cora understood.

"No men. I've had enough of them to last a lifetime."

"You'll bring the girl, Marie, to live here, too?"

Cora drew in a sharp breath. "It is my fondest wish, but it may not be wise, my lady."

"Why not?"

"Because people will talk." She made a helpless gesture with her hand. "If I bring Marie to live under your roof, people will think she is the laird's child. She has black curly hair and blue eyes. I had thought to board her with one of the shepherd's families."

Anne had never thought of Aidan having children. She took a thoughtful step before asking, "Is she his?"

"No! And I know it for a fact. Yes, the laird has a reputation with the ladies, but he is more—?"

"Circumspect?" Anne supplied hopefully.

"What does that mean?"

"Careful of the consequences."

"Aye, he was always careful . . . and gentle." Cora glanced away. "I shouldn't have said the last, but not all men care how they treat you."

Anne shook her head. "It is all right." There was a

beat of silence between them, and then Anne said with authority, "Go fetch your things while I finish these stalls. And you can bring Marie with you."

"I'll do the stalls," Cora volunteered eagerly. "You shouldn't be doing this. You're not used to this sort of work."

The offer was tempting. But her pride insisted she show Aidan she could do whatever task he set before her. Of course, that didn't mean she didn't want help. "We'll do them together."

"And have them done in no time," Cora assured her. The two women set to work.

On the other side of the wall, Aidan had listened to the entire conversation.

Anne's generosity at giving Cora a position humbled him. No other woman in the kirk would have done it. And there was something haunting about the words Anne had used when she'd admitted she'd known what it was like to be an outcast.

He did, too.

Had he not left London because he didn't fit the mold? Society was no place for a romantic medievalist with a traitorous ancestry.

He listened as Anne and Cora set to work cleaning the stalls. While they mucked and raked, Anne outlined to Cora what she expected of her. Aidan was impressed. Anne did know how to run a household.

He didn't worry about having Cora in his employ. The girl had been a momentary distraction and, if the truth be known, he'd crossed paths with too many former lovers to have a care about meeting one more again.

But he was concerned about what he would say to Anne. He eased out the side door and leaned against the limestone wall.

He shouldn't have eavesdropped. It had opened her up to him and exposed her vulnerability. She would not be happy if she learned of it.

Hugh found him deep in thought.

"Are you afraid it will fall down?" he teased.

"What will fall down?" Aidan asked.

"The wall. You act as if you are holding it up." Seeing Aidan wasn't in the mood for joking, he stated his business. "The Reverend Oliphant is here from Thurso. He had the chance to come early and is ready to hold the funeral so he can take himself home again."

Aidan nodded. "Is the grave dug?"

"Thomas and I finished it an hour ago," he answered.

"Then let us gather in the chapel."

"I'll tell the others."

Aidan stopped Hugh before he walked away. "Tell my wife, too, will you? She's in the barn."

If Hugh thought it strange Aidan didn't want to inform Anne himself when he stood mere feet away from her, he didn't comment. Instead, he did as bidden.

Aidan waited, listening to Anne's response. She

told Hugh she had one stall to finish and then she and Cora would come.

Thoughtfully, Aidan trudged his way to the chapel. Deacon fell into step beside him. "It's a stroke of brilliance!" he practically crowed.

"What are you talking about?" Aidan asked, irritated.

"Having the English lass clean the stables. You are a genius, Tiebauld. A strategic genius. With you in our rebellion, the English will never be able to outfox us."

"Deacon?"

"Hmmm?"

"Sod off." Aidan went into the chapel. It held less than twenty-five people. The inside had a pulpit, several rows of chairs, and not much more. The coachman was laid out in a hastily built casket in front of the pulpit. Several members of his clan drifted in.

A few minutes later, Anne arrived. He sensed her presence before he saw her. The very air seemed to vibrate and churn with her unique energy. Turning toward the door, he smiled. She'd taken a moment to tidy her hair.

Ever the proper Englishwoman, he thought with a touch of admiration.

And being such, she walked the short distance up the aisle to where he stood. She slipped into the chair beside his, but she was careful not to touch him in any way.

The Reverend Oliphant began the service. Aidan wasn't listening to the words of comfort and a promise of a hereafter. Instead, he thought about hair pins. Anne had said in the stall she wished for some. It was such a small thing, but the sort of item women liked and men never thought of.

It wouldn't take him a bit of time to ride to Wick and buy her a few. Might cheer her a bit.

Through the ceremony and the subsequent burial, he was aware of her genuine grief. She'd liked the coachman. He hovered close, in case she became emotional. But Anne didn't break down. She had too much pride. Her strength pleased him—until the ceremony was over and she turned on her heel and walked away, out the opposite side of the small row of chairs, without so much as a glance in his direction. Marching up to the Reverend Oliphant, she asked him to join them for lunch, an invitation heartily accepted, and then she left the chapel, heading for the kitchen.

Aidan hurried to catch up. "Anne?"

She stopped, her shoulders stiff. "Yes?"

He slowed. He had nothing else to say. He groped for words. "Are you all right?"

She softened then. "I'll be fine. Todd was a nice man. It was a sad passing. So sudden."

"A funeral is always sobering."

Her head nodded agreement. "It reminds us of how fragile life is."

Now it was his turn to nod.

"Well, I'd best talk to Mary about lunch," she murmured.

He let her leave. Usually glib around women, he hadn't been able to think of a single sensible word to detain her longer. Her eyes were what tied his tongue. Their gaze was so honest, so direct and forthright, they made him feel like a royal bastard. Why did he choose today, knowing the Reverend Oliphant could arrive, to prove his point and order her to clean the stables?

During lunch, Aidan felt left out of the conversation. The Reverend Oliphant liked Anne. The two of them actually had much to discuss. Of course, the topic was mainly religion. Aidan had nothing to add. The last time he'd set foot in a church for a Sunday service had been in London.

"I pray to see you in chapel, my lady," the Reverend Oliphant said.

"Of course, I will be there," she answered.

The Reverend Oliphant's smile was cunning as he said, "And perhaps you can get your obstinate husband to come say a few words to the Lord."

Anne didn't even look at Aidan as she answered, "I may try."

"I wish you success," the Reverend Oliphant answered.

Aidan hated being discussed as if he wasn't present. Still, that afternoon, he rode to Wick for hair pins.

Chapter 9

Anne spent the afternoon detailing to Cora what would be expected of her and seeing the young woman and her niece settled in the servants' quarters, a wing of rooms off the great hall and close to the kitchen. If anyone was surprised at the Whiskey Girl's change of status, they didn't comment.

She even liked Cora's niece, Marie, a silent child who at the age of seven was old enough to know what traffic her mother and aunts dealt in. Cora had been right to move her.

Norval took to the child immediately. "I've not had family of my own," he explained. "It's been rather lonely here."

Anne nodded. She understood loneliness, and if Cora and Marie's presence did a little something toward keeping him sober in the evening, then that would be a good thing, too.

Of course, moving the ale kegs from the courtyard and great hall and putting them in the kitchen where they belonged would also be a first step in the right direction. However, considering Aidan's fondness for ale, she didn't dare attempt such a thing—yet.

Later, Anne hurried to Aidan's bedroom to dress for dinner. She hung the periwinkle dress in the wardrobe to air and put on a simple ivory muslin trimmed in green ribbons. The ivory wasn't as richly detailed as the periwinkle dress, but she thought she looked rather fine after she finished her toilette.

It would be nice to pin her hair up, but a bright red ribbon gathering it at the nape served the purpose as well. Especially since she wasn't planning to muck out stalls that evening. She was almost to the point where she could laugh about the whole experience—*almost*.

Grabbing her Kashmir shawl, she left the room and stopped. Deacon waited for her in the hallway.

She was tempted to walk right past him but he must have read her mind. He pushed away from the wall where he had been lounging and placed himself in her path.

"I hear you hired one of the Whiskey Girls as a household servant."

"I did."

He sneered. "What do you hope to prove by hiring one of the village whores as a maid?"

"I don't have to prove anything," she replied

calmly, although inside she was shaking. Deacon would love to discredit her.

"I suppose not," he answered. "However, I think it is an accommodating wife who places her husband's dolly close by for his convenience. A Scottish wife wouldn't do such a thing."

For a moment, Anne couldn't speak. His barb struck the heart of her insecurities. But she'd never let Deacon see that.

"Well, I'm not Scottish," she said tightly, "as you so often remind me. I am one of the dreaded English, those creatures who strike fear in you."

"I'm not afraid of anything."

"Is that true? Then why does my simple womanly presence bother you so much? If Aidan wishes to send me away, he can."

"He's been trying to, lass, you're too stubborn to recognize it."

Anne took a step back, suddenly unable to breathe.

Deacon pressed on. "They are all laughing at you, every one of them. Even the women like Bonnie Mowat and Kathleen Keith. Go home, English-woman. Go back to where you belong." He turned and walked away.

Anne leaned back against the wall, her palms flat on the stone surface. She feared if she took a step in any direction the floor would disappear beneath her feet.

And here she had started to congratulate herself that all was going well.

She struggled for composure. She couldn't give Deacon the satisfaction of seeing how crippling his words had been. She stood up straight, twisted her neck to loosen the tightening in her shoulders, and with head high, went down for dinner.

Downstairs, Aidan and Hugh looked up as she entered the room. They stood by the fire drinking from polished tankards. Deacon had already taken his seat at the table.

"I was thinking, Anne," Aidan said without preamble, "the floors are cold without my mat of rushes."

She didn't pause, but walked straight to her seat at the table, which was on the opposite end from Deacon's. "Are you going to lay down fresh rushes?"

Her husband frowned. "No, I was thinking of one of those Indian carpets, something with a design in gold and blue."

She tensely smiled her assent. But the décor of the room was no longer of interest. She started to sit when she noticed a small package beside her plate. She glanced around the table. No one else had such a package. "What is this?" she asked, picking it up.

Deacon frowned, not even deigning to answer. Aidan and Hugh acted as if they hadn't seen it before.

Anne opened the paper wrapping. Inside were

twenty silver hair pins. A dozen thoughts hit her mind all at once. She looked up and caught her husband watching her closely.

Aidan didn't approve of the way she'd been wearing her hair. She knew he'd given her pins.

"What's in the package?" Hugh asked.

"Nothing important," Anne answered, closing her fist around the pins. She took her seat.

What was his game now? To embarrass her into returning to London? She tossed her hair defiantly and immediately wished she could crawl under the table and hide.

Aidan and Hugh took their places at the table just as Norval and Fenella started to serve. Fenella wasn't expected to serve, but even in her uneasy state, Anne noticed she favored Hugh by moving to him first.

Bitterly she wished the girl well. She herself had enough of love. Cupid's dart stung.

"Anne, are you feeling well?" her husband asked in a low voice.

She glanced up at him sitting beside her, their elbows inches from each other. He seemed genuinely concerned for her health, while uncaring for her feelings. The pain of his rejection was so sharp, it hurt to look at him. She lowered her eyes. "I'm fine."

"You're so quiet. And you haven't touched anything on your plate."

Anne picked up her fork. The dinner was peas and stuffed grouse. She made a pretense of eating.

She thought it would be enough, that he would leave her alone. He didn't.

"I haven't done something to offend you, have I?"

"No, nothing at all," she answered. "You've treated me like a crown princess."

Aidan leaned back, stung by her scorn. "What have I done to made you angry?"

"Nothing," she replied, stabbing a pea so viciously with her fork, it split the poor thing in half.

He checked on Deacon and Hugh to ensure they hadn't overheard anything. Hugh was too preoccupied watching the sway of Fenella's hips as she carried the serving bowl out of the room to have noticed a herd of elephants if they'd marched into the room.

But Deacon had overheard their exchange. He met Aidan's gaze with a level one of his own in commiseration and then went back to his meal.

Aidan knew he should leave the matter alone, but he couldn't. He covered his mouth with his hand so Deacon couldn't hear and whispered, "You don't like the pins?"

Her fingers tightened around her fork. "They are . . . lovely."

If she thought they were lovely, why hadn't she said so? And why did he have the distinct impression they were anything *but* fine?

"I couldn't get you gold ones. The shop didn't have any."

She swerved in her seat to confront him. "I expect nothing from you." Her voice was hard, tight as if she were held back stronger emotions.

"Anne—?"

"Excuse me." She cut him off. She lay her fork down and looked to Hugh. "I'm not feeling well. I fear I must go to my room."

She didn't wait for a reply, but pushed back her chair and dashed for the stairs. Aidan barely had a chance to rise.

He sat back down. She had taken the pins. She'd had them in her free hand all through dinner. So, she must like them—?

"Did you understand any of that?" he asked the room in general.

"Any of what?" Hugh answered, stuffing another slice of bread in his mouth.

"None of it," Deacon responded.

Aidan seized upon his answer. "So, you agree with me Anne was definitely out of sorts?"

"She said she didn't feel well," Hugh said.

Deacon drained his ale mug and set it aside before answering. "I take it you gave her a gift?"

"Oh, was the package from you?" Hugh asked, as if fitting together pieces of a puzzle.

Aidan didn't answer. He felt a bit silly, especially since the pins hadn't pleased her at all . . . and he was surprised at how much he had anticipated her pleasure in his gift.

"Tiebauld, forget it," Deacon advised. He sat back

in his chair and put one booted heel on the table. "Women are silly creatures. You can't credit anything they say."

"I thought you didn't like her because she was English. I didn't realize you felt this way toward *all* women."

Deacon frowned. "I like women well enough in their proper place." He grinned and added, "In the bedroom."

Hugh guffawed at the joke but Aidan didn't laugh. "You know, Deacon, you're a snob. I just never recognized it before."

"I'm no snob."

"Yes, you are," Aidan said. "Either that or you're mad at the world and want everyone to join you."

Deacon's chin lifted pugnaciously. "I admit to strong views."

"No, dogged views. There is a difference." Aidan stood. "Goodnight, gentlemen." He left the room.

Behind him, he heard Hugh ask, "What did Tiebauld mean by that, Deacon?"

Deacon didn't answer.

Upstairs, Aidan headed straight for his room. Anne could truly be ill and if so, he wanted to know. If not, he wanted an explanation for her behavior tonight.

But she wasn't in his room. In fact, her things had been moved out.

Puzzled, he went to the guest room. Carefully, he opened the door. The room was dark. He almost thought no one was there until he widened the door to let in light from the torch burning in the hallway.

Anne lay in the bed, sleeping soundly. The hall light fell on the curve of her hip as she slept on her side, her back to the door.

So, she had been ill. Aidan felt relieved. He didn't know why she had moved from his room . . . but it was for the best. He started to close the door when something on the floor reflected the hall light.

Curious, he opened the door wide enough to see it was one of the silver pins. They were scattered across the wash basin and onto the floor, almost as if she'd thrown them at the mirror.

Aidan eased back. He didn't know why she would do such a thing. But the image of those shining, lovely pins kept him awake long past midnight.

In the end, he decided the best action would be to take none. He'd let her come to him when she was ready.

The intricacies of the female mind were too complicated for his ken. His feelings for Anne were something he didn't know if he wanted to explore too closely.

With that disturbing thought, he fell asleep.

Deacon was in a disgruntled mood. The hour was late as he sat in front of the hearth smoking his pipe. He stretched his legs toward the fire, an empty ale glass in his hand. Smoke curled around his head.

Was he the only one left with sense? Couldn't

Tiebauld and Hugh see what the women were doing to them? Hugh was acting like a stud in heat every time Fenella MacEwan crossed his path.

He didn't want to think about what was happening to Tiebauld—although he had his suspicions.

A step sounded behind him. He turned. Cora McKay came into the room. She carried a lighted taper. Seeing him, she skidded to a halt. "I'm sorry. I heard a sound and came to check and didn't realize you were still up." She started to leave.

But he called her back, feeling a perverse sense of desire. He knew Cora, although he'd never lain with her. She was the youngest and shyest of the distiller's daughters.

She was also the loveliest.

"Did you want something?" she asked in her low, musical voice.

Deacon brought in his legs and patted his lap. "I want you to sit. Right here."

The color drained from her face. It pricked his conscience, or at least, what was left of his conscience after so much ale. He told himself he was imagining things. She was a Whiskey Girl and used to men talking rudely—and he had a strong desire to be "rude" with her right now.

When she didn't move, he prodded, "Come along."

She glanced into the darkness behind her. "We're alone," he said impatiently. "Don't worry, I won't tell Tiebauld or that English bitch."

A frown line formed across her forehead. He didn't know why; he didn't care. He had anger inside, frustration needing to be released in any form . . . and this was as good as any. Better, in fact.

She started walking toward him. He drew a long breath. Maybe if he had her, he wouldn't feel so dissatisfied.

Cora stopped beside him. Her lips were pressed tightly together like some prudish maiden aunt's. He knew how to loosen them up. "Unbutton my breeches," he said crudely.

But instead of giving him what he wanted, she turned the taper sideways. Hot wax fell on his crotch.

Deacon came up with a roar. He hadn't been burned, but he understood her intention. Nor did she wait to offer an apology but took off running in the direction of the servants' quarters.

He gave pursuit.

Her candle went out but they both knew the way—or at least he did, until they reached the servants' hallway. She'd run into one of the rooms. He'd find her, and when he did—

In brutal anger, he threw open a door. The room was dark. No Cora there. He tried another and another. He paused, thinking . . . and then noticed a light under the door at the far end of the hall.

On silent feet, he approached the light. With one shoulder, he threw the door open.

Cora was there, but she was not alone. A child

came awake at the noise of the door hitting the wall. She jerked up in bed, screaming. The little girl had doe-shaped eyes and long dark hair much like Cora's.

Cora threw protective arms around the girl and faced Deacon. "All right. I'll do what you want but not here. Not in front of the child. And I'll not let you touch her, do you understand?"

He pulled back, sickened Cora would think him capable of such a thing. "I wouldn't hurt her," he said. Then, "Is she yours?"

"No, but I'll not let harm come to her. I'll die first."

The child started at her words. She wrapped her arms around Cora's neck and held tight. "I won't let him touch you either, Auntie. I won't let him hurt you."

"I wouldn't hurt either one of you," Deacon protested thickly, sober now. What had come over him? He'd never forced himself on a woman before. It embarrassed him when he realized he'd been about to do so now.

Deacon stepped back. At one time he'd been a favored son in the proud clan Gunn. Now, he was chasing maids and scaring children.

It almost took all his courage to face the two of them. "This was a mistake. I'm sorry. Very sorry." He backed out of the room and closed the door.

In the great hall, surrounded by silence, he sat in

his chair and stared into the fire. He wondered when he'd changed . . . and if he could ever return to the man he'd once been.

If Aidan had thought Anne would immediately notice his quietness, he was wrong. Over the next several days, they were polite strangers. The only time she sought him out was to discuss improvements she wished to make. Otherwise, she left him to his own devices.

In keeping with his idea of what a truce between them should be, he pretended to ignore her . . . although he found himself lingering around the castle, waiting for her to notice him.

She didn't.

Instead, she was busy turning Kelwin into a home.

Over the years, he had worked to turn the lands into a thriving, profitable estate, but he had ignored the house. Now an herb garden was planted right outside the kitchen step. A chicken coop appeared almost overnight, stocked with hens and a crowing rooster. Mrs. MacEwan promised him a cake baked of the first eggs. His dogs were becoming better mannered and often ran right past him to greet Anne.

If anyone in his small community sensed things weren't right between him and his wife, they gave no indication. In truth, everyone gladly accepted

Anne. Even Deacon had given up hounding Aidan about her.

Actually, his friend had become very sober of late. He kept Aidan apprised of the watch for the Danish ship and his brother Robbie's rebel activities. Otherwise, he didn't seem to have much to say about anything—not even on the subject of Anne.

And Hugh was gone. He talked and walked and looked like the same old happy bachelor he'd always been—but everyone knew he was in love with Fenella MacEwan. He could barely think of anything else. Fang advised Aidan to push Hugh into a June wedding, "So he can get his wits back and act normal again."

Aidan didn't know if he should talk to anyone on matters of love. He'd discovered the one woman impervious to his charm and she was supposedly his own wife.

Granted, a marriage shouldn't be consummated if he was going to dissolve it, but a niggling thought wormed its way into his mind that sleeping with Anne might not be a bad idea. After all, she worked as hard as he did. And then maybe he'd be able to concentrate on something besides the swing of his wife's hips as she walked or the way her eyes crinkled at the corners when someone said something tickling her sense of the absurd.

If they consummated the marriage, he could find out what it was like to kiss her. Then perhaps he would stop fantasizing about her to the point at which he'd lost interest in other women.

At the very least, he could complain when she ignored him.

It was a sunny Thursday, one of those days when the sky is clear blue and the ever present wind is finally promising summer, when Aidan discovered his favorite mare was in foal. He was pleased. He'd bred her on one of Argyll's prized studs. The bloodlines were impeccable. Davey Mowat and his friends were happy with the news, but Aidan wasn't satisfied. He wanted to share it with someone who mattered.

In the past he would have searched for Deacon or Hugh. This time, he found himself walking toward the house to tell Anne.

She wasn't there. He called to Norval, who answered from the upstairs hall he had not seen "my lady."

Aidan charged out to the kitchen. "Mrs. Mac-Ewan, have you seen my wife?"

"She's on the beach," Mrs. MacEwan said.

"What the deuce is she doing there?" he asked, but didn't wait for an answer. He charged out of the kitchen.

Outside the door was one of many paths leading down to the rocky coast and a pebble and sand beach. At the rise of the cliff, Aidan looked down and saw Anne along with Cora and a group of children, Marie among them. They appeared to be dancing. Anne wore her ivory muslin, one of the two dresses she usually saved for dinner meals, and her hair fell loose and unbound almost to her waist. The others were also dressed in shades of white.

Curious, he started down the cliff path. He hadn't gone far when he came upon Deacon sitting amongst the rocks. "What are you doing here?"

Deacon pulled his gaze away from where the women played. He shrugged. "Passing time."

Aidan frowned. "Are you feeling all right?"

"Why do you ask?"

"You don't seem yourself."

For a moment, Deacon appeared ready to confide something, but then held the words back. "I'm fine." He stood and pushed by Aidan, taking the path up to the house.

Aidan glanced down at the beach. Cora had noticed Deacon. Her gaze followed him up the path. Then, seeing Aidan, she quickly looked away and said something to Anne.

By the time he reached the beach, everyone knew he was coming. Marie happily ran up to him on bare feet. He noticed she wasn't the only one. They all had bare feet, even Anne, and wore necklaces fashioned out of seaweed.

"We're dancing," Marie told Aidan joyfully, and made a pirouette in the sand. "We're at a sea ball."

He had to laugh. The child's presence in the castle had added a delightful new dimension to life at Kelwin. "With seaweed around your necks and in your hair, you all look like the Danish tale of a mermaid who grew legs."

Anne blushed and he was enchanted. "It's just such a glorious day," she said. "We decided to be a little silly." Marie's two friends skipped up to him to show off the necklaces "my lady" had made them.

But although Aidan pretended to admire the sea jewelry, he wasn't really paying attention. Instead, something about seeing these precious children laughing and vying to be close to Anne created one clear thought in his head—he wanted children. He'd always intended to have them—it was his duty, his obligation—but he had not felt the urge until this moment, when he was with Anne surrounded by prancing, laughing little girls.

"Can you dance, Laird?" Marie asked boldly.

Cora chastened her. "Marie, you don't talk in such a way to the laird."

"It is all right," Aidan answered. He knelt so he was on Marie's level. Her two friends, whom he now recognized as Ellen and Molly Keith, Hugh's twin nieces, crowded up beside her. "I don't dance," he confessed. "I'm clumsy. I trip over my own feet. They are very large, you know."

They laughed. "Lady Tiebauld will teach you," Ellen said. "She taught us."

Lady Tiebauld. No one had dared to use Anne's title in front of him. They referred to her as "my lady" but never by the title. He just realized the omission.

Cora had noticed the mistake. Anne, too. She watched him, waiting for his response. With her bare feet and seaweed necklace, she appeared as innocent as one of the little girls. Then the ocean breeze blew the hem of her muslin skirts and he couldn't help but admire the shape of her long legs, the womanly curve of her hips.

Aidan rose. "Perhaps Lady Tiebauld will teach me to dance." There, he'd used her title, too.

Her reaction was everything he could wish for. She wasn't ignoring him now. And she couldn't refuse his request without disappointing her young companions. He held out his hand. "My lady?"

The girls clapped their hands with delight.

Anne didn't move.

"We can't fail them," he prompted.

She sent a hesitant glance at the path leading up the cliffs as if ready to bolt. He eased over, blocking her path of escape. She actually edged back from him.

Had he really been such a great boor?

Realizing he must make the first move, he bowed with all the élan of a London ballroom. Anne's lips parted in surprise at his formal show of manners. The little girls giggled.

Anne considered him a moment, and then she curtsied in response, a deep, graceful movement. This time when he held out his hand, she placed hers in it.

If this had been a ballroom, she would have worn gloves and he wouldn't have known the warmth of her skin. Nor would he have been able to devise his own dance, one suitable to his purpose.

A step in, a step out, then circle the partner, a hand resting on her waist. It brought them very close. It forced them to move as one.

"I thought you said you couldn't dance," she said, her voice slightly breathless.

Could it be her pulse raced as fast as his? He shrugged. "I'm clumsy."

"I find you anything but," she said, as he took her hands and raising them over her head turned her in a classic *tour de main.*

The children loved the step and practiced it themselves. Cora watched thoughtfully.

"Perhaps I've grown out of it," he said.

She smiled. He moved near enough to smell the scent in her hair. Her breasts lightly brushed his chest. He longed to touch them, to feel their shape and taste them. His hand returned to the curve of her waist.

Their circle of steps came to a halt.

For a moment, neither moved. It seemed as if neither breathed.

Aidan lost all sense of time and place in the depths of beautiful sea-gray eyes.

The clapping of the children broke the spell. Anne pulled away. "I think they have the idea," she said to excuse herself, but she couldn't fool him. Something had passed between them. Something unfathomable. Something rare and vital.

Aidan turned to the girls and aped another bow, not at all displeased with his dance.

"We should go in," Anne said. "I'm sure Mrs. MacEwan has cold water or hot tea for us to drink."

"Oh, yes, and toast, too," Cora added. "Come, let me have your hands." She took the twins, who claimed to be "beyond hungry," and started up the path.

Aidan said, "Go along on with your friends, Marie. Lady Tiebauld and I will be along in a moment."

The poppet looked from one to the other, her bright eyes speculative, and then she raced up the hill after her friends as fast as her bare feet could travel.

Alone, Anne sidled away like a skittish foal. She moved toward a rock large enough to be a chair. Her silk stockings and those silly kid slippers were half buried in the sand beside it.

For a second, he hoped she'd put her stockings in front of him. He might even offer to help. But she didn't. She merely slipped her feet in her shoes.

"You need sturdier shoes," he said.

She made a noncommittal sound.

"Send a note to the cobbler in Wick," Aidan said. "He'll make a pair of shoes for you. You might need a new pair of dress shoes, too."

"Thank you," she said, and rose to her feet. She

still hadn't looked at him, not once. She started for the path.

Her studied nonchalance irked him. *Thank you? That was all she had to say?*

He reached for her arm as she passed him and brought her around. "Anne—" he started, and then stopped.

He didn't know what he wanted to say. And she wasn't going to make it easy. She frowned, waiting.

"You don't wear the pins I bought you." His statement sounded silly, but he did wonder.

Her gaze hardened and shifted from him to look out over the sea. Overhead, gulls rode the current of the wind, their harsh calls mocking. Before his eyes, the warm woman who had danced in his arms slipped away to an unreachable place, a place where he wasn't welcome.

Almost desperate, he ran his hand lightly up her arm. It was only a touch, and yet it made him yearn for more. "If you don't like the pins, I don't mean to press you. It wasn't what I came down here to say anyway."

"Why did you come?"

To see you.

Those words refused to pass his lips. If he said them, he'd be lost to something he wasn't certain he wished to explore.

"To tell you my mare Doublelet is in foal." It had been his true reason.

A beat of silence. "That's good news." Did she appear mildly disappointed? Had she wished for him to say something else?

"Yes, I have big plans for the foal."

He sounded like a country oaf! She'd be wise to walk away—but she didn't. Instead, she hesitated, her expression thoughtful, as if she could devine his thinking. She bit her bottom lip, debating.

Aidan leaned closer, wanting to hear whatever she said. Even if all she did was ask what plans he had for the horse, it would be an opening—one they could both accept. From there, they would talk about horses in general or about the castle, or maybe even other things that had nothing to do with the running of the estate.

But it was not to be. Before she could speak, Davey Mowat shouted for him from the top of the cliff, his tone desperate. "Laird! Laird!"

Aidan moved back on the beach so he could be seen from the cliff. "What is it, Davey?"

"Soldiers are coming! Hugh sent me to warn you."

"Soldiers?" Anne repeated. "Why would they be here?"

Aidan didn't answer. Instead, he took her hand and started up the hill.

In the courtyard all was confusion until Aidan appeared. "Go back to your kitchen, Mrs. MacEwan," he said. The cook immediately retreated, taking her daughter with her.

"Do you think—?" Hugh started, and then stopped when he realized what he had been about to reveal.

Aidan frowned. Deacon stood on the path leading to the stables. Several of Fang's sons surrounded him. "It's Lambert, Tiebauld," he called. "I feel it in my bones."

Turning to Anne, Aidan said, "You go in the house and don't come out, no matter what happens. Make certain Cora and the children stay there, too."

"Yes, Aidan, but—"

"Anne, this is no time to argue."

Chapter 10

Anne stared into his intent eyes and closed her mouth.

Dancing with him on the beach had been a magic moment. She knew he had pulled her close. His hand on her waist had lingered possessively, and in the depths of his eyes, she'd seen longing . . . longing for her. She'd despaired of ever meeting a man who would look at her in such a way. A man she could in turn love, honor, and respect. A man like Aidan.

But now, he was back to the domineering, in-control man who was laird of Kelwin Castle.

"Be careful," she murmured.

His proud, devil-may-care grin flashed at her. "I'm always careful. Now, go inside."

Anne submissively did as he'd ordered, herding Cora and the children in front of her. But once inside, obedience ended.

Aidan had secrets. She'd heard Major Lambert's

name before. In a second, she remembered: Sir Rupert had asked Lady Waldo about a Major Lambert. He'd been worried when he'd said the name. At the time, every one of Anne's senses had screamed a warning.

Now, a sense of foreboding even stronger than before shuddered through her.

"Take the children to the servants' quarters," she ordered Cora. "You'll be safe there."

"What about you, my lady?"

"I'll wait here." Cora started to leave, but Anne called her back. "Do you know why the army would pay us a visit, Cora? Who is this Lambert?"

Cora shrugged. "They may be passing through and need food and drink."

And pigs can fly, too, Anne thought; but she kept her comment to herself. "I pray it is true."

"I do also," Cora agreed softly, and then left the room with the girls.

Anne tiptoed back into the alcove and cracked open the front door in time to see a party of fifty soldiers march with a sense of purpose through Kelwin's arched gates. Sunlight caught and gleamed off of their fixed bayonets. It was a wicked sight.

At the head of their party rode a wigged officer. His boots shone with the effects of champagne blacking. His gold braid seemed brighter than the sun. He had a great hooked nose and an aura of aristocratic disdain.

In contrast, her husband was in his usual shirt

sleeves, leather breeches, and his well-worn favorite pair of boots. Still he appeared every inch the
nobleman.

The dogs were barking wildly. Aidan ordered
some of the lads to shepherd them up to the stables.

The officer signaled his troops to halt when he
reached the center of the courtyard. The smallest
dog, York, had escaped being corralled and stood
his ground close to Aidan, barking away.

Aidan swooped York up. "Here, now, stop yap-
ping."

The pup obeyed.

"Good morning, Lord Tiebauld," the officer said,
looking down his imperial nose at Aidan, who
stood defiantly before the castle door, his overlong
hair blowing in the breeze.

"Good morning, Major Lambert."

"Quite a menagerie of curs you have here," the
major observed.

His tart verdict irritated Anne. She was glad-
dened when Aidan said, "If you don't like my dogs,
you may leave, Major."

"Oh no, I can't do that," the major said, with a
touch of carefully feigned boredom. "I'm here
searching for a desperate fugitive."

"A desperate fugitive, running through Kelwin?"
Aidan shook his head. "You have a fantastic imagination, Major."

"I may or may not," the gentleman officer said.
His gaze drifted to search the crowd of curious on-

lookers lining the courtyard. "But I have it on good authority Deacon Gunn, brother of the rebel Robbie Gunn, is here. I am going to ask you to turn him over."

A hush ran through the courtyard at the mention of Deacon's name. Aidan's chin came up, a sign to Anne he was going to be stubborn. "On what charges?"

"Treason against the Crown," the major answered.

Treason? Anne had never imagined such a thing.

Peeking through the crack in the door, she had a clear view of Deacon standing with Fang's sons. He didn't even flinch when his name was spoken. The soldiers could not know what he looked like, else they would have arrested him.

She held her breath, waiting for someone to denounce him. No one did.

Worse, if he moved, he would call attention to himself.

Aidan said flatly, "I've not seen Deacon Gunn for weeks."

" 'Tis odd," Major Lambert said. "We have a report from a man who had recently traveled this way saying he'd seen you, my lord, and Gunn out for a ride."

"I won't deny he's my friend," Aidan answered. "But I have not seen him in recent weeks."

Every fiber of Anne's being tightened with tension as the officer frowned. Major Lambert was not pleased with his answer. The scene reminded her of another time, another place—when her own father had been marched away by soldiers. In the safety of the alcove, she kicked off her shoes and frantically started to pull one stocking up her leg and then another. She must be the model of propriety. It was the only thing British authority understood.

Outside, the officer was asking, "You won't mind then if we search your estate, my lord?"

"Yes, I do," Aidan said.

Major Lambert's eyes narrowed, but his voice was reasonable. "I don't know why. If he's not here, I'm certain we will find nothing . . . and your loyalty to the Crown will be duly noted."

"Searching for Jacobites, Major Lambert? Those days are long behind us."

"The Jacobite threat in Scotland is always present, Lord Tiebauld, as you well know as the descendant of one of the most notorious rebels in Scottish history."

Aidan laughed with genuine amusement. "My grandfather, named with the likes of William Wallace and Rob Roy? Major, Scottish history is full of rebels, one after the other, and it will be until England recognizes our right to govern ourselves without oppressive tactics like this one."

The set of Major Lambert's face hardened. "It is my sworn duty to rout out traitors wherever they may be . . . *whoever* they may be. Including you, my lord."

Anne could wait no longer—not after such a statement. Aidan was flirting with danger. Did he not realize it? If he wasn't careful, the major would take him in Deacon's place. Anne rejected the thought of Aidan being tried and hanged as a rebel. The people would be bereft.

She would be bereft, too. Yes, she pretended not to notice him, to remain unconcerned about his activities, but the truth was she was falling deeper and deeper in love with him. Each day she found something noble, admirable, wonderful about him.

She would remain here beside him even if he didn't love her, because she couldn't leave. He and the proud people of Kelwin were becoming a part of her soul.

Instinctively, she knew she had to create a diversion in order for Deacon to escape safely and defuse the tension between the man she loved and Major Lambert.

Anne smoothed her skirts, straightened her shoulders, and boldly threw open the door.

"My lord," she trilled at Aidan, "you didn't tell me we had guests." She infused in her voice as much aristocratic hauteur as possible. Snobbery would be something Major Lambert could understand.

Everyone's focus shifted to her. She smiled, hoping Deacon had the sense to take advantage of the moment and slip away. He'd probably delay leaving to watch her performance out of spite.

And quite a performance it was, too. Anne

shoved aside any hesitations and glided forward with the straight-backed poise every debutante had to master before being presented at Court. She slipped her arm around her husband's and complained, "How bad of you to have company and not tell me." She looked to the officer. "I've been here only a week and already I suffer *ennui*. I am anxious for civilized conversation." Squeezing her husband's arm, she said, "Aren't you going to perform introductions?"

For a moment, she feared Aidan would refuse, that he would be willing to further antagonize the officer. She pleaded with her eyes. He had to play his part. If he didn't, she feared the consequences.

He raised one bemused eyebrow, then shifted York to his other arm, reached for her hand, and gallantly kissed it. "My *dove*"— she almost laughed at the endearment—"Major Lambert is here on business," he continued. "I do not wish you to trouble your mind over it. He will be leaving."

The back of her hand tingled where he had kissed her, but she put on her best pout. "He mustn't. I *do* so wish for entertainment. Please introduce us."

Irritation flashed in the depths of Aidan's eyes, but he did as she'd requested. Not to do so would have seemed suspicious. "Very well. My lady, this is Major Lambert of one of the King's men protecting his interests in Scotland. Major, my wife, Lady Tiebauld."

"Your wife?" The words startled the major. He

dismounted, dropping the reins. "I had not heard you were married."

"I did not feel it necessary to send you an announcement," Aidan replied stonily.

Looking past the major's shoulder, Anne noticed Deacon had indeed shown good sense and taken advantage of her diversion. He'd slipped away, but he would need more time to escape the estate. She smiled at the officer. "We've been married for weeks."

Major Lambert appeared disbelieving. "But I had not heard you were even betrothed, Lord Tiebauld—and I would have heard such extraordinary news."

"Oh, it all took place in London." She simpered like a chit from the schoolroom. "No one knew about it up here in the Highlands."

The major persisted. "I had not thought Lord Tiebauld had been to London in years . . . or have you, my lord? Have you been dashing around on secret errands?"

"My comings and goings are not your business," Aidan answered.

He frustrated Anne with his coldness. Didn't he realize Deacon needed time? She stepped forward, pointedly ignoring his scowling face. "Would you care to join us for luncheon, Major? I can share the Town gossip."

Aidan said, "I'm sure Major Lambert has other things to do—"

"I would be delighted," the major answered. "My men have work to do here anyway."

"What work?" she asked innocently.

"They are going to search the estate for rebels," Aidan said briskly.

"Rebels!" Anne made a silly fluttering gesture of distress. "You won't find rebels here."

"He thinks I'm one," Aidan said quietly.

Anne looked at her husband. "You?" She started laughing and Aidan reluctantly smiled with her.

"You can see my wife finds the situation ridiculous, Major." Aidan placed York on the ground. The pup sniffed at the officer's boots.

"I have my duty," Major Lambert replied stiffly, shaking his foot to chase York away.

"Yes, yes," Anne said, worrying York might do something rude if provoked. "And you must do it, but we can enjoy ourselves during its course, can't we?"

Cora had approached. Anne said, "Cora, please tell Mrs. MacEwan there will be a guest for lunch." As the maid hurried to do her bidding, she said, "Come inside, Major." She waited for him to offer his arm and let him escort her inside. Aidan trailed behind.

"I don't imagine you know Lord Liverpool?" she asked.

"I've met him," Major Lambert replied, impressed. "Are you acquainted with him?"

"Oh, *la!*" Anne sighed. "I'm not, but my husband's sister, Lady Waldo, is very close to him." She didn't know if what she'd said was true, but felt it important for the officer to know her husband was not without friends, political friends.

Major Lambert gave search orders to his second-in-command and followed her into the great hall, where he had the good taste to exclaim over the windows.

"They are marvelous," Anne agreed. "My husband has worked to bring Kelwin to its former glory. He's a medieval scholar."

"Yes, I know," Major Lambert said. "We were in school together."

Anne's mouth almost dropped open. From their attitudes, she would have thought they'd never known each other before. "Is this true?" she asked Aidan.

"Oh, yes," he said, helping himself to a tankard of ale. "We even traveled in the same London circles for a time until I inherited my title. A title is something *Lambie* has always wanted. Tell me, Lambie, are you any closer to your holy grail?"

The officer stiffened. "I don't like that name."

"I know," Aidan answered, and smiled. "Lambie."

Anne positioned herself between them. "Do you wish a glass of ale, Major? My husband brews it himself. Or would you prefer wine?"

"Actually, I have no fondness for the local brews," Major Lambert said, condescendingly. "But my palate would appreciate a glass of wine, my lady."

Norval had come in to set the table with pewter dishes. Anne turned to him and brightly said, "Norval, please bring out a bottle of wine."

"Wine, my lady?" he asked, confused.

"I'll get it, Norval," Aidan answered. "I need to bring it up from the wine cellar." There was a touch of irony in his words because Anne had not found any such place and doubted it existed. But she assumed there must be wine somewhere, and she was right.

A moment later, Aidan returned with a very dusty bottle of red wine and two glasses. At the same time, a group of soldiers marched past the window on their way to the sea path. It chilled Anne to have them climbing all over the estate. She prayed Deacon was wise enough to avoid them.

Having sensed her distress, her husband pressed a glass in her hand. "Drink."

She lifted her gaze to his. "Thank you."

His fingers brushed hers and he leaned forward. *"Courage,"* he whispered in her ear.

"What did you say?" Major Lambert asked.

Aidan picked up the other glass and offered it to their unwanted guest. "I was reminding my wife of her unconventional jewelry."

Only then did Anne remember she still wore her seaweed necklace. With a sound of distress, she set down her glass and pulled it off. "You must think me silly," she told Major Lambert. "I was playing with the crofter children on the beach."

"I thought it was a touch unconventional," he admitted.

"My wife *is* unconventional," Aidan said, a trace of pride in his voice.

"And lovely," the major added. "I would not have thought you so fortunate, Lord Tiebauld." He raised his glass in Anne's direction as a toast.

"Yes," Aidan agreed, but a tightness had appeared at the corners of his mouth.

Flustered by the unexpected praise, Anne asked, "Are you married, Major?" She picked up her glass and took an unusually large swallow, needing the fortification.

"No, he's waiting for a rich wife," Aidan answered. He sat down at his place at the table. Through the windows past his shoulders, the soldiers trudged up the path—empty-handed.

"I do not have the luxury of your money, Tiebauld," the major said baldly.

"Or a *title*." Aidan couldn't seem to resist another dig. He smiled at Anne. "Major Lambert hopes to earn a knighthood by marching a horde of Scottish traitors to London. Even if he must fabricate them."

The soldier's hand tightened on his glass. "I don't have to create Jacobites in Scotland. Nor do I believe traitors should be allowed to keep titles."

Aidan wagged a finger at him. "Ah, those decisions were made long ago. They are out of our hands. And it was my great-grandfather, Lambie, not me who was the traitor. Don't confuse us."

"I won't—if you are innocent."

Aidan came to his feet in challenge.

Anne hurried up to him, saying, "It is almost time for luncheon. Perhaps we had best change the subject."

To her relief, Norval and Cora walked in, ready to serve. "Shall we sit?" She moved toward her place at the table. Major Lambert reached to pull out her chair, but her husband suddenly cut in and beat the officer to it.

Anne sighed. If she had anticipated this petty rivalry she would have let the soldiers carry Aidan off in chains! Instead, she was forced to play her role to the hilt, batting her eyelashes and recounting every party she'd ever attended in London, mentioning the name of every person she'd ever met.

Major Lambert hung on her every word. Aidan was right. He was an ambitious man whose father, she learned, was a solicitor and unable to further his plight in political circles. "But I have plans," he assured Anne. His gaze drifted toward her husband.

At last, one of the major's soldiers appeared to report they'd finished their search.

"Did you find anything?" the major asked, rising.

"No, sir. No evidence of Deacon Gunn or other traitorous activities."

Since they hadn't recognized Deacon when he'd been standing right in front of them, Anne was not surprised. She didn't dare look at Aidan.

Major Lambert turned to her, clicking his heels as he bowed in the Prussian method. "I thank you for your hospitality and conversation, my lady. You are a far more gracious and lovely woman than Tiebauld deserves."

She had to laugh. "I may agree with you, Major Lambert." She walked him to the alcove. Aidan stayed behind. She was conscious of his gaze on her every move.

Major Lambert bowed low over her hand one more time and then left. But she sensed they would see him again.

She stood where she was, listening until at last she heard the sound of the soldiers marching away. For a moment, she feared she would collapse. Releasing a deep breath, she turned—and gave a start.

Aidan's expression was so grim, it alarmed her. He waited for her on the dais. "Come here, Anne."

She didn't want to go. And yet she could not be a coward. "You are upset."

He pointed to a space on the floor in front of him. "Here."

Anne began walking toward him, feeling much like a guilty prisoner coming before a magistrate. She stopped at the base of the dais.

He stepped down and lifted her face up to him. "Why did you do it?"

She met his gaze. "I wanted to give Deacon a chance to escape."

"He did."

"Good."

His brows came together, and Anne sensed he saw more than she wished he did. He took her hand, his thumb lightly rubbing the inside of her wrist. "But there is more, isn't there? You were shaking all through lunch."

"I didn't!" she said with alarm. "I was so nervous, but I'd hoped he didn't notice."

"He didn't. *I did*." He paused a moment, then said, "I won't let harm come to you. When I tell you to do something, I expect to be obeyed. Do you understand, Anne?"

She looked past his shoulders out the window at the rolling sea. The image of the soldiers searching the beach where she and the girls had been dancing made her tremble.

He pulled her closer. "What is it, Anne? What frightens you?"

Her throat tightened. It almost hurt to speak. "You mustn't play games with men like Major Lambert, Aidan." She raised her face to him. "He can do what he threatens. He could have dragged you out of here today and all the way to London. In chains, even. And if you'd died along the road or in prison, well, so be it."

"Britain is still a nation of laws," he assured her.

"That are not always followed," she answered. "Especially when words like treason are bandied about. You aren't a traitor, are you?"

"Anne," he said, drawing out her name in a way to let her know she was being ridiculous.

She pulled her hand away. "Don't patronize me, Aidan. You have patronized me from the first moment we met, and I won't stand for it anymore. My father died because he believed in those laws. They said he was a traitor, too."

"What?" Now she had his attention.

She nodded. "He wasn't a traitor, but a doctor. A good one. I grew up on the coast like this. There was smuggling. One of the local men got caught by the excise men. There was a fight and he was knifed, but not before he killed one of the excise officers. The villager came to my father for help. He didn't tell Father how he earned his wound, and Father didn't ask. Instead, he treated the man and would have sent him on his way, except the excise men caught wind of where the smuggler was."

She rubbed her arms to vanquish the chill of memory. "People are funny, Aidan. You don't know whom you can trust when something like this happens. Someone told the excise men the smuggler was with my father. I was asleep and there was a loud racket. They broke down the door to our house. The next I knew, they were dragging Father out, while my mother begged and cried for them to

let him be." She frowned at Aidan. "The excise officer was an ambitious man much like Major Lambert. He was proud to deliver my father to London."

"What happened?"

"Father was tried and found innocent. But it took
almost all summer, as the summer passed we became poorer. There were nights when we had so little food, my mother would give me hers and other
nights when there was nothing at all."

"Did he return?"

"No. He became ill in prison and died before he
could come home. Mother passed on less than a
year later. My parents were very close. They held a
great fondness for each other. I don't think she ever
laughed after he left. And it was so unfair because
he was innocent. So I'm going to ask again, Aidan,
are you innocent?"

Instead of answering, he walked to her and
placed his hands on her shoulders. Slowly, almost
reverently, he kissed her on the forehead. It was a
chaste kiss, almost a benediction. He followed it by
rubbing the back of his fingers against her cheek.
"Brave, brave, Anne," he said softly, then turned
and left the room.

She stood quiet for some time, lost in her own
thoughts. Aidan had been telling her it was a question he would not answer and there was nothing
she could do for it. He would make his own choices.
He didn't love her, so her opinion, and her fears,
carried little weight.

But she worried she would be much like her mother. If something happened to him, a part of her would die, too.

Sometimes it hurt to dream of things one couldn't have.

Anne shook away her dark thoughts. Aidan wanted nothing from her. She could have no expectations.

Always practical Anne.

Always the one left alone.

She went to her room to fetch her shawl. It was late afternoon and the day had grown cloudy.

No one was in the upstairs hallway. She opened her door and left it open as she crossed to an old trunk she had found and cleaned to hold her belongings. As she opened the lid, she sensed she was not alone.

Anne turned as the door closed, revealing Deacon hiding behind it. She gave a little scream of shock.

He placed a finger to his lips. "I didn't mean to scare you."

"What are you doing here?" she asked, groping for her composure.

"I needed a place to hide where they wouldn't look." He paused. "Why did you do it? Why didn't you tell the English where I am?"

Anne straightened. "I do not wish you harm."

"I've wished you to the devil a hundred times since you first arrived."

"And I haven't gone, have I?"

He stared at her and then chuckled. "No, you are a most stubborn English lass."

The door flew open. Deacon moved just in time or he would have been smashed. It was Aidan. "I heard you scream," he said to Anne.

She pointed to Deacon and Aidan relaxed. "I wondered where you'd gone off to."

"Here all along," Deacon said proudly. "Right under Lambert's bloody English nose."

"Well, we'll have to find a place for you," Aidan said.

"I can't stay, Tiebauld. You are in danger with me here."

"I'm in danger with you anywhere. Lambert wants me. I might as well be hanged for a wolf as well as a sheep. Come along. We'll put you in the servants' quarters. Stay out of sight and everyone will believe you've escaped."

But Deacon didn't move. "Is it all right with your wife?"

"Anne?" Aidan asked in surprise. Deacon had been so set against her, his asking her permission surprised him. Aidan looked to her. "What do you say, Anne? Shall we hide Deacon?"

She considered her former rival a long moment. Finally, "I believe we must."

Aidan smiled his approval. "Come along then, Deacon."

His friend hesitated a moment. "You were bold, my lady. You saved my life."

Over the past week, she'd have loved to see Deacon humbled. Now, she understood why Aidan valued his friendship. The man was loyal, and she had proved her worth to him. He accepted her, his straightforward praise for her actions touching her deeply.

Anne waited until they left, and then she collapsed on the bed. She wanted to believe all would be fine.

She knew she was fooling herself—and yet she'd seen genuine concern on Aidan's face when he'd heard her scream. Always the protector. She smiled sadly, wrapping the yellow Kashmir around her arms and burying her nose in it. For the past few days, she'd pretended not to care. She didn't think she could live that way any longer.

And she was tired of arguing. She'd even offered herself to him, and short of parading herself naked in front of him, she didn't know what to do.

Perhaps the time had come to try that, too.

Aidan led Deacon to the servants' wing. "The only ones here are Norval and Cora, and they can be trusted."

Deacon didn't answer. Ever since the night he had propositioned her, he had not spoken to Cora. He'd been a coward.

Now, he was going to be practically living with her.

Aidan didn't notice his quietness. He made sure there were blankets and left.

Deacon sat alone in his room, listening. After an hour, he heard a woman's light tread. She went into the room next to his.

He rose from the bed and went out in the hall. The door to Cora's room was closed. He could knock, but she would not let him in. She'd barely looked at him since the night he'd attempted to attack her.

The handle turned, and before he could move, she opened the door. For the space of several heartbeats, they stared at each other.

She broke the silence first. "Lord Tiebauld told me you would be here."

He nodded, tongue-tied and ashamed. But when she started to move past him, he said, "Wait."

She stopped and looked at him expectantly. "Yes, my lord?"

He stalled. "Where is the girl?"

"Marie? She's up with Mrs. MacEwan in the kitchen."

They were alone. Deacon forced himself to say his piece. "I want you to know you don't have to worry about me." He made himself meet her gaze. "I won't harm you."

Cora shifted. "I'll not turn you in to the soldiers, if that is what you are afraid of."

"I'm more afraid of you than I am the English,"

he admitted candidly. It was true. Suddenly, awkward with his hands, he doubled them in fists at his sides and confessed, "I'd thought I was a better man."

Her mouth twisted into a rueful smile. "I've never had a man apologize to me before. I don't know if I like it."

"It doesn't matter if you like it. What matters is if you accept it. I've not had a drop to drink since that night, Cora. I'd like to blame the ale. I don't know if I can."

She raised her hand to her bottom lip, the gesture thoughtful and evocative all at once. "I can forgive," she said. "Thank you." She hurried away.

Anne didn't come down to dinner. She had asked Norval for a bath and had sent word to Aidan she didn't want to be disturbed. He worried. Lambert's appearance had stirred memories, memories she'd probably wanted to forget.

It bothered him that in her grief, she had turned from him.

Worse, now knowing her past, he had no right to let her become embroiled in his activities. She would only be hurt.

As he made his rounds of the stables and courtyard, Aidan found himself increasingly concerned. Maybe he should go to her. Maybe he'd lived with himself for so long, he'd forgotten how to relate to

another. Women were sensitive. She might even
now be up in her room, crying her eyes out.

He could picture it. His brave Anne overcome by
the loss of her father and mother and needing someone to hold her.

He liked the image.

But he was aware she could just as easily snub
him. Anne was a proud woman. She might not like
his offer of comfort.

She might even take offense in it. It seemed he
never knew how to do the right thing when he was
around her. He'd not had the problem before. He'd
always thought women easy to understand.

But Anne was a deeper, more intelligent woman
than he'd known. A headstrong lass who kept him
on his toes.

He hadn't ever thought he'd admire a woman
who challenged him. But he liked it. And he liked
her. Very much. Maybe even too much.

In the stables, he rubbed Beaumains' nose and
caught himself fantasizing about Anne. Her skin
would be as soft and velvety—and then he laughed.
Imagine comparing a woman to a horse's nose.
Anne would laugh, too. She had a sense of the
ridiculous . . .

Suddenly, Aidan wanted to see her.

He strode with purpose into the house. Impatient,
he bounded up the steps to the hallway. He knocked
on her door.

There was no answer.

He knocked again. "Anne?"

Nothing.

Puzzled, he opened the door. The room was dark but the light from the hallway torch showed the bed empty. Where could she have gone?

She could be in the kitchen or servants' quarters. It was also possible she could have gone visiting. In a short amount of time, she had integrated herself in the lives of his crofters.

She obviously wasn't upset.

He hit his head lightly against the door. He was fool. A fool who was in danger of falling in love if he wasn't careful.

He shut the door and headed for his room. It was all for the best. Tomorrow, he would put her on a coach for London if he had to tie her to it.

Aidan shoved open his bedroom door with one shoulder and then stopped.

Everything was as he liked it. A fire burned in the hearth. Several candles gave the room a soft glow and his torches provided light for reading. His soap was dry and in its place. His towel hung over the chair.

But there was one difference, and it was a huge change—Anne was soaking in the tub.

Chapter 11

Anne heard the door shut.

She and Aidan were alone.

Even though she dared not face him, the hairs on the back of her neck tickled with anticipation . . . and fear. Her courage abandoned her. *She was being a fool!*

She sat upright in the tub, hugging her knees to her chest to hide her nakedness the best she could. Pretending her presence was a mistake, she said, "I did not expect you to come to bed so soon. Please give me a moment's more privacy and I'll leave."

Her words sounded stupid to her own ears—but Aidan should do the gentlemanly thing and allow her a graceful exit.

He didn't. Booted footsteps crossed the stone floor to her. A heartbeat later, he sat in the chair by the tub.

Anne couldn't meet his gaze. She concentrated on the fire in the grate. "My towel, please."

Instead, he captured her hand in his and ran his thumb along the sensitive skin inside her wrist. It tickled, and yet she didn't laugh. She could barely breathe.

He lowered his head. She turned then and watched as he pressed his lips where his thumb had touched, right on the pulse spot. Suddenly, the room grew warm. Hot, even. His tongue brushed her skin and the fingers of her other hand moved to stroke his blue-black hair.

He raised his head. His gaze followed the curve of her breasts pressed against her knees, up the line of her neck to her face, lingering a moment on her lips before meeting her eyes. "You do like me, even a little?"

I love you. "Perhaps a little."

"A little is enough." He laced her fingers with his and started to rise.

Anne panicked. *What had she been thinking?* She wasn't ready to be naked in front of him. Her stomach coiled with anxiety. She grabbed the other side of the tub with her free hand. "It was a mistake. I meant to be gone before you came to bed."

He chuckled softly, not believing her excuse. "For the past four days you've managed to avoid me very well." He kissed the hand he held. "Trust me."

"What are you going to do?"

He reached for the towel. "Dry you off. Will you let me?"

Anne had never heard a more scandalous suggestion in her life—or a more tempting one. "I'm afraid."

"I know. You needn't be. I won't do anything you wouldn't wish."

"I know." But it still didn't make this step into the unknown easier.

Aidan didn't move, but waited patiently.

She released her grip on the tub and let him help her to her feet. Water dripped and ran in rivulets off her. The chill in the night air made her wet skin tighten. Her nipples puckered. Her instinct was to cover herself with arms and hands, but she wouldn't. No more hiding.

For one wild second, her arm floundered in the air and then she dropped it to her side. "I suppose there will be no secrets between us now," she said weakly, in an attempt to hide her embarrassment.

Aidan hadn't known what he'd expected, but it hadn't been this curvaceous, sensual creature who had risen from his tub. Her high-waisted gowns had effectively disguised what was beneath.

In reality, she was a sea nymph come to life with cautious gray eyes and silky hair down to a waist that was narrow enough that he could measure the distance with his hands. The curving flare of her hips gave way to long, long legs. The kind that could wrap themselves around a man and hold him tight.

But what really captured his attention were her breasts. Anne had plump, beautiful breasts with dark brown aureoles that aroused something vitally primal inside him. The tightened nipples begged for his touch.

He leaned forward, wanting to capture those impudent little nubs with his mouth. To taste their texture and warm them—

She jumped out of the tub and he kissed air. "I'm growing cold."

Only then did he come to his senses and remember his promise to dry her off—a promise he intended to keep. He slid his arm around her waist. "Let me warm you."

She was still skittish, her eyes ready to swallow her face. He started with her arms, relaxing the tension in them . . . but he couldn't help but move to her breasts next. He weighed them in his towel-covered hand. "You are beautiful."

She'd been studying a point in the corner of the room. Her gaze now shifted to him. "Do you mean those words?"

The doubt in her tone surprised him. "Anne, I've always thought you lovely, from the first moment we met."

"You couldn't have. My clothes were torn and my hair was blown every which way."

" 'Twas not clothes or hair styles that attracted me." He moved the towel down her back and over the curve of her buttock. Her skin was smoother than cream.

"Then what was it?" She asked the question almost fretfully.

He grinned. "It was your spirit. Not many lasses would have attempted to geld me." He referred to her whacking him with the stick.

Hot color flooded her face. In the haven of his arms, her gaze dropped to his chest. "I didn't mean to hurt you."

"Yes you did, but the damage wasn't permanent, as you will soon find out." He tossed the towel aside. It landed in the tub and he couldn't care less. He lifted her up in his arms, wrapping those lovely long legs around his waist, her breasts against his chest.

She looked up in confusion, her mouth opening, and he silenced any questions with a kiss. A kiss that let her know he was done with talking. A kiss that would seduce.

Instead, he soon discovered himself being seduced.

She was an innocent, new to the art of kissing. She started to pull back. He wouldn't let her. He held her as one would a child, an arm under her buttocks, a hand on her back to press her close, while he claimed her mouth, begging, pleading, schooling her into what he liked.

And she kissed back, a willing pupil. He broke off

the kiss, but her lips chased his. Her arms came around his neck and she took the kiss deeper still.

He stroked her with his tongue.

A low, happy laugh escaped her. They stared at each other, nose-to-nose and almost cross-eyed.

He nipped the tip of her nose and slid her body down a notch until she could feel the strength of his arousal against the most intimate part of her. Nothing separated them but the leather of his breeches. He could feel her heat.

For a second, her eyes widened and he watched, fascinated, as understanding dawned in them. He smiled. "I'm going to have you, Anne Black. I'm going to carry to that bed and make a woman of you. My woman."

She bowed her head. He thought she was laughing, but a tear landed on his chest.

Stunned, Aidan said, "Anne, is something wrong? What have I done?" She tried to duck her head to avoid his scrutiny, but he'd none of it. "Anne, what is the matter?"

"You've done nothing." She raised her head to look at him. Her nose was turning a little pink and her eyes were shiny with huge tears. "I'm just happy. That's all. I'm a goose, aren't I?"

He didn't answer. Instead, he carried her over to the bed and laid her down on the sable throw. "You are beautiful," he whispered, pulling his shirt off over his head. He threw it aside and with a leap landed on the bed beside her. The bed ropes bounced, rolling her against him. He caught and held her fast.

Her eyes were sparkling now with joyful laughter. It transformed her into a seductive creature. If she was like this from only a few kisses, what would she be like when he'd buried himself deep within her?

He knew without saying it was going to be good between them. They had been destined for this moment.

Almost reverently, he cupped her breast. Dear God, he wanted to inhale her. To taste and touch every inch of her—

A knock sounded on the door. Anne scrambled to cover her nakedness, but Aidan wouldn't have any of it. He caught her wrist. "Whoever it is can go to the devil. We've got other things to do." He pressed her back against the bed.

Someone knocked again. "Laird? It's Davey. Hugh sent me."

Mere inches from her parted lips, her body warm and pliant beneath his, Aidan froze. "Davey?"

The Danes had come. It was starting.

"Laird, they—"

"I'll be right there, Davey," Aidan said, cutting him off. It would not be good to say anything in front of Anne.

"What is it?" she whispered.

He sat up with a groan. The Danes' timing couldn't be worse.

"Are you all right?" she asked anxiously.

He looked at her. She'd pulled the sable up to hide nakedness, but her hair was tumbled and messy, her lips rosy and a little swollen from his kiss—and he wanted nothing more than to give her a quick one. But he couldn't. This would be her first time and it must be done right.

He'd have to wait.

He prayed his errant body could.

"I'll manage." He tore his gaze from her and went to his wardrobe. He pulled out a black shirt and threw it over his head.

"What could Hugh want that is so urgent?" she asked.

"The horses," he answered noncommittally. "I asked Hugh to keep an eye on Doublelet. You must be careful when a horse is in foal."

She nodded, accepting his excuse. It made him feel ill-at-ease to lie to her.

He crossed to the bed and gave her a great bruising kiss. "You wait here and we'll finish what we've started when I come back."

"Don't be long," she whispered.

Sweet, sweet Anne. He left the room, the sooner to return.

Anne stretched out on the bed, her body still stimulated and humming with excitement. The fine, thick fur felt good against her bare skin. She hoped nothing serious had happened to Doublelet. Everyone at Kelwin knew Aidan anticipated great things from her foal.

Perhaps she should join him in the barn. It would be easier than waiting.

And she could be close to him.

She rose from the bed and started dressing. Fussing over her hair, she hurried to his wash basin by the windows where she'd left her pins.

It was cloudy but the moon was full. A lover's moon, she reminded herself. It came out from behind the clouds just long enough to wink at her. She almost laughed at it, she was so happy, but then she noticed movement.

Anne peered into the darkness. There, on the cliff path, were walkers. Who would be out at this time of night? The cloud shifted again, and she recognized Hugh.

And Aidan was with him, as were several of the other men from the clan.

A sense of foreboding came down on top of her, crushing her earlier well-being.

Why would Aidan tell her he was going one place and then go to another?

Anne backed away from the window. She should go back to bed. But she wouldn't be able to sleep.

And when he returned—?

For a moment, she wavered in indecision. She didn't know if she could stand the pain of discovering his passion was nothing more than a ploy to hide his subterfuge. A successful ploy.

The suspense of waiting for him to return was unacceptable. She wanted answers now. Hurrying to her room, she changed into her blue cambric dress and followed her husband out of the castle and down the cliff path.

Her kid slippers were not the best for climbing down a rocky path at night. She had to walk slower than she wished lest she slip and give away her game.

Halfway down the path, she could see a group of men on the beach. What were they doing? She traveled as closely as she dared. Fang's middle sons served as watchers but they weren't doing a good job of it. They were more interested in what was happening at some point out at sea.

Anne strained her eyes to see what they saw. All was inky darkness . . . and then she heard a sound of oars in the roiling water.

She settled behind a rock and waited. A few minutes passed like hours. Against the sand of the beach where she and the girls had danced the morning away, a dinghy was pulled to shore. She caught sight of her husband's tall form. He helped land the boat as men jumped out of it. They greeted him in a language foreign to her but which Aidan knew passably well.

They didn't talk long, but set to work unloading

small kegs. He's smuggling, Anne realized, and didn't know whether to be relieved or worried.

Another dinghy came ashore and the Scotsmen quickly helped to unload it. The line of kegs along the beach rapidly grew.

Aidan called his lookouts to the beach. Anne moved closer. She had to know what was in those kegs. It couldn't be brandy. Aidan had no taste for it and he was wealthy enough through his family. What could he need with smugglers' booty?

The dinghies pulled away from shore, their cargo unloaded. In the distance, Anne could see the lights of a ship she'd not noticed before. The Scotsmen waited, it seemed, until the boats were too far out to see what they were doing. They lifted the small kegs on their shoulders and started to walk toward the far cliffs.

Anne knew there was a path there leading along the coast, but they didn't go toward the path. They seemed to disappear.

She frowned. She had to get closer.

Aidan's watchers were busy helping to carry the kegs, and she took advantage of it. She even dared to go all the way up to the nearest one. She sniffed. Besides the smell of salt air, there was the scent of something acrid. It made her nose tingle.

The men were coming back empty handed. She dashed to cower behind some rocks close to the water. The edge of her dress started to get wet, but she didn't dare move.

Three times she watched the men perform their task. She strained her ears for any clue for what could be in the kegs and where they had stored them, but they were grimly quiet.

Her vivid imagination took over. There must be a cave in those cliffs. A smuggler's cave. A shiver went through her that had nothing to do with the chill in the water lapping at her hem.

When they'd finished, it was as if they vanished into the night. One moment they were working, the next they were gone back to their homes and families.

But where was her husband?

"You can stand up now, Anne."

Aidan's voice startled her. She looked up and found him looming over her rocky hiding place. He held out his hand.

Slowly she came to her feet, pointedly ignoring his hand. "How did you know I was there?"

"The scent of the soap. What are you doing here?"

"I wanted to know what was going on. Obviously it has nothing to do with a pregnant horse."

"For what purpose?" There was a testy note in his voice.

Well, she could be testy, too. "My husband sneaks around in the dark. Is that not reason to want to know what he is doing?"

He took hold of her by the chin, raising her gaze to his. "And what did you find out?"

Anne tried to pull away. She couldn't. "You know my history. I don't like smuggling."

Footsteps ran along the path. It was Davey. "Hugh said the gunpowder is covered with a tarp . . ." His voice trailed off as he realized Aidan was not alone.

Alarmed at what he'd said in front of her, he began backing up the cliff. "I'm sorry, Laird."

"Go on, Davey. Go to your bed," Aidan told him curtly.

The boy took off running.

Anne was stunned. "Major Lambert is right. You are planning a rebellion."

"It's not what you think." He reached for her arm but she shook him off, backing away from him.

"You have stored gunpowder in the cliffs. In what? A cave? Are you mad? Do you realize what Major Lambert will do to you if it is discovered? *What he could do to all of us?*"

He grabbed her arm above the elbow, his hold tight. "Quiet, or you'll wake all of Caithness."

"I thought I saw all of Caithness on the beach helping you." She shook her head. "How could you bring Davey into this?"

"I didn't, Anne. He came with his brothers."

She almost collapsed. "Does their mother know? It will kill her if any harm comes to her sons."

"I know." His voice didn't sound like himself, full of confidence and certainty.

"Aidan, are you saying you question this course of action?"

"Yes!" The word shot out of him as if he'd held it too long. "But I have no choice, Anne, and I don't expect you to understand."

"Then explain it to me. What is so important that it would drive you to rebellion?"

He sat on the rock she'd hid behind. "I've tried to avoid it, Anne, but Deacon is right. You saw Lambert. He wants my blood whether I am innocent or guilty."

"He could hang you guilty at this moment," she said crisply.

It surprised a laugh out of him, a laugh she didn't understand. "What is so funny?"

"I realized you are correct." He stood. "You've heard of the Clearances, haven't you?"

She shrugged. "No."

"Well, some call them 'improvements,'" he said sarcastically. "A landlord gives his tenants a week to clear out. Whether they do or they don't, the homes are burned and the land is used for grazing."

"Why?"

"It's more valuable with sheep on it than it is with people."

"Where do the people go?"

"Who cares? Or at least, that is the attitude. Some move in with family, others go to Ireland, and still others are forced to emigrate even further."

She frowned at the sand, digesting what he'd told her. "I suppose if they are renting, then they should expect to be asked to move on?" It was hard to believe people would do such a thing to others.

"I forget how English you are," he said softly. "Anne, people are being burned out because they are poor. But their families have lived on the land here since before the days of the first earl of Tiebauld."

"And those are the ones who wish to rebel."

"Yes, those who hate the English."

The moon came out from the clouds. Its light tipped the waves. It was so beautiful here. It would be hard to imagine it all destroyed.

She looked to him. "Aidan, do the Clearances bother members of our clan?"

"No. So far I've been able to protect them. My money has buffered them from the likes of the 'improvers.' But Deacon's family lost everything."

"Then let him and his brother fight—if they are foolish enough. This is why he tried to get me to leave, isn't it?" She didn't wait for his answer, but went on, "They do not have to drag you into their fight. The stakes are too high!"

"Anne, it's too late. For years I've tried to straddle two worlds. On one side are the other gentry, many of them more English than Scottish. On the other, my fellow clansmen. It is hard for you to understand the ties that bind us, ties that cut across social class. It's the old ways. I can't ignore them any longer. But I've said I will help only with the gun-powder. This is the end of my role."

"No, because they will continue to need you, just as the smuggler needed my father."

"You don't understand. I must do this."

"I understand what will happen if you are tried for treason and found guilty." She railed at his stub-bornness. "Do you? Have you any idea what it will be like?"

His expression could have been set in stone as he said, "I've made my decision, Anne."

"You will die!"

"Perhaps. But it is my choice."

His words wrapped around her heart like a vise. She took a step back. His actions were treasonous. The Crown would hang him.

She doubled over, the burden of grief almost more than she could bear.

He reached out. "Anne?"

"No, don't touch me! *I loved you.*" She recoiled from him. "But you are going to destroy yourself and everything here. The castle, the people, every-thing you've built. This isn't a game, Aidan. Or a lit-tle 'healthy danger' like stalking a mad wildcat." Tears stung her eyes. The words choked her as she said, "It'll be gone . . . all . . . gone."

"Not if I'm careful—"

She cut him off. "You can't escape it. And I can't watch it." She turned and ran.

He called after her but she did not stop. She

couldn't. She was in danger of crying and no good came of tears. He chose his fate. He chose to leave her.

Her foot slipped out of her kid shoe. She picked it up and kept running, heedless of stones on the path. She couldn't feel them.

She couldn't feel anything right now.

At the top of the cliff, Anne bypassed the house and ran for the stables. There, all was peaceful and quiet. It smelled of straw and hay. Familiar scents, comforting scents. The horses were asleep. Not even the dogs who had chosen the stables for their bed seemed surprised at her appearance. The animals didn't know what the future held. They had no fears, no worries.

Finding an empty stall, she closed herself in, went to the furthest corner, and slid down the wall. Then and only then, when she was alone and need not fear being heard, did she release the huge hiccupping sobs of her grief, letting them overcome her.

The smallest dog, York, scratched at the stall, whining to come comfort her. But she couldn't let him in.

She couldn't let anyone in, not anymore. It hurt too much.

Helplessly, Aidan watched Anne run. She'd need time to understand. If she loved him, she must accept the man he was.

Love.

The word shimmered in his mind. He etched it in the sand with his toe, but the "L" turned into an "A" and he wrote the letters of her name instead.

She had to understand.

He walked up the path, words forming in his mind to convince her. And if they didn't work, he'd kiss her into submission. His pace picked up. Yes, that was what he would do.

But inside, he didn't find Anne in his room. "So, we're back to that," he muttered, and strode to the guest room door.

He pounded hard on it three times, and then shoved it open. She wasn't there.

Aidan returned to his room. He told himself he should let her be, and yet he couldn't. The sable throw still carried the imprint of her body. Her pins were on his wash stand.

Her very presence was woven into the fabric of his life.

A sound in the hallway made him race to the door. He threw it open and there was Anne. She was about to enter her room. Her dress was streaked with dirt and mud. She carried her shoes.

"Anne!"

She paused, a hand on the door handle. For a long moment they stared at each other, and he could almost imagine he was looking into the eyes of a stranger.

The expression on her face was strained, her complexion pale. His poor Anne.

He held out his hand. "Come, let us talk."

She went in her room, shutting the door firmly behind her.

Frustrated, Aidan closed his own door. He'd let her sleep on it. In the morning, she'd see sense— even if he had to shake it into her.

Unfortunately, sleep was a long time in coming.

When he did wake, the day was more advanced than it usually was when he woke. Swearing softly, he started to dress and then stopped. Someone knocking on the door was what woke him.

"Who is it?" he barked, pulling on his breeches.

"Cora, my lord."

He cracked open the door. "What is it?"

The maid appeared nervous. "Lady Tiebauld insists upon leaving."

"Leaving for where?"

"*London*, my lord," she answered with exasperation. "Deacon said you would want to know."

Aidan opened the door wide. "Don't let her leave."

"We won't. But when everyone refused to do as she asked without permission from you, she marched off to the stables saying she would saddle her own horse."

She spoke to the air. Aidan was already getting dressed. He threw on his shirt, not even bothering to tuck it in, and shoved his feet into his boots.

He charged toward the stables.

Chapter 12

Hugh, Deacon, and Mrs. MacEwan waited for Aidan in the great hall. Even Norval worriedly paced a line from the dais to the staircase and back.

"It's about time you woke," Hugh snapped.

Aidan frowned at Deacon. "What are you doing here?"

His friend held up his hands in a gesture of surrender. "I was attempting to talk sense into your wife."

Since when had Anne and Deacon become chums? "Get back into hiding. I'll take care of my wife."

Mrs. MacEwan rubbed her hands anxiously. "You will stop her, won't you, laird? She is so insistent. I told her she couldn't go riding off alone but she says she doesn't need an escort."

"She's being stubborn," Aidan answered.

"Aye, she is, but I wouldn't tell her that to her face," Mrs. MacEwan agreed, and then lowered her voice to add, "Not if you want her back."

Aidan didn't waste any more time on conversation—especially if they were going to become lectures! He stormed out the front door. Norval stepped back just in time or else he would have bowled him over.

Out in the courtyard, Kathleen Keith, Bonnie Mowat, the other women, the children, and even some of the men stood waiting. He frowned at having Anne's tiff aired in such a public forum. "Don't any of you have something to do with your time this morning?"

Mrs. Keith raised her chin and scowled right back at him. "We've been waiting for you to get your arse out of the bed and come stop her . . . my lord," she added with belated respectfulness.

Aidan gave her a glare that sent her scurrying behind Mrs. Mowat.

"You will stop her?" Davey said, trotting alongside Aidan.

"I intend to." He headed for the stables.

The others fell in behind him, following as closely as they dared. Aidan knew they were there—and he also knew he couldn't prevent them from nosing into his business.

Not without making the matter worse!

His long legs ate up the path leading to the stables. He stopped in front of the double doors. Davey's friend Jamie dashed forward, the dogs trailing at his heels.

"I kept a watch on her like Davey told me to,

Laird," Jamie reported. He confided, "She doesn't know much about horses. If she leaves, she won't go far."

"Good lad. Now, run along with the others and let me talk to my wife."

"She doesn't want to talk to anyone," Jamie informed him officiously.

"She'll talk to me."

"To burn your ears off," the boy muttered, moving to join Davey, who stood on a stone wall.

Aidan took a step toward the door. The dogs went along with him. He stopped. "You stay here, too, laddies."

Was it his imagination or did they actually act chastened? However as he approached the doorway, York pranced right past him and up to Anne, who stood in a patch of sunlight, her back to Aidan. She was having a devil of a time saddling an antsy roan mare, Hugh's hunting sack, presumably holding her worldly possessions, at her feet.

She still wore her blue dress. What with her straw leghorn bonnet and jaunty yellow shawl, she was sure to be a sight riding on the road. Aidan doubted if she would make it to Wick, let alone London.

The pup pushed against her legs, and when that didn't gain her attention, he barked. Ignored again, he sat and looked helplessly to Aidan for assistance.

The problem was, Aidan didn't know what to do.

So he spoke honestly. "No one wants you to leave, Anne. Not even York."

She stiffened at the sound of his voice, and for a moment he thought she'd ignore him, too. Then, "He's a pest."

"Pest. It might be a good name for him. We could change it."

Her hands stopped moving. She squeezed the cinch strap she'd been buckling tightly. But she did not answer him.

Behind him, the good citizens of Kelwin had edged closer, the better to hear their conversation. All too aware of them, Aidan crossed over and shut the barn door.

Putting the bar in place, he said, "They'll probably peek through the windows anyway."

Anne had not moved, but at his words a sound escaped her that sounded half-laugh, half-sob.

He walked to her. He would have taken her in his arms, yet something about the set of her shoulders warned him to go slowly.

"I don't want you to leave, Anne." There, he'd said it. He meant it.

"I can't stay." She righted herself and gave the cinch one last tug to ensure it was tight enough.

Her insistence made him angry. "Well then, you'd best put a bridle on the horse," he said brittlely.

"Yes, I mean to do that." She moved to fetch one from the saddle room.

Aidan moved between her and the horse, his

hands on his hips. "Hugh may not want you to ride off with his hunting sack. He'd only lent it to you temporarily."

She came out of the saddle room and for the first time met his gaze. He was surprised how hard her eyes were. They seemed to look right through him. "I'll send it back. Here, you can take this now." She pulled her wedding ring off her finger and offered it to him.

He refused to take it. "Don't expect my sister to help," he said harshly. "She wanted a baby from this marriage."

"I don't want her money or yours. Some things cannot be bought." She closed her hand over the ring and tucked it into Hugh's hunting sack.

"Then what will you do?"

"Take a position as a lady's companion. I believe it will suit my temperament."

He almost laughed. "Not hardly. You are a stubborn and proud woman, Anne Black."

"*Burnett,*" she corrected. "My name is Anne Burnett. I'll have the marriage annulled in London."

She started past him to the head of the horse, but Aidan reached out and turned her around so her back was against the roan's body. He held her trapped with his arms, his hands on the saddle. The horse shifted restlessly.

"You can't leave me, Anne. Not now."

"*I must.*" The urgent words sounded hoarse, as if she had to force them past her lips.

He tried to make her understand. "You've interrupted all our lives. You are one of us now. We can't let you go."

"We?" she asked sadly.

"Me, Anne. I don't want you to go."

Her lower lip trembled, but she steadied herself. Her hand came up to rub the side of his face. "You haven't shaved yet."

"I rolled out of bed, heard the news you were leaving, and came here."

Her fingers traced the path of his jaw to the curl in the hair around his collar. "And you need a haircut," she said softly.

"Is this why you are leaving me? My grooming habits? My hair?" He released her and went to the saddle room, where he kept a box of tools. He took out a pair of shears. "Here, Anne," he said, offering them to her. "Cut it. It means nothing to me." He added quietly, "Nothing means more than you." The moment he said them, he realized the words were true.

She drew in a shaky breath. He pressed on. "You've bullied your way into my life. You can't leave."

Her gaze dropped to the shears and then to the floor. She shook her head. "I can't stay. I can't watch what will happen."

"You can see the future?"

"I don't need to be a seer. I know what will happen. You are defying the *English government*! All of this, everything, will be destroyed."

"Not if I can help it. It is only the gunpowder. After it is delivered, I will not be involved."

She stared at him as if he'd spoken gibberish. "You cannot turn your back on your friends. Deacon's presence alone is enough to have you tried for treason. Aidan, you are involved. You've made your decision."

He took a step back, the reality of his actions sinking in. He closed his eyes, wishing it could be another way and knowing he had no choice. "You're right," he said, breaking the silence. "I have sided with the rebels. There is no turning back." He reached out rubbed the roan's muzzle. "It must be in my blood."

"No, a love of fairness is in your blood, Aidan. A belief in letting men live with respect for each other. You are the most revolutionary man I've ever met . . . and one of the most successful. I love you. I will always love you. I could love no other."

It was on the tip of his tongue to ask her to stay again, but he knew she wouldn't. "And I shall always love you, Anne . . . Burnett," he added sadly.

She nodded, studying the floor. Aidan understood how she felt. For the first time, he had discovered his heart . . . and now, it was breaking.

"Well," he said, more to end the silence. "I, uh, don't think you should ride alone to London. Give

me a few hours and I will have a hired chaise here."
It was hard to look at her. He ran his thumb over the
curved handle of the shears. "You can give Hugh
back his hunting sack. You can have the trunk in
your room."

"Thank you."

There, it was resolved. But neither of them
moved. So close to each other, and yet so far apart.

Someone pounded on the stable door. Aidan was
about to wish them to the devil when Hugh's voice
shouted, "Tiebauld! Major Lambert's men are riding up the road. There is a party of them, all on
horseback."

"What the bloody hell do they want now?" he demanded irritably.

She took hold of his arm, her expressive eyes
wide with fright. "They've come for you, Aidan."

"Or Deacon."

"No. It's *you* they want. I can feel it." She pulled
him toward the saddle room, where there was a
door leading to the outside. "You must run. If you
hurry, you can escape to one of those small boats by
the beach. They won't catch you if you are out at
sea."

"Anne—"

She ignored him, her mind busy with a plan. "I'll
go and tell them you are . . . are ill. I'll refuse to let
them see you, and that will buy more time for
you—"

"Anne!" He took her arms, the shears still in one hand. "Listen to me. I'm not going to run."

"You must! They will put you to death."

Aidan shook his head and pulled her into his arms. She offered no resistance. He kissed the top of her hair. "Oh, Anne. They'll expect me to run." He held her tight, giving her a moment to calm herself. "Now listen, you must be brave and do what I tell you, even if you wish to argue with me." He drew back to see her face. "We are going to greet the soldiers like the most loyal subjects the King has."

"What if they arrest you?"

He smiled. The panic had left her eyes. Her courage was back. Her practical mind working. "You will weep and rail and pretend to be the dutiful wife. Then you will go to my room and look in the bottom of my clothing trunk at the end of the bed. Inside it is a false drawer. There you will find gold. Take it and return to London. Go to my sister. She will know what to do."

"Can she save you?"

He almost laughed. Alpina would be furious if she knew of his activities. She barely thought of herself as Scottish. But he couldn't tell Anne that. "She will do what she can. Now, put a good face on it. For all we know, Lambert dropped one of his gloves and has come to retrieve it."

"I doubt it."

"We'll see, then." He offered her his arm.

Anne looked down at it and smiled. "Very well. Let us pretend all is normal."

"It is—for us!"

His wise observation surprised a laugh out of her as he'd intended it to. He escorted her out of the barn, York trotting proudly beside them, and there they were greeted by what appeared to be all the tenants of Kelwin.

It took them both aback to be an object of such speculation. Mrs. Mowat and Mrs. Keith stood with raised eyebrows. Even Fang was there. He spoke for the group as he always did. "Well?"

"Well *what*?" Aidan asked.

Fang's eyes rounded like an owl's. "What is the matter with your brains, Laird? We all want to know if she is staying."

Anne pulled back, fearing the answer to such a question. Aidan placed his hand reassuringly over hers resting on his arm. "For now," he said.

A cheer the likes of which he'd never heard went up from the crowd. The women congratulated each other as though they had accomplished something. Some of the men were less pleased. Aidan thought he saw money change hands and realized there had been a wager or two.

All he could do was laugh. If a demonstration of such affection was not enough to will her to stay, well, it had to soften her resolve a bit.

"Come along," he said briskly. "We have company."

His reminder sobered everyone. "What do you want us to do, Tiebauld?" Hugh asked.

Aidan gestured with the hand holding the shears. "Be yourselves. Nothing is amiss. But let us not go down into the courtyard together. Some of you take the cliff path." He nodded to Davey. "Take care of my lady's horse." The boy ran to do his bidding.

Aidan turned to his wife. "Shall we?"

She nodded, almost as if not trusting her voice to speak. They were almost to the courtyard when she said, "Do we look like a lord and lady coming in from a stroll?" She rearranged her shawl on her shoulders.

"Possibly. Remember what I told you about the trunk and keep your wits about you. Here they are." He led her to stand on the castle's front step while he walked out to greet the party of some twenty men.

The soldiers rode through Kelwin's majestic gate, their red coats a bright splash of color on an overcast day. Major Lambert was not leading them. Instead, his young second-in-command was in charge.

Around the courtyard walls, the people of Kelwin gathered to watch in spite of Aidan's warning. The day before, their mood had been cautious. Today they were hostile. Aidan noticed Fang's two oldest sons carried pitchforks, as if they'd just come in from the fields.

He prayed the hotheads would keep their tempers.

The officer rode up to Aidan and dismounted. Bowing, he said, "Lord Tiebauld?"

Aidan nodded.

"I am Lieutenant Fordyce. I apologize for calling on you so early."

Not liking the man's forced politeness, Aidan asked bluntly, "What business brings you back to Kelwin, Lieutenant?" They might as well have it out in the open.

The officer licked his bottom lip, a nervous gesture. There was a note of regret in his voice when he said, "Major Lambert has requested the company of Lady Tiebauld as his dinner guest this evening. We are to escort her to his headquarters in Lybster. I have a horse for her to ride." He nodded to one of the soldiers, who came forward with a steady-looking bay.

For a second, Aidan didn't believe he'd heard the officer correctly. "My wife?"

A low murmur ran around the courtyard among his clansmen. They, too, were surprised.

Aidan snorted his answer. "What is Lambert doing, planning a dinner party? She shall not go."

"Major Lambert feared you would object. However, my lord, I have my orders. Last night, it was my good fortune to be with him when he captured the Jacobite rebel Robbie Gunn. The major wants me to assure you it will be only a matter of time until he has arrested all the rebels."

Robbie Gunn, imprisoned. Aidan had no doubt

Lambert would do everything in his power to squeeze out the names of his compatriots. But the Gunns were a tough lot. Lambert could kill him before he'd speak.

Although shaken by the news, Aidan said almost pleasantly, "I wish him luck."

"Thank you, my lord." The lieutenant looked past Aidan's shoulder. "My lady, will you be so good as to accompany us? Time is of the essence."

Aidan stepped forward. "She will not."

"Yes, of course I will," Anne countermanded. "Give me a moment, please, Lieutenant, to gather my things. I may also change." Head high, she turned and walked into the house.

Aidan wanted to swear. Was there ever a more stubborn woman than his Anne? "One moment," he practically snarled at the officer, and rushed into the castle to shake sense into his wife.

Chapter 13

Anne knew Aidan would be right behind her. He caught up with her as she gave Cora instructions to fetch Hugh's hunting sack from the barn. "And don't let the soldiers see you," she warned.

The maid hurried to do her bidding, but Aidan stopped Cora and cautioned her in a low voice, "Don't let Deacon know his brother has been captured. He'll do something foolish."

Bleakly, Cora nodded and left.

Aidan didn't wait to see her gone, but headed for the stairs, grabbing Anne by the elbow as he passed and steering her up to the hallway, where they could be private. "You are not going," he said, when he was sure they were alone. "It is too dangerous."

"A little danger is a healthy thing," she quoted, calmly walking into her room.

He swore violently at her using his own words to argue. She untied her straw bonnet and threw it, along with the Kashmir shawl, on the bed.

"I won't let you go," Aidan commanded. He stood in the doorway, blocking her way.

Anne glared at him a moment, frustrated by his refusal to see what was happening. "How are you going to stop Lieutenant Fordyce from carrying out his orders to fetch me for supper, Aidan? His men are armed. Of course, it's a trap. They expect you to fight them over this—this *dinner* invitation. It sounds so silly." She crossed her arms, a chill going through her. "Are you ready to fight? Hugh, Fang, and his sons will take up arms. They will battle to keep me here. Of course, any of them could be killed and their families destroyed. The English government will sanction Major Lambert's actions. Worse, it will brand all of you as traitors. On the other hand, if I go with him, you have time to escape."

Aidan pounded his fist against the door so hard the wood bounced. "I won't run, Anne." He gestured with the shears he still held in his other hand. "Lambert knows I won't go anywhere as long as he has you. You will be his hostage to ensure I'm available after he's tortured a confession out of Robbie."

"Tortured?" Anne felt her heart stop. "He wouldn't do such a thing. He couldn't . . ." Her voice trailed off. Pictures of her father's haggard, bruised face rose in her mind, pictures she'd attempted to erase from memory. Of course, the major would beat Robbie. The Crown expected him to use whatever means necessary to ferret out traitors.

"Lambert wants a knighthood. Ever since our

days at University, he's lusted for greater things. Marching the great-grandson of Donner Black to London in chains for treason will earn him the right to a title."

"He won't hurt me," she insisted stubbornly. "I'll be safe, and once you are away, I'll contact your sister—"

"No, Anne. I won't let you be dragged into it."

"I already am," she replied curtly. "Besides, I will play on Major Lambert's honor. He's a gentleman. He can't be completely ruthless to a woman."

"Any man is ruthless when he wants something."

A footstep sounded in the hall and Aidan leaned back to see who approached. It was Cora. "I beg your pardon, but here is the sack my lady ordered me to fetch."

Anne reached for the hunting sack. Her hand shook. It embarrassed her. She wanted to be brave— but she was frightened.

"Leave us," Aidan said to the maid. He waited until she'd gone down the hall. He stared at Anne a moment and then came to a conclusion. "All right, we must think." He began pacing the length of the room.

"Think of what?"

"A plan." He paused. "We must be more clever than he is."

"Aidan—"

"I'm going with you."

"No! Then he has you where he can get to you if Robbie Gunn confesses." Was he mad?

"Cut my hair." He held out the shears to her.

His abrupt change of subject caught her off guard. "What? Why are you worrying about that now?"

He sat on the edge of the bed. "You said it was overlong. Do it up. Something currently in fashion. Make me a gentleman again." He considered things for a moment. "Style it like that of the poet all the women swoon over in London."

"Byron?"

"Yes, him." He sat waiting.

She took a hesitant step. "Is this part of a plan?"

Aidan frowned. "Of course . . . although I haven't thought the plan through. It will come to me. Cut my hair."

"I don't know if I can," she admitted baldly.

"Then now's the time to find out."

"Aidan, this is absurd."

He sighed in exasperation. "For once, Anne, can you do as I ask without argument?"

His words jabbed her conscience. If he wanted his hair cut before she left, what did it matter? She crossed to the bed and started snipping. She'd cut her cousins' hair a time or two, and her own, on occasion. She did have some talent for it. However, cutting Aidan's hair was different. It was so thick, and as she clipped, the shorter ends curled around her fingers.

Cora came up to tell them Lieutenant Fordyce sent word he was growing impatient. Aidan cheerfully wished the officer to the devil, a message Cora could not deliver. Anne rephrased his message to one begging the lieutenant's patience while she finished dressing.

"Yes, tell him, my lady is at her toilette," Aidan agreed, and then chuckled, rubbing pieces of his own hair between his fingers.

When she was done, Anne had to admire her handiwork. The shorter style brought a masculine strength to his face. "You look very handsome."

He grinned. "Change your dress, Anne. Wear your finest. We are going to take a trip. I must shave." He bounded out of the room with an energy she didn't feel.

Anne put on the muslin dress trimmed in green ribbons she'd worn the day before. She pinned up her hair and put on her bonnet, tying the ivory ribbons under her chin. She did not have gloves. Such small items had been lost in the coach accident and she had not had time to replace them.

The last thing she did was reach into the hunting sack and pull out her wedding ring. She ran the pad of her thumb over the engraved stag before slipping it on her finger. The band's weight felt good.

She left the room. Aidan was still in his room, dressing. She could hear him humming. There were times she thought her husband sane . . . and times she was certain he was mad as his reputation had suggested. She feared this was going to be one of those "mad" times.

Lieutenant Fordyce waited in the great hall. Gathering her courage, Anne breezed into the room with a casualness she didn't feel. "I hope I haven't kept you waiting overlong?" she asked with her best "hostess" smile.

"No, my lady," he responded dutifully.

The thought dawned on Anne that she and the lieutenant could leave immediately before Aidan came down, but a footfall on the step warned her she was too late.

She turned to her husband—and her jaw dropped. Stunned, she backed into the room.

Aidan followed her, but not as she'd ever seen him before. Gone were the leather breeches, the open-necked shirt, and scuffed boots he habitually wore in his role as laird of Clan Dunblack.

Instead, he wore a riding coat of Spanish blue superfine. The color brought out the sharp cobalt color in his eyes and made his shirt seem almost blinding white in contrast. Beneath it was a vest of gold brocade. His boots appeared almost lacquered, they were so black and shiny. Buff-colored breeches hugged his horseman's thighs, and he carried a top hat made of the finest beaver skin.

He was the very image of a gentleman of breeding. A Corinthian. An Out and Outer with the dev-

astating good looks of a rake . . . for no amount of
tailoring could have faked with padding the powerful strength in his shoulders.

He moved into the room with his usual athletic
grace and even Lieutenant Fordyce was given
pause. It was one thing to round up a Scottish rebel;
it was another to bring in a titled lord who could
have walked the streets of London—and have
friends in power.

Anne found her voice. "You *do* know how to tie a
neck cloth, my lord," she said admiringly.

Laughter danced in his eyes. "I always keep
starched ones at the ready." He swung his attention
to the officer. "I had Norval send word I wanted my
coach readied. I prefer my own conveyance because
it will be a more comfortable ride for my wife."

"Yes, my lord," the lieutenant responded, cowed
by the wondrous change in Aidan's appearance.

Aidan offered his arm. "Shall we, my lady?"

She smiled, completely charmed. She'd travel to
hell with this man. "Yes, my lord."

The good people of Kelwin still waited outside for
them. They craned their necks to get a better view of
their laird. Anne was reassured to know she wasn't the
only one taken aback by his transformation.

Aidan nodded to Hugh, but did not speak. Fang's
oldest son drove the coach up. Aidan opened the
door and offered Anne his hand.

"Wait one moment, if you please," Lieutenant
Fordyce said. He cast a frown at Thomas Mowat

and then said, "I think it best if one of my men drives."

"However you wish," Aidan said easily.

Thomas jumped down from the box and a burly soldier climbed up. The lieutenant ordered one to ride postillion and stationed another on the roof.

"Cautious, isn't he?" Aidan said to Anne in a low voice. He helped her into the coach and climbed in after her.

Lieutenant Fordyce mounted his own horse and gave the signal to leave, obviously uneasy surrounded by the disapproving clansmen.

The coach was very narrow inside and not well sprung. Aidan's large frame took up most of the space. After the second bone-rattling bounce as they rode through the gate, Aidan said, "I haven't used it in ages. But Lybster is not far. We should be there in an hour or two." He smiled and waved at Davey and his friends, who ran along the road after them.

Anne leaned back against the hard leather seat. "So, what is your plan?"

"I haven't thought of it yet."

She made a choking sound. "Is that why you dressed up?"

"A man should look good for his hanging." He immediately apologized when he saw she didn't find his quip funny. "Ah, Anne, don't frown. It was my poor attempt at a joke. Something will come to me. What is important is that we are together." He reached for her left hand. "You put your wedding ring back on."

"I felt it completed the costume," she murmured, not wanting to commit herself to more.

"It does. Come here." He pulled her to lean her head on his chest. His hand rubbed her arm, warming her. "Have courage. I'll think of something."

"You are running out of time."

He laughed. "My best ideas come when I am forced to improvise."

Anne closed her eyes. She could hear the steady beating of his heart.

His hand stopped moving. "Are you sorry for coming to Kelwin? For agreeing to this marriage?"

She raised her head. His expression was somber. And she told him the truth. "No, I'm not sorry. I wouldn't mind if our lives were a bit more dull . . . but I won't regret the marriage, Aidan. I never will."

"Promise? No matter what happens?"

"Yes."

He smiled then and she placed her hand against his smooth, hard jaw. "I love you."

Hugging her close, he didn't answer but held her as he studied the passing scenery out of the window on her side. They followed the coast road. On her side was the wild North Sea and its rocky coast. Anne felt a pang of disappointment. She wished he'd echoed her words. She knew he cared for her, but she wanted love, the kind of a commitment that promised a forever.

"What are you thinking?" she asked, keeping her voice deliberately light.

He shook his head. "I was wishing there was another way to solving the differences between England and Scotland."

"You want to stop the Clearances."

"It would go a long way to creating harmony in my country."

Anne mulled over his words. "You should take the matter up with Parliament."

He made an angry sound. "What good would it do?"

She sat up. "They could stop the practice. They could make a law against it."

"Anne," he said with exaggerated patience. "The men making the laws are the same ones who stand to gain from the practice."

His words didn't sound right to her. "What you say may be true for the House of Lords, but not for the House of Commons. And Aidan, people are more aware of social injustice than they have been in the past."

"Society in London is completely selfish," he replied crushingly. "They feel they control the world and have no care for anyone else. They aren't interested in problems outside their small social sphere."

"There are those who are as you say. But Aidan, there are others, persons of intelligence, who question the old order of things. Those are the people you should talk to."

"No one would listen to me."

"Why not?"

The corners of his mouth turned down. "You don't understand the ways of the world."

A flash of anger sparked Anne's pride. "And you haven't been to London in years."

"Has it changed that much?" he asked, with a hint of sarcasm.

"Yes. Aidan, the ending of the war has opened up a wealth of new ideas and new thinking. At the same time, people in London don't realize what is going on here in the North and how it hurts the innocent. You have an obligation to use your title and your family's power to make them care. You have a seat in the House of Lords, don't you?"

"I do, but Anne, I haven't been to London in years and I have no desire to go back."

"Not even to prevent a rebellion? Someone has to speak for the Scottish. They can't do it for themselves. They need you. You are the laird."

"It's too late, Anne."

She leaned against the far corner, frustrated by his stubbornness. "It's not too late. Until the gunpowder is used, it can be stopped."

He shook his head. "I don't know. If Lambert kills Robbie Gunn or marches both Robbie and me to London, the Highlands will burn with rebellion."

He was right . . . but so was she! "Aidan, I don't want there to be a war. I don't want Hugh to die before he and Fenella can be happy. I don't want Bon-

nie Mowat to cry for her sons. I've already told you,
I can't watch you die."

Reaching for her, he pulled her close. "Anne, have
faith. Trust me."

She nodded, unable to speak.

They rode in silence. Then Aidan said, "I could
plead the crofters' case against the Clearances in
Parliament, but they won't listen."

Hope rose inside her in spite of his stubbornness.
"You will make them listen. And if they don't hear
you, you'll go back and tell them again the next
year."

He laughed. "And the year after that?"

"Yes." She ran her hand down the line of pewter
buttons on his vest. "You must tell them until they
listen."

"It could take years, Anne."

"How long has it been going on?" she said.
"Years?"

He didn't answer, but the mulish set of his mouth
told her she'd made her point. "You may not be able
to save everyone, Aidan, but you know that already.
You've managed to keep your people safe. Now you
must use your connections to speak for those who
don't have a voice."

"Enough, Anne. Enough." He turned to the window again. She watched him, her hands in her lap.
He was thinking.

Then, he said, "I vowed never to return to London. I never felt as if I belonged there."

"So you created your own world here."

"Yes." He shot her a defiant glance. "Is that wrong?"

"No . . . except that now your people need you to return *for them*."

He didn't answer, but broodingly stared out the window, although she doubted he noticed the passing scenery. He was lost in his own thoughts and she would have to have faith he would make the right choice—provided they escaped Major Lambert.

The coach started to slow and change direction. Aidan straightened. "We're in Lybster."

Anne remembered the quaint fishing village. They veered off the main road. At a crossroads, the military party had to wait for a funeral procession marching to the church. The view on her side of the coach was of the church graveyard and the freshly dug grave ready for its occupant.

"A grim omen," Aidan muttered. She nodded. He waved a boy over. "Who died?"

"Packy Gilbride," the youngster answered.

Aidan leaned back in the seat. "Did you know him?" Anne asked.

"Aye. He was a character. Had hair the color of Deacon's and a temper to match."

Lieutenant Fordyce rode up. "It won't be much longer, my lord," he reported officiously, as if theirs was a pleasure trip. "Major Lambert's headquarters is over the next hill, about a mile south." He was the model of respectful courtesy.

"Thank you, Lieutenant," Aidan said dryly. They exchanged a few other words and then the officer left them. He laced his fingers with Anne's. "No matter what happens, you must take care of yourself first, even if it means denouncing me and telling Major Lambert what you know."

"I would never do that."

He faced her. "You must. If I am to have peace, it will only come from the knowledge that you are safe."

His face was so close to hers that she could see texture of the shades of blue in his eyes. "Promise," he whispered.

She nodded, but silently vowed it was a promise she would not keep.

The coach started moving, and before she was ready, they arrived at the country manor that served as Major Lambert's headquarters in Lybster.

"Courage, Anne," he whispered, as they drove up the tree-lined drive.

Major Lambert greeted them himself. He was dressed casually in a white shirt, long vest, and riding boots. His neck cloth was slightly askew, as if he'd been pulling on it. He'd left off his wig, and his close-cropped hair gave him a relaxed, almost festive, air. His cheeks were ruddy with good humor, and drops of mud seemed to have splattered along the front of his vest and on his sleeves. He carried a riding crop in his right hand.

"Welcome," he cheerily greeted them, as Aidan

helped Anne down from the coach. "I had hoped you would join us too, my lord."

"You knew I would," Aidan said.

"I had anticipated the prospect." He clapped his hands together, a happy man. "My asking you here on such short notice wasn't too much of an inconvenience, was it? Of course, it doesn't matter if it was."

"We appreciate your concern," Aidan returned. He kept his hand on Anne's arm and she was grateful for the support.

Major Lambert laughed, enjoying his sport.

"My lady is tired," Aidan said. "Do you have rooms for us?"

"Of course, of course," Major Lambert answered. He brushed one of the flecks of mud on his shirt with a hint of irritation. "But first, I have someone I'd like you to meet." He didn't wait for their response, but took Anne's free arm and walked her in the direction of the stables. Two armed soldiers fell into step behind them.

Aidan's hand slid down her arm. He gave her hand a reassuring squeeze. *Courage.*

Major Lambert led them toward a stone cellar built into the side of a hill. He would have hurried Anne faster save for Aidan, who refused to walk past a pleasant stroll. Anne felt a pawn between two kings.

There was a guard at the door of the cellar. As Major Lambert approached, he came to attention and then stepped back. "Come in," Major Lambert invited.

"My lady will stay here," Aidan said and Anne was relieved. She sensed she would not like what the major had to show her.

But Major Lambert would have none of it. "I insist," he said.

Aidan would have protested but intuition told her the major wanted exactly that. It was not enough to crush a rebellion: Major Lambert wanted a pound of flesh from an old rival. "Of course, I will go in," she murmured.

Her husband didn't like it. "I'll go first." And she was happy to let him do so.

The good-sized cellar had a stone floor. A torch provided light. The air was dryer but no cooler than outside. However, instead of the potatoes, onions, and hams whose scent still lingered in the air, there was a single chair in the middle of the room. A man was tied to it, else he would have slumped over onto the floor.

The prisoner had been beaten severely to the point he was unrecognizable. It wasn't mud that stained Major Lambert's shirt, but blood. This man's blood.

Anne could picture her father in that chair—or, God help him, her husband. Her stomach roiled. Aidan's hand came around her waist and he pulled her close, shielding her face with his chest. "What joke is this?" he said in a low, dangerous voice.

"Why would you show such a thing to my lady, Major?"

"What?" the officer asked with a mild show of concern. "Oh, beg pardon, does it upset her? Here, then, let me do the introductions and we'll be done."

"What game are you playing, Lambert?" Aidan demanded bluntly.

"No game, my lord. This is anything but a game." Lambert smacked his boot with his crop for emphasis.

"Are you questioning my loyalty to the Crown?"

"I've always questioned your loyalty to the Crown," Major Lambert said simply. "Soon I will have the evidence I need. You recognize him, don't you? Robbie Gunn?"

"I have never seen him before," Aidan lied.

Anne didn't know how anyone could identify him. His battered, swollen face made almost all of his features indistinguishable—save for the hair. His wasn't as carrot colored as Deacon's, but it was red all the same.

"I'd wager you have." Major answered. "Gunn is a Jacobite and a traitor. I believe you are, too."

"Then you must prove it. But I warn you, *Lambie,* there are laws in this land. I am not without friends. You will not further your own ambitions on the person of my wife. You will leave her out of any of your schemes. I insist she be sent to London."

Aidan was sending her away, to safety. She

started to protest, but his arms around her tightened, cautioning her to silence.

"I can't let her go," Major Lambert said apologetically. "Because, Tiebauld, whether you like it or not, you are a rebel symbol in this country."

Her husband exploded. "For God's sakes, man! This is 1814, not 1745. My ancestor's heyday is long over."

"Is it?" Major Lambert attempted to lift Gunn's head with the end of his crop. His prisoner did not move. Lambert looked up. "No, my guess is that if you join forces with the Gunn brothers, the highlands will go up in flames. Everyone is waiting for what you decide, you know."

"I know of no such thing."

"Turn over Deacon Gunn and I'll believe you."

"I haven't a clue to Deacon's whereabouts. You searched my estate. You saw for yourself."

Major Lambert walked around them. The sound of his crop hitting his boots went right through Anne—and yet almost defiantly she stared him down.

"It is only a matter of hours before I get what I want from Gunn," the Major said slowly. "I can wait. You'll wait with me." He nodded to a soldier to open the door. As he proceeded them outside, he said, "Colonel Witherspoon will be joining me this evening. He is very interested in what Gunn will have to say."

"Then you'd best keep him alive," Aidan responded. "Because right now, if he dies from your beatings, Scotland *will* go up in flames, and *you* will be known in London not as the man who ended a rebellion, but the man who started one."

Major Lambert had not considered that twist. He hesitated, uncertain. "I know my responsibilities," he chided, but some of the bluster had left him.

"Very well," Aidan said, his voice cool. "In the meantime, my wife and I would like to be shown to our rooms. Hopefully, they will be better than the ones you've given Gunn. And I meant what I said, Lambert. If you hurt my wife, I will use every means at my disposal to ruin you."

"You'll find your wings clipped if you are in Newgate," Major Lambert said stiffly. He led them into the house.

Inside, soldiers' boots clumped on the fine wood floors. The furniture had been moved and pushed at angles for the men to talk or laze about. As the major walked through, they came to attention. He ignored them. Instead, he charged up the stairs and stopped at the room at the top. He opened the door.

"This is where you will be staying." The room was comfortably modest. The walls were a green wash, the curtains heavy white damask. A four-poster double bed with a peach cotton spread took up the majority of the floor space.

Anne entered, pretending all was normal. "Is there water?"

"It will be sent up," Major Lambert answered tightly.

"Then this will do very well," she said.

"A guard will be outside the door." He crossed to the single window and looked out. "Sound carries. We can hear everything you say." He smiled, the expression chilling. "You will dine with me?"

Aidan said coolly, "I'd sup with the devil before I'd sit at a table with you."

"You may receive your wish," Major Lambert countered and laughed at his own small joke. He left the room and Anne collapsed on the bed.

"I've never seen anyone hurt the way Robbie Gunn was," she whispered. "How can he still be alive?"

"He has a strong spirit."

"Like his brother?"

Aidan smiled. "Aye. They are equally obstinate. Lambert doesn't know who he is threatening. Robbie will die rather than give him names."

A knock sounded on the door. At Aidan's call, a soldier entered with warm water and linen towels. Another soldier set to guard them peered in with curiosity.

Aidan stood and said a few words to both men. He sounded perfectly at ease. Once they were alone again, he walked to the window alcove. He stood for such a long time, she asked what he was watching.

"I can see the cellar from here," he said, his voice low. "Lambert has sent some men with food and water," he observed. "He's taking my advice to keep Gunn alive to heart."

"Or is he planning to prolong the man's agony?"

"Perhaps a bit of both." Aidan turned from the window and there was a wicked gleam in his eye.

She stood. "You have a plan," she said, with a conspirator's eagerness.

"Yes."

"What is it? What are we going to do?"

He took another look out the window a moment before saying, "We're going to make love."

"You're joking." She couldn't have heard him correctly.

He smiled. "Anne, I've never been more serious in my life." He began to untie his neck cloth.

Chapter 14

"*We are surrounded* by British soldiers," Anne reminded Aidan as he hung his neck cloth over a chair in the corner of the room.

"Yes, I know." He sat down in the chair and pulled on the heel of his boot.

He couldn't seriously be going through with this! "You're mad."

"It's been rumored," he agreed. He tugged again at the heel and then looked to her in frustration. "Come play my valet, will you? I need help removing these damn boots. I don't wear them enough."

She dropped her gaze to his offered foot and back up to his face. He appeared almost comical, sitting in such an awkward position. "You don't want to make love to me."

"On the contrary, I haven't been able to think of much of anything else since last night."

"Well, you've done an admirable job of hiding it," she answered briskly.

He put his foot on the floor. "Anne, come here."

She frowned and took a step back. He rolled his eyes heavenward. "I should have known." He held out his hand. "Please, Anne, come to me."

Almost with a will of their own, her feet moved around the edge of the bed. She hesitated a moment.

"Trust me, Anne."

"How can I, when you come up with such ridiculous notions?"

"Afraid?"

"Yes!" she admitted. "Yes, yes, *yes!*"

He shook his head. Coming to his feet, he walked the short distance between them. His large, capable hand cupped the side of her head. "My Anne, so bold, so brave, and yet so timid of what is right and natural."

The beat of her heart accelerated. It always did when he stood this close. "And you are a fool—"

His lips covered her mouth, effectively silencing her. For a moment, she couldn't think. She could only react—and she did, by kissing him back.

Suddenly, she was tired of fighting. This felt good. It felt right.

His hand slipped around her waist. He pulled her body up against his. His lips left hers as he nibbled a trail along the line of her jaw. His other hand cupped her breast. "Anne," he whispered.

She answered by melting against him. Pleasure. Her body quivered with needs she hadn't known before his touch.

He lifted her up and carried her the few steps to the bed, where he lowered her to sit on the edge.

The sudden motion made Anne dizzy because of her racing pulse. She started to sit up, but he kissed her down—with demanding, possessive, hungry kisses—and Anne responded in kind. This time, when his tongue stroked hers, she opened eagerly to him.

Her senses were full of him. Sandalwood and citrus. Warm, masculine man. Her lips tasted his skin, reveling in the texture. She didn't ever want to stop kissing him, not even for breath.

His hands moved with purpose now. His fingers loosened her laces before pushing her sleeves down her shoulders. The kiss stopped while she had to slip first one arm and then another free, his hands already greedily dipping into the bodice of her chemise and cupping her breasts.

At the first touch of his skin on her flesh, Anne cried out in a combination of surprise and relief. She'd wanted this. She longed for it.

Still, she must have had some semblance of sanity, because when a footstep sound outside the door, she struggled for conscious thought, coming up on her elbows. "It's the middle of the day."

"The best time for love," he murmured, kissing the line of her hair down to the tender skin beneath her ear. His fingers scattered her silver pins onto the mattress.

"Aidan, people will hear us." Her voice ended on

a squeak as he touched her ear with the tip of his tongue. The feel of his warm breath on such a sensitive spot almost sent her reason through the ceiling like a shooting star.

"We'll be quiet." His words hummed through her ear.

She moaned. "I don't know if I can be."

He brought his face round to look her in the eye. His were twinkling with laughter. "Then make as much noise as you'd like, love. We're married. We're newlyweds. Everyone expects us to do this."

Love. "Did you hear what you called me?"

He grinned. "Aye." He brushed her nipples with his thumbs. "Love," he repeated with more meaning.

Anne laughed out of nervousness and wonder. "Love," she whispered.

He pushed her chemise down to her waist until her breasts were completely free of confining material. He weighed them in his hands.

Doubts, uncertainties, and reservations all fled. For one shining moment, she let herself believe he loved her. With blinding insight, she realized she'd withheld a part of herself from him out of fear of being hurt and abandoned. Everyone she had ever loved had left her. The need to protect herself from the pain of abandonment had been the driving force behind her desire to leave Kelwin that morning.

Now, she released all apprehension. She wanted

only to live in the moment. She wanted to feel his skin against hers. She wanted to give herself freely and completely to the man she loved. Joyfully, she threw her arms around his neck, almost knocking him back, and kissed him as if her life depended upon it.

Aidan laughed, falling onto the bed and rolling her with him. The time for words was past. His hands skillfully untied her garters and pushed her stockings down her legs. She curled her toes, letting her shoes drop softly to the floor.

His lips left hers. She objected, but her indignation turned to a happy sigh when his mouth closed over her nipple.

Anne practically jumped off the bed as he drew it into his mouth. The pull of his mouth on her breast did strange things deep inside to the woman's part of her. It raised a need . . . and a knowing, both as old as time.

His hands slid up the inside of her thighs and he touched her in the most intimate place of all, mimicking the movement of his tongue. Anne was lost, captured in a haze of driving, spiraling emotion she'd never known before.

"Aidan, what are you doing to me?"

He lifted his head and grinned, his eyes so blue they took her breath away. "Loving you."

She held out her arms. "Please, be with me."

Aidan undressed himself down to his breeches.

He made quick work of it and had no trouble removing his boots. His muscular body was a work of art in the late afternoon light.

Reaching up, she ran her hand down his chest, marveling at the flat planes and hard surfaces.

Her dress was around her waist. Laughing, he drew it over her head and tossed it aside. She was naked.

For a moment, Anne moved as if to cover herself, but his hands on her shoulders steadied her. His expression intent, he combed her hair with his fingers until it curled down around her shoulders, the ends almost touching her breasts.

"I've pictured you like this," he said. "It is how I want to remember you."

His words reminded her of where they were, what could happen to them, but before she could respond to fear, he stood, one knee on the bed, the other foot on the floor. "Unbutton me, Anne. Show me you want this as much as I do."

Her anxiety disappeared, replaced by startled bemusement. He expected her to be a willing participant. She'd assumed a woman's body was nothing more than a vessel for a man to do whatever it was he wished.

This was new. This was exciting.

She scooted to the edge of the bed. Her fingers trembled as she unfastened the first button. She could feel the length of him beneath the fabric. She slipped another button from its hole and another.

His fingers brushed her hair as she worked. At last, she'd freed the last button. "Take it out, Anne," he said, a hint of laughter in his voice.

"It?" she asked, uncertain. The other night she had discreetly averted her eyes from this very male part of him. She wasn't anxious to touch it.

"Oh, it is a bold and hungry creature."

"You're teasing me. I've heard it described as a stick. Sticks aren't bold."

He laughed with genuine amusement. "More a staff than a mere twig. Go along, Anne. See for yourself."

She met his challenge, pushing his breeches down, and drew a sharp breath. "Oh dear." It wasn't what she'd expected . . . and yet it was more than she'd imagined.

"Touch me."

"I don't know."

His hand took hers. "You liked it when I touched you?"

"Yes."

"Then return the love, sweetheart. Feel me." He placed her hand on him and she was taken aback at how soft and smooth he was. But hard, strong. She ran the back of her fingers along velvet skin and he almost purred with appreciation.

She lifted her gaze. "You like—?"

Aidan kissed her, pressing her back on the bed, suddenly very serious, very focused. He shoved the covers aside and leaned forward, pushing her to the mattress. The sheets were cool against her skin. He climbed on top of her, his lips not leaving hers, his skin rough and smooth against hers.

Her body understood better than her mind what the next step would be. Her legs opened to cradle him against her.

He kissed the line of her neck. His hands molded her to him. His whispered words of praise and encouragement that like an elixir robbed her of all will save his.

Anne forgot where she was or even who she was. The world ceased to exist beyond the bedroom doors, beyond the boundaries of the bed.

Aidan spoke. "I can't wait any longer, Anne. I'll try not to hurt you."

He'd been moving his body against hers. But his next action was foreign, unanticipated. It stirred her from the languorous haze of desire. He entered her.

She stiffened. "Aidan?" Her hands gripped his shoulder.

"It will be all right, love." He thrust deeper.

Anne felt a sharp pain, like the prick of a needle. It shocked her and she jerked, attempting to move away from him.

He held her in place. "Give it time, Anne. Let your body adjust to me."

She met his gaze, wanting to trust him. "Does this mean the marriage is consummated?"

His lips curved into a smile. "Absolutely."

"Then it is worth it." She drew a steadying breath. "I think I'd like to get up now."

"Get up—?" He pressed his head against her forehead and looked nose-to-nose in her eyes. "Anne, we haven't even begun."

"Do you mean there is more?"

He nodded. "More pleasure."

She didn't know if she believed him. This was such a strange position. Almost too intimate.

And then he started moving.

Holding herself still, she planned to wait it out until he was finished. But something happened. His movements sparked a responding sense of need. He pushed deeper and she felt the return of desire, only this time, it came with more force.

The ache became a distant memory. Her body moved to meet his. He was driving harder now, even as she reached to respond.

This was making love. Emotion guided her now. She strained to meet him, searching for a point inside her she didn't understand. Aidan talked to her, kissing her and encouraging her to meet his every thrust.

Then, suddenly, she crossed a threshold she'd never known existed. One moment she was in the present, her body as tight as a bowstring; in the next she was flying.

Anne cried out, holding Aidan close. She couldn't let go. She'd never let him go.

He buried himself deep inside her. Once, twice, a third time . . . and then she felt him release. His life force filled her, branding her, making her truly and completely his.

Anne fell back on the bed, drained. She closed her eyes, reveling in the weight of his body covering hers. "I didn't know anything could be like that."

"I didn't either."

The touch of amazement in his voice caught her attention. She opened her eyes. "Truly?"

"Yes, truly," he echoed. He kissed her then, gentle, feather-light kisses on eyes and cheeks.

Cool air hit her skin. She'd been so involved in the heat of their own making, she had not noticed the chill in the room.

He rolled from her and pulled the heavy spread and sheets over them. His legs entwined with hers and she snuggled down next to him. "Are you all right?" he asked. "I didn't hurt you, did I?"

She laughed. "I've never felt better."

Visibly relieved, he said, "I got a bit carried away at the end."

"I liked it." She let her hand stray to his chest where she marveled at his hardness, his strength. "For the first time since my parents' deaths," she whispered, "I feel safe."

His arms cradled her close. "I will do everything in my power to protect you."

"This is enough," she answered, and pressed a kiss against his collar bone before yawning. She relaxed into the bedclothes. "I could sleep for a week—"

A footstep outside the door was their only warning. The door was flung open even as Anne ducked further under the covers. For a second there was no sound, and then Aidan said coolly, "Was there something in particular you wanted, Lambert?"

Anne peeked from the shelter of the bedclothes and her husband's body. Major Lambert's eyebrows could not have risen any higher up his forehead. "The guard said he'd heard strange noises."

Aidan smiled. "Not *so* strange, I would hope."

Major Lambert struggled for understanding. "You've been making love?"

"How else did you expect us to pass the time?" Aidan said. "Wringing our hands with worry while you trump up charges by beating a man to death?"

"Have you no respect for my authority?" The major raised his voice, conscious as a very embarrassed Anne was that Lieutenant Fordyce and some of the other soldiers craned their necks to witness the confrontation between the two men.

But Aidan answered calmly, "I am well aware of how much authority you wield, Lambert. You have the power to destroy me whether I am innocent or guilty. But I am a recently married man." His hand beneath the covers clasped Anne's. "I have a pretty young wife who is being dragged into your schemes against her will and against all that is right and noble. If I choose to spend what may be my last hours loving her, then it is no business of yours."

The major frowned. Anne sensed he wanted to throw Aidan's words back at him—but there was nothing he could say. Especially in front of his men, whose sympathies obviously rested with her and Aidan. She could see it in their faces. They had wives and sweethearts. They must have known there was bad blood between Aidan and their commanding officer.

"Very well," Major Lambert said at last. "While away the hours, my lord. Enjoy yourself." He slammed the door shut.

"Touchy fellow, isn't he?" Aidan said thoughtfully.

Anne sat up, holding the sheet in place over her breasts. She pushed her hair. "Is that what this was about? You wanted to make him angry?"

He turned, surprised. "I enjoy tweaking the fool's nose, but this—" He placed an arm around her and drew her back down onto the mattress with him. "This has nothing to do with Lambert . . ." He kissed her neck. "Or anyone . . ." He kissed beneath her chin. "Or anything outside this room." He kissed her lips.

She fell under his spell. It was as if she were a torch and he the spark. He rose up over her. "Can you do it again, Anne? Is it too soon? I don't want to hurt you."

Her answer was to open herself to him, offering what was only hers to give. As he settled himself on top of her, she pushed back his hair from his face and asked, "You do love me? Even a little?"

His eyes darkened. "I love you very much. Am I pleased with Alpina for her high-handedness? No. And yet, you have come into my life and changed it in ways I hadn't thought possible. I was waiting for you, Anne. I didn't know it—"

"And it took you a while to recognize the fact."

He laughed, the sound vibrating through her. "Aye, Anne. But how can one ignore a tempest?" he asked. "But I know how to tame it." He kissed her so thoroughly, so completely, she was his willing slave.

This time their pace was slower, more leisurely. They explored each other and Anne learned Aidan was a generous, considerate, sensual lover.

Now she understood the mysteries of love lauded by the poets. She discovered why a woman would forsake all for love.

There was nothing she wouldn't do for Aidan. Nothing.

As afternoon faded into night, in a bedroom surrounded by English soldiers and facing an uncertain future, Anne became a prisoner of her own heart. When they weren't making love, they talked about everything, and about nothing, making up for wasted time.

Occasionally, he would cross to the window or pace in front of it. His actions worried her, but she wasn't going to ask any questions, fearing the answers.

At one point, he noticed the soldiers delivering a tray of food. He came back to the bed satisfied. "Lambert is listening to me. He's working to keep Robbie alive."

"He may be too late," Anne said soberly.

Aidan shook his head. "The Gunn brothers are a tough and hardy lot. Robbie has had a beating, but he won't die yet." His lips twisted into a grim smile. "He'll just look like he has." With that, he let down the curtain, and with one wild leap, jumped into the bed beside her.

Major Lambert left them alone. There was a great deal of traffic outside their door, since the room was at the top of the stairs, but Anne ignored it. She didn't even care that dinner had not been sent up to them. She closed her mind to everything but her husband.

Aidan seemed perfectly capable of both devoting himself to her and keeping an ear attuned to the activity around them. He was the one who noticed that Colonel Witherspoon, Lambert's commanding officer, had arrived. He watched their movements around the cellar from his window vantage point.

"What do you think?" Anne asked.

"I don't know." He lifted a lock of her hair spread out on the pillow and curled it around his finger as he worked some problem in his mind.

"Aidan?"

Her voice brought him back to the present. He smiled and pulled her to him.

Later, as they lay tangled with each other and the sheets, she thought Aidan had fallen asleep. Lying with her back against his, she ran her hand over her flat stomach. An intuition as old as time told her his seed had taken root deep within her. She would have his child.

The mattress shifted. Aidan rose, moving in the dark to dress.

Anne came up on one arm, her hair hanging over her shoulder. "What are you doing?" she whispered.

He placed a finger to his lips, warning her to silence while he checked out the window. Satisfied, he crossed to the bed and started molding the bedcovers and feather pillows into a wall beside her.

She sat up. "Aidan—" His lips closed over her mouth.

"No questions, Anne," he said, when at last he broke the kiss.

"Where will you be?"

"I'm going to save Robbie."

"Aidan, you can't." She reached for him. "Please, stay here."

He sat on the bed and put his arms around her. "I must try. Lambert will take me to London no matter what unless I can outwit him."

Anne started to climb out of the bed. "I will go with you. I can help."

"You are helping right here. You are the decoy. If someone should come in, pretend to be asleep. They will assume I am on your other side." He came to his feet.

"Aidan—?"

He pressed his fingers to her lips. "Take care, Anne. Be brave." With those words, he crossed to the window, opened it, and slipped out before she could protest.

Anne jumped from the bed, wrapped a sheet around her, and hurried to the window. The wind blew the curtains. She knelt to avoid being seen by any guards on the ground. But the only one she saw was a soldier guarding the cellar.

Meanwhile, in spite of his size, her husband moved quietly as a cat along the slippery shingled roof. Again clouds covered the full moon. He stayed close to the shadows and she didn't think she would have noticed him if she had not known he was there.

Even as she worried, the guard appeared to look in the direction of her window. Anne pulled back quickly, ducking to avoid being seen.

Her heart pounded in her ears as she waited for the soldier to call an alarm; but no such warning came. When at last she dared to look out the window again, Aidan was gone. It was as if he'd disappeared into the night.

She closed the window.

The room seemed empty without his presence. Numbly she walked to the bed and lay down, pulling his pillow to her. It smelled of him.

She rested her hand on her belly and flattened her palm. She imagined a tiny pulse already beating there. A piece of the man she loved.

So she did the only thing she could do—she prayed.

Chapter 15

Aidan didn't dare tell Anne the details of his plan. He wanted her completely innocent of what he was doing in case he was captured . . . and also, because it was almost too fantastic to work.

His practical wife would recognize immediately his foolishness and not believe it could succeed. He wasn't certain, either.

Swinging down to a portico on the first floor, he allowed his body to hang over the edge a moment before releasing his hold. His feet hit the damp, spongy spring earth. His left ankle buckled, reminding him he was growing too old for such tricks.

He wished he could have stayed beside his warm, willing wife. Who could have imagined Anne was such a passionate creature? His reason to succeed this night was driven by his desire to return to her bed—forever.

Stepping back into the shadows, he glanced up at the window where he'd left her. She'd shut it. Good.

He ran along the line of the house, moving with the stealth of a hunter. One soldier guarded Robbie's cellar, but Aidan knew Lambert had posted others.

Light came from the first floor dining room. People were seated at the table eating and drinking. Aidan knelt below the window casement and listened to Lambert entertain his superior officer, Colonel Witherspoon. From the sound of it, they'd had a good deal to drink, and Lambert was doing everything in his power to promote his suspicion of an impending Scottish rebellion. He mentioned Aidan's name, pounding the table so hard the china and silver rattled. Aidan couldn't catch Witherspoon's low-voiced reply.

Fortunately, it appeared Lambert's men did not share his vigilance. The two guards who were supposed to be walking the perimeters stood in the shadow of a tree, gossiping. As Aidan moved around the house and across the yard, he caught another asleep against the rustic stone barn.

Aidan skirted him and the outbuildings. Lambert's dislike of dogs served Aidan's purpose. There wasn't one on the property to bark an alarm. He slipped unnoticed along the line of a thicket fence toward a copse of trees and walked off the manor estate without a cry being raised. His long legs ate the mile or so distance to Lybster. He had hunted in this area. He knew the backways and paths followed only by the locals. Lambert's men did patrol a distance from the manor house, but they were watching for an armed force of men, not a lone walker taking the back ways.

Aidan prayed he could play upon Lambert's faults. Within half an hour, he found himself on the grounds of the church at the crossroads where they'd stopped earlier in the day for the funeral procession.

It was the dead of the night. The good people of Lybster were sleeping soundly in their beds. Sheltered by dark, shadowy hemlocks, the cemetery lay on the opposite side of the church, away from the village, so the superstitious need not see the ghosties in spite of it being holy ground.

The hemlocks protected him from discovery while the same moon that had helped him smuggle in the gunpowder now let him find the freshly dug grave. He located a shovel and pick in an unlocked shed attached to the church. It took him approximately another hour to dig up the body.

He'd have to move faster.

Packy Gilbride, the man in the grave, had been a good-humored character known for his love of a prank. He also hated the English.

Aidan used the pick to lift the lid off the coffin. For a second, what he was about to do threatened to overwhelm him. He looked down at Packy Gilbride's moon-shadowed outline. The man was peaceful in his repose without the lively skepticism that had marked his spirit when he was alive. "I'm sorry to disturb your peace, Gilbride, but I need you. Do you understand?"

A cloud passed the moon. In the changing shadows, Packy seemed to smile.

It was benediction enough. Aidan hoisted Gilbride's body out of the grave and lifted him up on his shoulders. The body's deadweight would not be hard to carry, not for a man as strong and desperate as Aidan.

A sheet wrapped around her toga style, Anne anxiously paced the length of the room taking care to avoid the window. It had been impossible for her to climb back into bed and pretend all was well.

She'd started to dress and then had changed her mind. If by some chance Major Lambert barged in, she could not be fully dressed—not after the man had caught her naked in bed with her husband.

Of course, if the major discovered her "husband" was nothing more than a mound of bedclothes, Anne didn't know what she was going to say. She'd worry about it later.

The soldier guarding her door barely made a sound. She discovered why when she overheard soft snoring, which came to an abrupt halt as heavy boots clumped out into the downstairs hall.

Major Lambert had been right: sound did travel in the house. The conversation he and his guest were having flowed all the way up the stairs, waking her sentry and alerting her.

Quickly she hopped into bed, giving the door her back.

Lambert's voice bounced off the walls. He slurred his words a bit, as if he'd been drinking. Her heart almost stopped when she heard him mention Tiebauld. Then the men walked outside.

Anne scurried over to the window, anticipating their direction to be the cellar. She was right.

Major Lambert's guest was a trim officer probably no taller than herself. The two men disappeared inside the cellar. About five minutes later, they came out, but she couldn't make out their expressions, except that the guest was talking earnestly to Major Lambert. She didn't know what any of it signified.

Anne rushed back to the bed, expecting Lambert to check on her at any moment. The memory of the door to her childhood home being rammed opened with a splintering crash the night the soldiers had come for her father echoed in her ears.

She willed the memories away. This was no time for panic.

Checking the shape of the bedclothes to make sure it would appear Aidan was there, she lay down, her back to the door. She closed her eyes.

The front door into the house opened. Booted steps started up the stairs.

Anne tried to breathe evenly. It was impossible.

Major Lambert and his guest paused right outside her door. "Tiebauld is in here, Colonel," Lambert said. His voice lowered, but she could still hear him say clearly, "He and his wife have been going at each other like bloody rabbits."

"Rabbits?" the colonel questioned.

"You know, sir," Major Lambert averred. "The poke and tickle?"

There was a beat of stunned silence and then the colonel started laughing. "Here? With your men all around him?"

"It surprised me, too," Lambert said. "I knew Tiebauld in school. He was the laugh of Eton. He couldn't walk across a room without tripping over his own feet. But after his performance today, I would describe him as a horse."

Anne's cheeks grew hot at such coarse talk. But a niggling insecurity in the back of her mind wondered at what Major Lambert had said. She wanted to believe Aidan had turned to her out of love. But could he also have been orchestrating a ruse to trick Major Lambert?

"And you could hear it all?" the colonel was asking.

"You couldn't avoid it," Major Lambert said. "Isn't that right, Williams?"

"Aye, sir," the sentry dutifully answered.

"Well, he's quiet now," the colonel said.

There was a thoughtful pause. "Almost too quiet," Major Lambert said. Anne could picture him putting his ear to the door, so she wasn't surprised when the door opened without a knock or preamble.

She held her breath.

"Well, he is still there," Major Lambert said as if he'd always suspected that was the case. He shut the door. "The man had to wear out sooner or later." He started to laugh, but when the colonel didn't join him, his voice trailed off. "Is something the matter, sir?" he asked stiffly.

The colonel moved away from the door. Anne rolled over, listening intently.

"Major, Lord Tiebauld is well respected amongst the gentry and by the people. If Gunn doesn't confess his name, you can't charge him with treason. Otherwise, you will create a situation I will be forced to divorce myself from. Am I clear?"

"Gunn will talk."

"So you say—and yet he isn't going to say anything tonight. The man in the cellar appears half-dead."

"I was a bit overzealous today," Major Lambert conceded. "Sergeant Fullerton can be heavy-handed. Gunn will recover."

"You'd best hope so. Or you will find yourself apologizing to Lord Tiebauld, who can make my position in this country very difficult. If that happens, I will sacrifice you."

"I would expect you to do no less, sir," Major Lambert said, but some of the cocksureness had left his voice. "At the same time, sir, I will also look forward to your full support when my suspicions are found to be correct."

"If that is the case, Lambert, then your career will

take a new and very fortunate turn. I believe you know of what I speak."

"Yes, sir."

They parted company then, presumably to go off to bed . . . but Anne didn't sleep.

Every fiber of her being centered on Aidan. He had to succeed. The alternative was unthinkable.

Aidan had never killed a man.

He stood over the body of the sentry who had been guarding the cellar door gripped by a coldness he had never felt before.

He had not meant to kill him. His intention had been simply to render him unconscious.

However, just as Aidan had been about to attack, some inner sense had warned the soldier he was not alone. He'd turned and would have cried out except for Aidan's quick action. He'd snapped the man's neck.

For a moment, Aidan imagined the guard's soul passing through him. Something, something he couldn't name, pricked the hair on the back of his neck and tore at his conscience.

Anne was right. War meant hundreds—thousands, even—of men dying. He could not live with the responsibility of their deaths on his shoulders. He understood her fears now. Just as he slowly, painfully accepted the fact he'd had no choice but to take the sentry's life.

At the same time, an idea of how to use the man's

death to his advantage also came to him. He'd left Gilbride's body on the other side of the cellar in the shadows. He could let it be for now.

The cellar door did not have a lock. Aidan pushed it open and pulled the soldier's body through it. Inside, the torch still burned, giving the room its only light. He kicked shut the door and lay the body on the floor.

Robbie Gunn could have passed for dead himself. He slumped in the chair, his chin on his chest. He appeared not to be breathing—but Aidan sensed the spirit of the man was alive.

"Robbie? 'Tis I, Tiebauld."

A choking sound was his only answer. It was enough. Aidan knelt at his side. "God, man, can you stand? Because if you can't, we'll both be swinging from a tree."

Robbie moved, lifting his head with difficulty. His swollen lips formed a crooked grin. His eyes were battered shut, his face discolored from bruises. "Have you come to save me, Tiebauld?" He sounded as weak as a wee lamb. Even his body seemed to have been shrunk by pain.

"Only if you are much tougher than you look like right now."

Pride shone in Robbie's eyes. "Death alone will make me heel."

"Good, lad. Now listen, here is what I have planned. I want you to play the soldier."

"And guard myself?" Robbie asked with a hoarse laugh.

"Exactly," Aidan answered seriously. He began working to loosen the knots binding Robbie to the chair. "I want you to put on the guard's uniform. Wear his hat low on your head."

"Are you telling me you don't have armed men outside waiting to help?"

"Aye, I brought all the kitchen women. Bonnie Mowat is going to conk heads with her washboard."

His quip earned a rusty laugh from Robbie. The knots finally untied, Aidan placed a hand on his shoulder. "It's us and us alone, lad. If you can't do it, we're damned."

"For my freedom? I can do it," Robbie said proudly. He attempted to sit straight and winced. "It may take me a moment."

"Aye, you'll manage," Aidan said, more to reassure himself than Robbie. If Robbie failed, they were all doomed. There was no turning back. He continued explaining his plan.

"The watch will change at four. The night grows cloudy. I'm wagering whoever comes on for you will be sleepy. Keep quiet, walk straight, and you could pass."

Robbie rubbed his legs, attempting to get the circulation going, a painful process. "Pass for the guard?"

"Aye."

"And then what?"

"Then you walk off the estate."

Robbie stared slack-jawed. "Have you been drinking?"

"No. I just did it myself. Lambert thinks you important, but his men prefer the show of soldiering to hard work. They lounge in the house and enjoy heavy meals. If they are on guard for anything, it is an armed force coming from the road."

Robbie considered his words a second and then he smiled as he realized freedom was within his grasp. Aidan was glad to see this surge of renewed spirit.

"So, you're joining me, are you?" Robbie said softly.

Aidan frowned. "What do you mean?" he asked in a low voice.

"You are leaving Kelwin for the rebel's life. It is glad I am to have you beside me."

Aidan rocked back on his heels. "I can't leave Kelwin." He couldn't. It was where he belonged. Yes, it was his birthright, but it was also the haven he'd created for himself.

"You can't stay, not after killing Lambert's guard. They'll hunt you down."

"If my plan works, Lambert will never know you are gone."

Robbie snorted his disbelief. "He'll know. Granted, you believe Lambert's men thick, but

don't you think the bastards will recognize their
own mate sitting in my place?"

"It won't be the same man."

"Who will it be? You?"

"Packy Gilbride."

Robbie's eyes widened. "Gilbride? I know he has
a rebel's heart, but I didn't think him a fool."

"He's not. He's dead." Aidan knew his words
were blunt, but he didn't have time to sweeten them.
However, he didn't anticipate Robbie's reaction.

"They've not killed him, have they?" Robbie rose
with a surprising amount of strength, ready to do
battle.

"No, no," Aidan hastened to assure him.
"Gilbride died of old age and obstinacy as we all
knew he would. But I've a plan to pull a switch, one
I think Old Packy would enjoy playing a part in."
Quickly, he told Robbie what he intended. "I'll bury
the soldier in Gilbride's grave. There won't be any
loose ends."

"Sooner or later, someone will miss the soldier."

Aidan shook his head. "Lambert will think the
soldier deserted. They desert all the time, especially
around planting season."

"But Packy and I don't look anything alike."

"Have you seen yourself lately? Dead Gilbride
looks better." Aidan stood. "You're both about the
same height, and the grayness in the red hair may or
may not be noticed. I warned Lambert he dare not

let you die or there will be a war. If my plan works, I'll advise Lambert to bury you as quickly as possible else word gets out the English killed you."

"I don't—"

Aidan cut through his protest. "It's the only plan I have. We must risk it and time is wasting." He began stripping the soldier. "If you want freedom, get into this uniform."

Robbie began disrobing. While he changed, Aidan fetched Packy Gilbride. Packy's body had shrunk in death. Robbie's shirt and coat fit him. Aidan didn't bother with the rest of the clothes but tied Packy's body to the chair.

In all, he'd spent ten minutes in the cellar, but at any moment someone might notice the guard on the cellar was missing. The time had come to leave. "Hurry," he urged. Robbie nodded that he was ready.

Aidan said, "When you leave the estate, go to the Widow Ewing's house. Do you remember her?"

"How could I forget Mavis? We've romped under the covers more than one night."

Aidan couldn't help but smile. Robbie was sounding more and more like his old self; he was beaten, but he was a survivor. "Tell her I will make it worth her while if she takes you in for a stay. She'll do it for me."

"She'll do it for *me*," Robbie refuted.

"Just see you don't let any harm come to her,"

Aidan answered, and hurried him toward the door. "You go first, I'll follow."

Robbie took the guard's post. Aidan waited the space of several heartbeats and then lifted the guard's body on his shoulders. He cracked open the door, listening, and was about to slip out when he heard voices. The watch! Probably the two men who had been gossiping under the tree.

Aidan took a step back so that if someone entered, he would be behind the door. He waited.

The guards said something to Robbie, who grunted his answer. Robbie's response must have been enough, because a moment later, he knocked on the door, a signal it was safe.

Aidan slipped out. "They didn't notice?"

"They've been drinking," Robbie whispered with disgust. "I'd shoot any of my men who drank on watch. Well, now, go on. Hurry . . . and God be with you, Laird Tiebauld."

Aidan didn't answer, but started back to the village. The sun would soon rise. It was close to three in the morning when he found himself in the graveyard. He made quick work of burying the guard and carefully put the shovel and pick back in the shed where he'd found them.

If anyone noticed anything out of place, they'd probably think it spirits and ghosties. The idea gave him no amusement.

He had to make his way back to Anne without

tipping off the guards, and he was running out of time.

Anne thought she'd been alert and wakeful, but when the door opened, she gave such a start, she knew she'd been dozing. She threw her arm over the mound of pillows masquerading as Aidan and pretended to sleep. The door closed.

"It's me, Anne," her husband whispered.

She rolled over on her back and then scrambled up, tucking the sheet around her. Aidan closed the door, his shadowy presence almost larger than life.

"What are you doing coming in the door?" she whispered. "I thought you'd use the window."

"I didn't have the strength to climb back up and I decided at this hour of the morning, no one would expect me to walk right in. So I removed my boots and tiptoed up the stairs. Our guard is asleep. Both he and Lambert snore."

Aidan appeared exhausted. He walked past the bed to peer out the window. Night was passing, re-placed by the first hazy glow of dawn.

"Weren't there guards anywhere else?" she asked.

"Major Lambert's men are a lazy lot," he an-swered, his voice subdued. "He has patrols out but they are easy to dodge." He set his boots down and crossed to the wash stand.

"The major checked on you. The ruse worked." She told him of Major Lambert's conversation with the colonel. While she spoke, he poured water into the wash basin. Carefully, he splashed water on his face and hands. Then he began lathering with the soap. Over and over he kept washing his hands.

Anne's voice trailed off. She stood, wrapping the sheet around her. "Are you all right?"

He didn't answer, but kept rubbing the lather over his knuckles, along his fingers.

"Is it Robbie?" she whispered. "Could you save him?"

"It is too soon to tell." He stopped washing his hands and stared at the lather covering them as if he couldn't quite comprehend how it had gotten there.

Anne crossed to him. Lifting the pitcher, she rinsed off the soap.

Aidan didn't look at her. "My clothes are filthy. Dirt. Everywhere."

"I'll brush them off. Here, remove them and let me have them."

It seemed to take several minutes for her words to sink in. Almost absently, he began to undress, but got lost in the motions.

Gently Anne guided him to the bed and pushed him to sit, sensing he needed this moment of quiet. She undressed him. Sweat and dirt stained his shirt. Fortunately, the streaks of dirt on his breeches could easily be brushed out.

"Your neck cloth and coat will hide the soil on your shirt, at least long enough for us to get away."

He nodded.

His strange manner was unsettling.

She knelt in front of him. "Aidan, has something horrible happened?"

He made more of an effort then. "It's been a long night."

"When will we know if you've succeeded?"

Shrugging, he asked, "What time is it?"

"Almost four, I suspect."

He nodded, but when he didn't speak, she took his hand in hers. "Let's return to bed. It is out of our hands now. You have done everything you could."

"Yes."

Expecting him to lie down, she started to rise, but he caught her by the shoulders. He pulled her into his lap and hugged her close, his arms like strong bands around her. He held her tightly.

"Aidan, what is wrong?" she whispered in his ear.

"I killed a man, Anne."

The words were etched in such deep regret they were almost painful to hear. She brought her arms around him. "You had no choice?"

For the first time since he'd entered the room, Aidan's gaze met hers. "I had no choice."

She cradled the side of his whiskered jaw with her hand. Tears welled in her eyes. She felt his anguish as if it were her own. "My poor love. My poor, poor love."

For a long time they sat this way . . . and then he began kissing her. "I need you, Anne. I need you." His hand loosened her sheet.

"I know." She shifted so the sheet could slip down around her waist.

His fingertips lightly outlined her lips. "You are right. No one wins at war."

She didn't know what to say. No words were adequate. Instead, she opened her arms and he came to her. She hugged him close, her fingers combing his hair.

"Anne," he whispered against her breast. His tongue flicked the sensitive nipple before he lowered her onto the mattress.

They made love. This time, it was different than it had been during the joyful afternoon when they had been enamored with the excitement of discovery.

Now their lovemaking was a solace, a search for meaning in a world that often seems senseless. A bonding.

When they were done, he was able to sleep.

But Anne couldn't. She held him in her arms and kept watch, praying his sacrifice was enough to free them—knowing that if it wasn't, she would follow him anywhere, even to death.

Well past dawn, Anne heard shouting. Aidan woke. They both lay still, listening.

Booted footsteps bounded up the stairs and pounded on the room belonging to Major Lambert. He summoned the messenger in. A second later, he swore with frustration.

She strained to hear what was being said but there was too much noise. Aidan rose from the bed and crossed over to the window, heedless of his nakedness.

"What is happening?" she asked.

"I don't know—yet." He turned from the window and gave her a inscrutable smile. Aidan's smile. Whatever had haunted him the night before had passed. The ends of his newly cut hair stood up every which way, and he needed a shave.

She didn't think he'd ever appeared more handsome.

Colonel Witherspoon was now awake. He stopped outside their door in the hall. "What is it, Major? What is going on?"

Anne reached for Aidan's hand, uncertain of what to expect. Aidan was as tense as she was.

"It's the prisoner," Major Lambert said, lowering his voice. "Robbie Gunn is dead."

Chapter 16

"The devil you say," the colonel snapped. Aidan pulled Anne away from the door.

"Get dressed," he whispered. He reached for his breeches hanging over the back of the chair.

"But Aidan, they've killed Robbie Gunn." The implications of their act overwhelmed her. The Highlands would be set aflame with war and strife. Kelwin and all the people who made it special could be destroyed.

"Anne, get dressed," he ordered. He was already buttoning his breeches.

"Aidan—?"

Suddenly he was in front of her, silencing her protest with a kiss, his hands gripping her arms. He broke the kiss, his gaze intent. "I ask you to trust me. *Now, do as I say. We don't have much time.*"

Woodenly, she moved to obey. She reached for her chemise at the end of the bed and dropped the sheet to the floor. Aidan pushed his head through the neck of his shirt and shrugged on his vest, buttoning the front so the worst of the dirt stains were effectively hidden. Then, without warning, he threw open the door.

Anne grabbed her dress and scrambled to hide behind the door.

Her bold, outrageous husband confronted Major Lambert. "Did you say Robbie Gunn is dead?"

Quickly pulling on her clothes, Anne peeked through the crack. Major Lambert frowned, his lips clamped shut, but Colonel Witherspoon, who still wore his nightshirt over his breeches, nodded.

"That is what the major is telling me." He made a short bow. "I am Colonel Witherspoon, Lord Tiebauld. We have not met before, but I have heard much about you. I wish our introduction could be under more fortunate circumstances."

"I didn't choose the circumstances at all, Colonel Witherspoon," Aidan said coldly, every inch the affronted lord. "I fear Major Lambert has overstepped his boundaries. Of course, you realize, Colonel, his single-handed decision to take Robbie Gunn prisoner and torture him may cause rebellion."

"Gunn was a Jacobite—" Lambert started, but Aidan cut him off.

"Every Scotsman is a Jacobite at heart. It goes with the romance of our country, and we are all romantics. Gunn was vocal about the Clearances. His family lost everything—their land, their heritage— all stolen by those with money to do it. But if you intend, Lambert, to arrest and beat every man who stands against the Clearances, you will be very busy."

"I'm certain Major Lambert had good cause to arrest Gunn, my lord," Colonel Witherspoon said.

"No, he didn't," Aidan answered crushingly. "He took after Gunn as a way to settle an old score against me."

Major Lambert declared, "What a ridiculous statement!"

Aidan said, "You knew Gunn and I were distant cousins. Ever since we were in school together, you envied my title and my family's prestige."

Anne formed an "O" with her lips. Aidan's words echoed the major's from the night before, words he had spoken to the colonel.

"Oh, yes," Major Lambert said sarcastically. "And I would trump up charges of treason to discredit you? There is no basis for such wild conjecture. Gunn was plotting rebellion."

"If so, where is your proof?" Aidan asked coolly. "And I'll expect something more solid than rumor or snippets of conversation overheard in tap rooms."

Major Lambert's face turned a livid red. "He would have confessed."

The seeds of doubt had been planted. From her hiding place, Anne had a clear view of Colonel Witherspoon's face. He slid an evaluating glance in Major Lambert's direction. Ambitious men must always be cautious, she realized. The colonel could not afford to be linked to Major Lambert's mistakes.

Then Aidan changed tack. It surprised both Anne and the major. "But Gunn's death is history. The important question is, what needs to be done now?"

"Who needs *you* to do *anything*?" Major Lambert practically snarled.

"You." Aidan nodded to the guard. "Is he necessary?"

"No," Colonel Witherspoon said, before Major Lambert could speak, and dismissed the man. Once they were alone, he asked, "What do you believe should be done, my lord?"

"He's one of them!" Major Lambert protested. "You can't listen to him."

"Lambert, you are a fool," Aidan answered with a flash of temper. "In your ambitious arrogance, you have jeopardized all of us. Sutherland, Argyll, myself"—he paused before adding quietly to the distinguished list of titled gentry—"and Colonel Witherspoon."

The colonel shifted, obviously ill-at-ease.

"Gunn is not that important," Major Lambert retorted disdainfully.

"A moment ago he was the key to an insurrection," Aidan said. "You can't have it both ways, Major."

"And do you feel Gunn was important?" Colonel Witherspoon asked Aidan.

"Fiery Robbie Gunn had the devil's own temper.

He could be a suspicious pest in life, but in death he will take on the status of a hero. As the descendant of a Scottish rebel, I understand the power of legend. We must prevent such a thing from happening."

"How can we?" Colonel Witherspoon asked, edging closer to Aidan.

"Bury him. Now, quickly, before word spreads."

"He can't just disappear," Major Lambert replied, echoing the question that had popped into Anne's mind.

"Yes he can," Aidan said. "Everyone knows the Gunns had little to their name. We'll put it about that he escaped and left the country." He shrugged. "Whole families are leaving now, driven out by the Clearances. Robbie's leaving would make sense."

"To go where?" Colonel Witherspoon asked with genuine interest.

Aidan considered a moment. "France, Denmark—it doesn't matter."

The colonel tested the idea in his mind. "Why not? The Frogs adore rebels. They'd probably have made him a minister of state."

"Robbie Gunn would have liked such a role." Aidan asked Major Lambert, "Who knew he was here?"

The major didn't want to answer the question. He clearly resented Aidan's intrusion. But a sharp comment from Colonel Witherspoon forced Major Lambert to answer. "Few."

Aidan snorted. "What does that mean?"

"Yes, Lambert, what does that mean?" the colonel parroted.

"A tavern keeper and a maid we paid to keep their mouths shut."

"Will they talk?" Colonel Witherspoon asked.

"Not if they value their lives," Major Lambert said. "I wanted Gunn's whereabouts kept quiet. I didn't have enough men to defend him if—" He broke off and looked away.

"Defend him if what?" Colonel Witherspoon prompted.

"If his brother or Lord Tiebauld attempted to rescue him."

"And jeopardize everything I own?" Aidan laughed, and Anne quietly laughed with him. His protest rang with truth. "Lambert," he continued, "you are living in a world of your devising. I have business interests and a responsibility to the Crown. A better jest yet is to think of what sort of force I could raise among my sheepherding clansmen."

"But your great-grandfather—" Major Lambert started.

"Is dead," Aidan finished. "I was raised in England. My sister married an important statesman—"

"Who is that?" Colonel Witherspoon asked.

"Lord Waldo," Aidan answered.

"Lord Waldo?" the colonel repeated in reverent tones. "I did not know you were related to him."

"Yes, he was a great man," Aidan said off-handedly.

"He helped arrange my commission," Colonel Witherspoon said.

Anne could have shouted "Hallejuah." As it was, she leaned back against the wall, almost over-whelmed by their good fortune.

Aidan quickly capitalized on the connection. "My sister was his second wife."

"Ah, yes, I met her in London. A gracious woman," Colonel Witherspoon said. "In fact, now I recognize the family resemblance between the two of you."

"And can you see her attacking the Crown?" Aidan asked with a thin smile.

"Lady Waldo? Absolutely not," Colonel Wither-spoon answered.

"Then pass the word on to Major Lambert, and perhaps at last he will believe rebels don't lurk be-hind every rock in the Highlands." Aidan didn't wait for a response but added with lordly contempt, "I'm done here. You have threatened my wife and damaged my honor. Gentlemen, Robbie Gunn's blood is on your hands. The problem is of your own making. I wash my hands of the lot of you." He started to close the door, but Colonel Witherspoon placed his foot in its path.

"I didn't know Lambert was going to beat the bloody man to death."

"It won't matter," Aidan answered. "It happened under your command." He shut the door.

A hundred questions jumped to Anne's lips. Aidan shook his head, warning her now was not the time. They listened. A second later, Major Lambert said, "I did not act irresponsibly. I know Gunn was raising an army."

"You heard Tiebauld," the colonel said. "Gunn had no money. What was he going to raise an army with?"

"Tiebauld supported him," Major Lambert said, but some of his bluster was gone. He obviously realized how weak his reasoning sounded.

Colonel Witherspoon sighed heavily. "There is always a rebellion being planned in Scotland and Ireland. The rabble are never happy." There was a pause and then, he said so quietly Anne had to strain to hear, "You are relieved of your duties, Major."

"What?" The word burst out of Lambert. Aidan's arms around Anne tightened as they listened to the major recover himself. "I beg your pardon, sir, but shouldn't you take a moment to consider?"

"I've considered," the colonel said bluntly, "and have decided it best for you to leave immediately. Return to my headquarters and I will see letters are drawn up to have you reassigned from Scotland."

"But there is nowhere to go!" Lambert said. "Other than Ireland or the West Indies."

"Where I'm certain you will find a suitable post." The colonel started walking back to his room, but Lambert must have stepped in his way.

"I am not wrong about Gunn."

"Well, we'll never know, will we? Gunn is dead, and Tiebauld is right! If word gets about how we caused his death, then we will have a riot on our hands, a riot of your making."

"I kept you informed of my every action," Major Lambert countered.

Colonel Witherspoon's voice became steel. "I did not order you to hold Tiebauld. Perhaps your jealousy blinds you."

"I am jealous of *no man*." Major Lambert spat the words out.

"It is of no difference," Colonel Witherspoon answered. He raised his voice. "Lieutenant Fordyce?"

"Yes, sir." His voice came from a distance, as if he stood at the bottom of the stairs.

"Hand pick a detail of men known for their closed lips. See that the prisoner is buried immediately."

"Yes, sir," the lieutenant answered. A second later, Anne and Aidan heard the door to Colonel Witherspoon's door shut while the lieutenant left the house to do his duty.

Only Major Lambert was left. Anne could feel the heat of the man's frustration even through the hardwood—

A fist slammed into the heavy door. Anne couldn't stop a small cry of surprise. She waited for the major to charge into the room; instead, he marched down the stairs.

Aidan released a breath of relief. "Let us leave as quickly as possible." He didn't need to repeat the suggestion; she was already searching for her stockings.

He tightened the laces of her dress as she shoved her toe in the tip of a rolled-up stocking. "You've been brave, Anne, my darling. Keep it up. We are almost free."

"Is Robbie Gunn truly dead?"

He brushed a quick kiss on her head. "Later." He finished dressing himself in an economy of movement.

She tied her garters and slipped on her shoes, thinking she and Aidan worked almost as a team. Rising from the bed, she helped him tie his neck cloth. The starch had long gone out of it . . . and he looked tired.

She pressed her hand against his cheek. "You've done the best you could."

"I pray it is enough." He took her arm and led her to the door. Outside, the guard had not come back.

They went downstairs. Colonel Witherspoon sat at the dining room table; Lieutenant Fordyce was with him. The colonel rose upon seeing Anne and Aidan. "Ah, so you have decided to take your leave, my lord?" he said jovially, as though they'd been overnight guests and not prisoners.

"I'm afraid I must," Aidan answered with classic understatement. He handed Anne her straw bonnet. She wandered into the sitting room, where there was a mirror by the door, and tied the bow.

"I've taken the liberty of ordering your coach

around," Colonel Witherspoon said. "One of my men will drive you."

"I appreciate your offer," Aidan said, "but I believe I will drive my own coach. It has been a long time since I've had my hands on the ribbons."

"Then an escort?"

"Unnecessary. Thank you."

Their dialogue jarred Anne. They could have been two old friends at a house party. It made her uneasy.

Aidan came into the room where she was. "Are you ready, my lady?" For a second, he almost appeared a stranger rather than the man she'd fully and completely accepted as her husband—and she realized there were two sides to Aidan. One was the arrogantly confident Scotsman who enjoyed hard labor and good fun.

The other was the man waiting for her. A man with polished manners. Urbane, sophisticated . . . in complete control.

Then he held out his hand and the two became one in her mind. Her Aidan. The man she loved.

She placed her hand in his. He said his final farewells to Colonel Witherspoon, even offering a friendly comment to Lieutenant Fordyce. They went out the door.

The coach waited, the horses stamping with impatience. "Have you ever ridden in the driver's box?" Aidan asked.

Anne tried to say no, but found her mouth too dry.

"You'll enjoy it," Aidan answered pleasantly.

They could be preparing to take a ride in the park—instead of hoping to escape with their lives. "Here." He helped her up.

The box seat was narrow. Being up this high made her dizzy. She started to sit. As she did, she glanced in front of her and froze.

Two soldiers marched into the woods carrying a canvas-wrapped body between them. They were followed by a third man who lugged shovels.

Suddenly her trembling legs could no longer support her weight. Aidan had said he'd killed a man.

Would he have sacrificed Robbie Gunn to save their lives?

She didn't know. Aidan could be ruthless when necessary.

A hand on either side of her, Anne gripped the edge of the hard board seat so tightly her knuckles turned white.

Aidan settled in beside her, the reins in his hands. He'd removed his hat and tossed it inside the cab. He hadn't shaved yet. His roughened beard gave him a dangerous look. She caught herself staring at him with uncertainty.

"Safe trip, my lord," Colonel Witherspoon said from the front step.

"And to you, Colonel," Aidan said. "Please visit when you are in the area of Kelwin."

"Not up your way very much," the colonel answered. "Too far north."

Aidan laughed and snapped the reins. The wheels rolled forward with a jolt and they were on their way home.

Anne's body swayed with the movement of the coach. Aidan put his arm around her for support. "Watch it now," he warned.

She nodded. He turned his attention to the horses. He had a better hand on the reins than the soldier who had driven them to Lybster. They rode in silence. Anne didn't dare speak until she was certain they were not being followed.

At the crossroads where they'd run into the funeral procession the day before, she remebered Aidan commenting it was an omen. She glanced at the stately hemlocks guarding a small cemetery and felt a pang of remorse that she didn't understand.

They turned onto the coast road. The day was windy but mild. Heavy, puffy clouds drifted across the sky. The North Sea battered the rocky shore as it did every day, over and over again.

Aidan broke the silence. "You are very quiet, Anne. What is bothering you?"

She could contain herself no longer. "Did you kill Robbie Gunn? Was he the man you murdered?"

Her words startled Aidan so much he pulled on the reins. The horses stopped in the middle of the road. His eyes narrowed. "No," he said firmly. "I didn't kill Gunn."

"Then who did?"

"No one." Flicking the horses to go, he told her the story.

When he was done, Anne released the breath she'd been holding with a sigh of relief. "I wanted to believe you couldn't do it, and yet we were desperate. I didn't know what was happening."

"I didn't want you to know. The less you knew, the safer you were."

"I would never betray you, Aidan."

He looked down at her. "I know you wouldn't. It is not in the fabric of your being to deceive anyone. You are too honest, Anne."

"I wish I were different," she said softly. "I wish I did not care. When you care, you can be hurt."

"You know no other way to be." He studied the horses' heads a moment and said, "We are alike, the two of us. We can't be molded into what other people want us to be. But here, together, we are the people we want to be."

"Perhaps."

He frowned. "What is it, Anne?"

She hesitated and then said, "Why did you choose yesterday afternoon to consummate the marriage? Why then?"

He question startled him, then he grinned. "Do you mean why, when it appeared my neck was about to be stretched by a noose, did I want to make love to my wife?"

"Were you truly afraid?"

"Yes," he replied soberly. "I believed Lambert was going to win."

"And so you made love to me as a ploy to throw him off guard. It worked. Lambert described you to Colonel Witherspoon as a horse, and he readily accepted the idea of you sleeping soundly after so much activity."

"He did, did he?" Aidan laughed, but Anne didn't see anything funny.

He prodded, "Come along, Anne, I was jesting."

She studied her hands in her lap, her feelings too new and unsettled to define.

"I wanted you safe. Consummating the marriage would ensure you would be taken care of in the event I couldn't outwit Lambert."

She raised her gaze to him. "That is all? You wished me to be taken care of?" For a second, she was tempted to push him off the coach. She could visualize him tumbling to the road, head over heels. "I was hoping for a different sort of confession," she admitted. "Something with passion."

"Like my saying I love you?"

Anne went very still. "Only if it is true."

His gaze met hers. "I love you, Anne. I believe you are the most irritating female of my acquaintance . . . and also the half of me that has been missing. I've waited for you. I consummated the marriage because I want us to be as one."

"Truly?" She held her breath. Years of being shuttled from one relative to another warned her to caution.

He smiled then, understanding in his eyes. "Yes, Anne. I love you. Truly. Forever and ever."

"Till death," she added softly.

A gleam came into his eyes. "And after. Kelwin is our home. Your place will always be by my side."

Anne didn't know whether to laugh or cry. She did both, while throwing her arms out to embrace him with such force, she almost *did* knock him off the coach.

She hugged him tight. "There never will be anyone but you."

"And my pledge is to you and no other."

"Not even a Whiskey Girl?" she asked, round-eyed.

"Well . . ."

She kissed him then, a full-bodied, giving-him-all-her-love kiss. And when she was done, he said, "Who needs a Whiskey Girl when I have a wife who can kiss like this?" They both laughed. "Come along, Anne, let's go home."

Home. She remembered the first time she'd heard him call Kelwin that. Now she knew home was by his side, wherever he was.

Aidan clicked the horses and they were off. Anne snuggled against him, loving the wild freedom of the North Sea and the rugged country that was becoming a part of her soul.

Before they caught sight of Kelwin's turret tower, Fang's son Thomas hailed them from his guard post. He slid down the knoll to the road. "'Tis good to see you, laird. We've been watching and waiting."

"Come along," Aidan told him.

Thomas clambered up to the top of the coach and they drove him the rest of the way down to the castle. As they approached the gates, Thomas started shouting, "The laird is back!"

Hugh, his mother, Kathleen, Fang, and Bonnie Mowat were all waiting in the courtyard when they arrived. Soon others came from all corners of the estate to welcome home the laird.

Aidan halted the horses and jumped down. He was immediately surrounded by his people. They clapped him on the back and begged for news of his adventures. The dogs came running up, barking and adding to the general welcoming confusion.

"Wait." Aidan held up his hands for quiet. "Let me help my wife down."

"Your wife?" Kathleen Keith challenged in a carrying voice.

Aidan faced her. "Yes, my wife!" he said, in a tone loud enough to rival hers. He put his hands around Anne's waist and swung her to the ground. "My beautiful, valiant wife."

Everyone began cheering. Anne's glance went from one happy face to another. She blinked back tears. This was her family.

"Thomas," Aidan said, "take the coach up to the stables. Fang and Hugh, I must talk to you. Where's Deacon?"

"Where he should be," Fang said.

"Safe?"

"Aye."

Aidan nodded. "Let us go inside. The rest of you, go about your business. All is safe. You need have no fears." Clasping Anne's hand, he took a step toward the house when a shout went up.

Davey and his friends had been on the tower wall, waiting for Aidan. They now shouted there was another rider approaching. An English soldier.

A hush fell over the crowd. Aidan strode to the front so he would be the first to confront this uninvited visitor. His clansmen took their places behind him, the men first, the women behind them, the children shushed and ordered into the castle. Anne worked her way to the front to stand beside her husband.

Seconds later, Major Lambert tore into the courtyard. He sharply reined his mount, causing the horse to skid on the smooth, aged stones. He jumped off.

He was hatless and wigless. His eyes burned with anger. "Tiebauld." He spat on the ground toward Aidan.

Aidan didn't move. "What is it you want, Lambert?"

"Do you mean what is it I want besides your head up on a pike beside Deacon Gunn's?"

A murmur ran among the women. The men stood stoic and proud, but jaws tightened and their fists clenched in preparation for a fight.

"I had Gunn," Lambert continued, "but you did something. I know you did."

Aidan said, "Give it up, man. It is done between us."

"Not yet," Lambert denied. "It is not done yet. I demand satisfaction." He began to unbutton his uniform. "Are you gentleman enough to give it to me?"

"I'm the one with the title," Aidan said quietly.

They were the right words to inflame Lambert's outrage.

For a moment, Anne could have sworn the major had gone mad. He hissed through his teeth, he was so furious. Fang's two oldest sons, standing close to her, laughed nervously.

The laughter died when Lambert grasped the hilt of his sword and pulled it from its scabbard, the sound of metal razoring metal ominously cutting the air. He held the sword in front of him. "You've ruined me, Tiebauld. *You*, an unimportant Scottish nobody whose family boasts one of the greatest traitors to the Crown in the last hundred years."

Hugh and Fang started toward Lambert, but Aidan held up a hand, staying them. "This is between the two of us. You'll not harm him." He confronted the former officer. "What is it you want, Lambert?"

"Satisfaction, Tiebauld. I demand satisfaction."

"And you will have it." Aidan looked to Hugh. "Go fetch my sword from its case in the great hall. The rest of you, move back." The others did as he'd commanded—save for Anne.

"Aidan, don't do this," she pleaded. "He is not sane."

He ran his thumb lightly across her bottom lip. "Would you have me run? Now, here, it will be all right. Help me remove my jacket."

She was tempted to tell him no. But she couldn't. She reached up and helped him pull one arm out—

Fang shouted a warning a second before Lambert charged both of them. Aidan whirled both of them around. Anne felt the sword blade whisk right by her before Aidan pushed her to safety.

Major Lambert stumbled when he missed skewering one of them, but he pivoted, ready to attack again.

This time, Aidan was ready for him. He wrapped his jacket around his arm to use as a shield. His eyes glittered like shards of glass. "Come, Lambert. I accept the challenge."

"To the death," Lambert growled.

Aidan's answer was to laugh, the sound bold and challenging.

Chapter 17

Aidan's laughter enraged Major Lambert. He charged again. Aidan neatly side-stepped him.

Fang had helped Anne to her feet. She started forward, ready to intervene, but Fang's grasp on her arm tightened.

"There is bad blood between them and has been for years," Fang said. "You can't stop it now, my lady."

"But they'll kill each other," she protested.

"Aye, and a grand fight it will be." Fang wasn't the only one relishing the battle. His sons, neighbors, and even the women watched avidly. Anne wondered if the whole world had gone mad.

Hugh burst into the circle forming around the two combatants. "Your sword, Tiebauld!" He tossed the weapon in Aidan's direction.

Lambert moved to intercept the sword, but Aidan was quicker. He caught it neatly in one hand and faced his opponent.

The major's mood changed dramatically, now that Aidan was armed. The two men circled each other. "I remember you as an indifferent swordsman," Lambert taunted. He jabbed out. Aidan feinted. Steel met steel. The sound grated against Anne's strained nerves.

Lambert attacked, swiping the air viciously. He moved forward, each stride forcing Aidan backward.

"Come on, man," Fang said under his breath. "Cut the bastard to ribbons."

His words shocked Anne—and yet she too was frustrated. Aidan must not lose to Lambert.

Suddenly her husband parried. His sword ran along his opponent's and the two men were upon each other where Aidan's superior strength could be used to advantage. But the major jumped back, disengaging.

Aidan grinned. "Not so easy, is it?"

"Child's play," Lambert answered, but he breathed heavily. He thrust and the fight was on.

Anne had once witnessed a demonstration of swordplay performed by several gentlemen who touted the art of fencing as a skill. The fight between Aidan and the major held none of the structure or finesse dictated by the *Manual of Arms*. It was a battle of brutal strength and cunning. Lambert was obviously the more experienced swordsman, but Aidan's natural athleticism gave him an advantage.

However, Aidan had been without sleep. Anne prayed his strength would hold out.

They hacked away at each other, grunting at the exertion each time their swords clashed. Sweat beaded their brows. The air rang with the clang of vibrating metal.

Then Aidan stumbled over a loose stone in the courtyard. Losing his balance, he hit the ground heavily, becoming an easy target for his opponent. Lambert brought his arm down, the blade aimed at Aidan's chest. The sharp-edged blade sliced the material of his shirt. Blood appeared. Lambert pulled back his arm to spear Aidan's heart.

Again Anne had to be restrained lest she jump into the fray. She couldn't bear to watch; she couldn't turn away.

Aidan rolled an instant before the major's sword point dived into the ground right where he'd been. Lambert's sword tip got caught between the smooth cobbles. Before he could pull it out, Aidan whipped his sword around, and even at such an awkward angle, struck the major's sword with so much force the handle went flying from Lambert's hand. His sword flipped one end over the other to clatter on the courtyard stones.

Lambert held his hands out to show he was unarmed.

It was over. Aidan rose to his feet. "Satisfied?"

"No." He nodded to indicate his sword.

To Anne's astonishment, Aidan shrugged and let him pick it up. She searched the faces around her. Did anyone else think this a ridiculous form of generosity?

No, they were all involved in the battle.

Worse, Aidan read her mind. He gave her an apologetic smile before he was forced to pay attention to Lambert's renewed attack.

For another quarter hour the men fought. They were both slowing down. Dueling was hard business.

Lambert's sword whacked Aidan's blade against the courtyard's stone wall. To everyone's surprise, the steel broke and Aidan found himself holding the hilt and little more than four inches of blade.

Aidan held out his arms as Lambert had done earlier to show he was unarmed, but instead of retreating the major lunged straight for Aidan's chest. Her husband swore, dodging in time, but Lambert had seen that trick before. He swiveled, ready to strike the death blow.

Aidan ducked, coming up under Lambert's arm and plunging the stump of his blade into the man's side.

It happened so quickly, it took everyone a moment to realize what had transpired.

Aidan stepped back, a look of horror crossed his face. "Lambert, I didn't—" His voice broke off. He drew out his blade. Blood poured from the major's wound.

The officer stared at the puncture as if surprised he'd been injured. Slowly, he tilted his head to Aidan. "You have beat me."

"Lambert—" Aidan started, but the officer's knees buckled. Aidan caught him before he hit the ground. Lambert tried to push him away, but Aidan would have none of it. He lay his adversary on the cold, hard stones and removed his own shirt to attempt to staunch the flow of blood.

Fang released Anne's arms. She ran to her husband to see what she could do to help.

Aidan whispered to Lambert, "I didn't mean to kill you," he whispered.

"I wanted to see you bloody dead," the major sneered.

The unbridled hate shook Anne, as it apparently did her husband. "Why?" he asked. "What did I ever do to you?"

Lambert coughed and blood ran in a rivulet from the corner of his mouth. "I know you are a traitor," he said with difficulty.

"It wasn't worth your life," Aidan answered sadly.

The major's eyes met his. "Tell me . . . I was right . . . I knew . . ." He coughed again and added, "Honor."

He died.

Anne placed her hand on her husband's shoulder. He released his breath with a shudder. "I didn't want to kill him, Anne."

She nodded. She knew. "It could not have ended any other way," she said softly.

Aidan lowered the body to the ground. He started to rake his hand through his hair and then stopped when he saw the blood staining his palm, his fingers. He rose to his feet. "He was right, you know."

"I know." She put her arms around him, resting her head against his shoulder. "But I am glad he is the one on the ground and not you."

"Aye, Anne, but his death is on my conscience."

"Aidan—"

"Bloody good fight!" Deacon's voice echoed off the stone walls in the silence of the duel's aftermath. He stood on the path leading to the stables. Now, he made his way to them. The sun chose that moment to come out from behind a cloud, highlighting his brash red hair. "You bested him, Tiebauld. It wasn't pretty, but God, man, it was neatly done."

"What are you doing out here?" Aidan asked. "You are supposed to be in hiding."

"I had to watch the fight." He kicked the bottom of Lambert's boot with his toe. "One Englishman dead. Soon there will be others," he vowed to the clansman crowded in the courtyard.

"Do you want to know of your brother?" Aidan asked coldly.

Deacon grinned with his customary cocksureness. "I assumed because you were here and Lambert was deadly angry with you, Robbie is free. Am I right?"

Aidan's hand found Anne's. He clasped it tightly. "Yes."

"Where is he?" Deacon asked. "We have plans to make. The time has come to strike."

"The English think Robbie is dead," Aidan answered.

The news startled Deacon as it did the others. The men moved closer to hear the tale.

Deacon burst out laughing. "Dead? How did you manage that, Tiebauld? It must be quite a story."

A frown formed between Aidan's eyes. "It is." He paused and scrutinized the people around him. Anne tried to see what he saw. There were all the familiar faces of those who had become like family to her. The children had come outside. They hovered close to their parents, occasionally sneaking a brave peek at the major's body. They would never forget this day as long as memory served.

Aidan had become a legend.

Anne could see it in his people's expressions. They expected him to make everything right, to protect and guide them.

She felt the weight he carried upon his shoulders. It had become her burden, too.

"I'll tell you everything," Aidan said. "But what I say must not leave these walls. Robbie Gunn is alive. However, he's in bad shape. When it grows dark, Hugh and Thomas will fetch him."

Fang spoke up. "Tell us the tale."

"I will," Aidan promised. "But first, come into the hall and help yourself to ale. There is something I must do." He nodded to two of the shepherd lads. "Take the major's body to the chapel. We shall send word to the English he is here."

"Why not throw him over the cliff and say good riddance?" Deacon asked. "Let them worry over where he's gone. Mayhap they will think he's deserted."

Her husband physically recoiled from his suggestion. "We're not animals. We"—he amended the word—"I owe the man a proper burial."

Still holding Anne's hand, he started for the castle. The others fell into step behind him, chattering with excitement. They felt free to discuss the duel now. Each had seen it from a different perspective and wanted to share his or her thoughts.

Deacon bragged that the swordfight had been an omen—and the young men around him agreed. They declared the English would be vanquished just as Aidan had defeated the better trained officer.

Only Anne and Aidan were quiet.

She wondered what her husband was thinking. She could not judge his mood. He released her hand when they entered the great hall. Norval met Aidan at the door with a fresh shirt.

"It was a grand fight, Laird," he said with new respect. "I've never seen the like."

Aidan didn't answer, but threw the shirt over his head and tucked it in.

Meanwhile, his clansmen filled the room. Some moved straight for the keg. Others gathered in groups, laughing and talking, the atmosphere festive.

However, Aidan did not join them. He grabbed a wall torch from its sconce and lit it off the fire in the hearth.

"Here's ale for you, Tiebauld," Deacon said, offering a foaming tankard. "And here is our first toast. To Laird Tiebauld of Clan Dunblack. He has returned the clan to its proud former glory!"

His words were quickly hailed and seconded, but Aidan didn't acknowledge them. Instead, he started for the side door leading to the kitchen walkway, the flaming torch held high in one hand.

"Where are you going, Tiebauld?" Deacon asked, each fist holding a full tankard.

"To destroy the gunpowder," Aidan answered, and walked out the door.

It took a moment for his words to sink in, and when they did, Deacon was the first to react. "Are you mad, Tiebauld? You can't do it!" he shouted, but there was no answer. Aidan had already left.

With a strong oath, Deacon tossed aside the tankards. He started after Aidan, slowing his step long enough to look at Anne. "It's your fault," he told her. "From the moment I clapped eyes on you, I knew you would do what you could to destroy him." He raced out of the room after her husband.

Everyone else stood rooted in stunned silence, except for Anne. She understood. She knew what Aidan was about to do and she would help him.

Lifting her skirts, she ran after the two men, only steps behind Deacon. The others followed.

Aidan made his way along the rocky path, heading for the cave. The torch's flames danced and flapped in the strong wind off the water.

As he skirted the edge of the beach, Deacon caught up with him. He grabbed Aidan's arm and swung him around. Anne was not far behind. She stopped. Up above her, along the cliff path were all the others—Fang, Hugh, the clan.

"Tiebauld, what is the matter with you?" Deacon shouted.

Aidan wanted him to understand. "War isn't the answer. It will destroy us all."

"We are already being destroyed," Deacon retorted. "The Clearances are costing people their homes. Taxes and laws eat away at us. If we, the highlanders"—he thumped his chest for emphasis—"are to survive, we must fight back."

"You can't win, Deacon, not this way."

"Of course we can win!" Deacon shouted, gesturing wildly. "Look at what you've done! You single-handedly walked into an armed English camp and rescued Robbie. If you can do that, Tiebauld, then with an army of loyal Scotsmen behind you, you can defeat the English. You can run them all the way back to London just as the great Donner Black did! It's in your blood."

"Deacon, England is the strongest country in the world. She will crush us, just as she did at Culloden. But this time, her vengeance will be a hundred times more terrible than it was in '45. There will be *nothing* left."

If he had hoped Deacon would listen to reason, he was disappointed. His friend's eyes burned with righteous pride. He caught a glimpse of Anne from the corner of his eye and pointed at her. "You would not desert us—not on your own. It is *her*, she has weakened you."

"No," Aidan answered. "You told me yourself, I must choose. In the last twenty-four hours, I have killed two men. *I will kill no more.*" He dashed up the rocky trail toward the cave. Argument was futile. The time had come for action.

He'd made it halfway to the cave before Deacon yanked him back. "I can't let you do it, Tiebauld. Robbie and I have worked too hard for this." He knocked the torch out of Aidan's hand.

But Aidan was taller, stronger. He easily pushed Deacon aside and lunged for the torch wedged against a rock. He picked it up and had gone four steps when Deacon called out, "Tiebauld! Halt, or I'll slit your wife's throat."

Aidan froze. Slowly, he turned. Deacon held Anne captive, the honed blade of his knife pressing into the tender skin of her neck. A bead of blood appeared.

The people of Kelwin were stretched out behind them. Some were on the beach. Others had climbed the rocks for a better view of what was happening.

All were soberly silent.

Aidan lifted his hand, palm out. "Deacon, no. You mustn't hurt Anne. She is an innocent."

"You were on our side before she appeared," Deacon told him roundly. "Don't think of her as guiltless. She has hobbled you, man. She's taken away your fire."

"She's my life," Aidan said quietly. "If you hurt her, then you hurt me."

"I don't want to hurt you," Deacon said. "We're friends, cousins. But I can't let you destroy the gunpowder—"

Anne interrupted him, her clear voice carrying so all could hear, "Aidan, destroy the gunpowder. Destroy all of it. It's the only way."

"Shut up," Deacon ordered.

Suddenly, a child screamed. It was Marie, Cora's niece, who stood with several other children on an outcrop of rocks. Her eyes wide with fright, she cried to Deacon, "Don't hurt my lady!" When he didn't move, she turned to Cora, who was already hurrying up from the beach to reach her. "Do something, Cora! He's going to hurt my lady!"

Cora quickly swept the weeping child up in her arms. "Deacon, let Lady Tiebauld go. Please." When he didn't move, she pleaded, "For us, Deacon. Please, *for us*."

"I can't," he said. "If I do, Robbie and I will have nothing left."

"If you kill my lady, it will be murder, Deacon, and I'll have nothing to do with you. You told me you wanted to be a better man, and yet look at you."

"Cora, you don't understand," Deacon said.

"I understand you want something you can't have. Your land is gone, Deacon. Gone. All that's left is revenge."

"And my pride!" he fired back.

Cora shook her head. "You can't build anything on pride."

Aidan looked from Cora to Deacon. His gaze met Anne's. Brave, stubborn Anne. She even smiled at him. "There must be a better way to fight the wrongs done us than war," he said. "I'm going to explode the gunpowder."

"But what of Anne?" Deacon asked.

"I'll kill you with bare hands if you hurt one hair on her head."

Anne added, "He will, too."

Her plucky response startled a laugh out of the onlookers. Aidan grinned with pride. "If you weren't made to be a laird's wife, I've never met one who is," he told her.

"Oh, no," she countered gamely. "I was meant to be a *countess*. Now, blow up the gunpowder. And, Marie—?"

The child in Cora's arms said in a watery tone, "Yes, my lady?"

"Have courage."

"I love you, Anne," Aidan said.

"I love you, Aidan Black," she echoed as he started up toward the cave.

He then shouted to those of his clan on the beach and up and down the paths. "Run, all of you. I don't know what will happen when the gunpowder explodes." He turned and charged the cave.

"Tiebauld!" Deacon shouted.

But Aidan wouldn't stop. Inside the cave, the roar of the sea echoed in the cavern. He kicked open one of the kegs of gunpowder. The smell of sulfur and salt peter twitched his nostrils. He lifted the broken keg and started back toward the entrance, a trail of black powder behind him.

Suddenly, the torch was yanked out of his hands. He turned. *Deacon.*

For a second, the two men stared at each other. Between them had been many good nights of camaraderie, of laughter, of sharing of dreams, hopes, and plans for the future. If he had a brother, it was this man.

"Your wife is not harmed," Deacon said. "I

couldn't hurt Anne. Now go. I'll set the fire. This way, when Robbie asks who the traitor is, I can say it was me."

"Then let me—"

"No." Deacon backed away. "Cora makes me think." He studied a point past Aidan's shoulder, his words measured. "I don't know what is right or wrong anymore . . . but she makes me believe there could be something better. Something more. But I can't stay here. Not if I do this."

"Then let me do it."

"No, I need to recover myself. I wouldn't have hurt Anne."

"I know." Or at least, he'd hoped.

Deacon nodded a moment, his mind working other problems. "Robbie will be angry." He straightened. "But it is my choice." His gaze met Aidan's. "Thank you for being my friend, even when I've been a fool."

Aidan held out his hand and Deacon clasped it. "We've both had our moments. Now, listen closely, I don't know what will happen when it explodes."

Deacon grinned grimly, rising to this new challenge with his customary bravado. "Then you'd best be a long way off."

"Are you sure?"

Deacon said, "Go on. We don't have time to waste."

Drawing a deep breath, Aidan accepted the inevitable. "Move quickly once you light the powder."

His friend snorted. "That was your plan? Light and run?"

"Run like the hounds of hell are at your heels," Aidan corrected ruefully.

"Well, it sounds like a good plan to me. I'll give you a count of ten."

"Right."

Aidan headed for the cave entrance, but Deacon added urgently, "If something does happen, tell Cora I love her. I've not said it to her."

Aidan turned to his friend. The threat of tears burned his eyes. "You can say it yourself when this is over," he promised. "Now, don't forget to run."

"Aye, like the hounds of hell."

"Maybe faster," Aidan advised. "I'll see you in a few minutes." He left the cave and began running.

Behind him, Deacon started the count. "One . . . two . . ."

The clansmen had all left for safe hiding places—save Anne. She waited for him on the beach, shouting his name when she spotted him.

He swore softly. She had to be the most stubborn woman he'd ever known.

No wonder he loved her.

In the next second, the cave exploded and Aidan went flying through the air.

Chapter 18

Anne's ears rang with the force of the explosion. The earth shook. Dirt and rocks flew through the air. She closed her eyes and fell to the beach, covering her head with her arms. Cold sea water washed the shore, covering her outstretched leg and dampening her skirts.

The explosion echoed along the cliffs, and then all went silent. Not even the ever-present gulls and terns gave a cry.

Her first thought: *she was alive*. Was Aidan?

Anne pushed her hair back from her face and lifted her head. The cave had collapsed and a good portion of the cliff now rested in the water.

Hindered by her wet skirt, she struggled to her feet. "Aidan!" His name reverberated in the stillness. She'd last seen him running down the cliff trail.

Now, the trail was gone ... and there was no sight of Aidan.

Fang, Hugh, and the others emerged from hiding. They stared as she did at the havoc the explosion had wrought on the coastline. Fang was the first to arrive at her side. Cora, the second.

Her throat closed with the pain of grief, Anne said, "I don't see him. I don't see either of them."

Tears streamed down Cora's face. Marie reached up to capture her hand. Together they searched for Deacon.

Fang walked by them. "They are both hearty lads. They made it through." Neither Anne nor Cora answered him.

Anne reached for Cora's free hand, and together the women and child started to climb the rubble of what had once been the trail. Fang followed.

Then, a man standing on the cliff shouted, "I see a body."

Anne feared her heart would stop. She scurried over the rocks in the direction the man was pointing. Hugh joined her with Fenella right behind him. He quickly outdistanced Anne and reached the spot where the man pointed.

"It's the laird!" Hugh called over his shoulder. Anne lifted her skirts and climbed the outcropping of rocks where he stood.

Aidan was regaining consciousness by the time she reached him. Dirt covered him. His face was badly scraped, his clothes torn—and he'd never appeared better to her. She threw her arms around him. "You're alive," she repeated over and over.

His hand took hold of her arm to free him long enough to kiss her—right there in front of everyone. He tasted of dirt, sweat, and Aidan. Wonderful, wonderful Aidan.

He broke the kiss off, lightly brushing the side of her face with his fingers as he managed a weak smile. "I think I've had enough danger to keep me for a while," he admitted in a voice hoarse from the dust.

Anne, Fang, and Hugh laughed. Fang liked the comment so much, he shouted it to the others. Tears ran down Anne's cheeks. She was so happy.

Aidan said, "Here, Hugh, help me up. I feel as I've broken every bone in my body."

When he was up and standing on his own, a cheer rose from the people. He was badly bruised, but otherwise uninjured.

Smiling with relief, Anne turned and saw Cora standing up the hill from them. Her smile faded.

Aidan asked, "Where's Deacon?"

The mood turned suddenly somber. "We don't know," Hugh answered.

Aidan started toward Cora. Anne helped him, taking his arm and putting it over her shoulder. "He can't be dead, Anne," he whispered. "I can't have another life on my soul. Not Deacon's."

She said nothing. She dreaded the worst.

Slowly Cora faced them. "I can't find him." She closed her eyes. "For so long, I couldn't rid myself of him, and now I don't think I can live without him." Marie buried her face in her aunt's skirts.

Aidan pulled away from Anne. "He must be here." He walked past Cora, Hugh and Fang following. They started climbing the rubble, shouting Deacon's name. The gulls were back. They squawked an answer, hovering in the air above and surveying the damage.

Anne picked up Marie and placed her arm around Cora. "He's too stubborn to die," she said aloud.

"Aye," Cora agreed quietly.

And yet there was no sign of him.

Aidan stiffly climbed a mound of rocks, the better to see. He called, "Deacon!"

Marie lifted her small voice to shout Deacon's name, as worried as any of them.

"Wait." Aidan held up a hand, signaling for quiet. "I saw movement. Over there." He stepped down from the rocks and clambered to a point not far from where he'd stood.

Then Anne and everyone else noticed what Aidan had seen. A hand in the loosened rock and dirt. The color drained from Cora's face. She grabbed Anne's arm.

Aidan had reached the hand. He fell to his knees and began digging. Hugh and Fang hurried to help. Thomas and his brothers came scurrying down the cliffs to join them.

Marie wiggled, wanting to be free to help. Cora took the child from Anne and held her close. "Not yet, sweet." Anne knew Cora feared what the child might see if she got too close.

"But I want to see Deacon," the child argued.

"Wait," Cora said firmly, and there was something in the way she said the single word to make Marie behave. She put her arms around Cora's neck.

Then Aidan shouted. "He's alive."

Aidan and the others shoveled the dirt from Deacon with their bare hands.

Deacon's head emerged from the rubble. He drew a wavering breath and released it on a soft moan.

"Hold on, man," Aidan said. "We'll have you out in a few minutes." He took a moment to brush the dirt from Deacon's face.

"Thank you," was Deacon's reply, laced with his usual irony. But then, he turned serious. "I can't feel my legs," he said, hesitantly.

The men laboring over him exchanged glances. "Give us a moment," Fang answered. "There is a fair amount of rock here. Don't try to move yet."

The men worked quickly. At last, Deacon's torso was free, but a boulder rested on his legs. Fang organized the men to move it.

Deacon looked to Aidan. "I should have let you light the charge."

The quip caught all of them by surprise. Aidan stared into the dirty, sweat-stained face of his friend, knowing he himself didn't look much better, and burst into laughter.

Deacon joined him, and Fang and Hugh. The boys couldn't. They didn't understand. But the men did.

It was sweet to be among the living.

Deacon nodded to where Anne and Cora stood. "They will think us mad."

"We already have the reputation," Aidan answered.

"All right, let us move this rock off his legs," Fang said, taking command. He organized where each would stand, and when he gave a count of three, they put their weight to it. "Careful now. Bring it straight up, else we injure him more."

With the number of men helping, they lifted the rock without due difficulty. Deacon grunted in pain. Sweat beaded his brow. "How bad is it?" he asked Fang.

The older man shook his head. "'Tis a nasty break. We'll set it, but the laird may want to send for the surgeon in Inverness."

"I don't need a surgeon," Deacon responded.

"Would you rather lose your leg?" Aidan countered.

Deacon waved a hand to Hugh and Thomas. "Here, help me up."

They did as he'd requested. His other leg was twisted, but not broken, and he was able to balance himself, although with great pain. Aidan was about to argue over the surgeon again, but Deacon no longer listened to him. Instead, his gaze shifted to focus on Cora. He forced his lips to twist into a smile and was rewarded by Cora's sob of relief and Marie's shouting his name.

"Do you think she'll have me?" he asked.

Aidan didn't need to ask whom he meant. "I think she'd be a fool to let a stubborn rogue like you trail after her." He met Deacon's startled look and added, "But she loves you. You're a lucky man, Deacon Gunn, and you'd better value her love."

Funny, but he would not have said those words as little as two weeks ago. Back then, the quality of love held little value to him.

Now, it signified the world.

Deacon glanced around at the men who were his friends. "But will she love me if I can't walk?"

"You'll have to ask her," Aidan answered.

Deacon drew a deep breath. "Well, come, lads. Take me to her."

Hugh and Thomas made a seat of their hands. It wasn't the best way to transport Deacon, but it was all they had at the moment. They'd only taken a few steps when Cora began running toward them, Marie in her arms.

"I think she'll take you any way she can have you," Aidan told Deacon softly, the moment Cora arrived in front of them.

Deacon and Cora's eyes met. Something passed

between them. Even Aidan could feel the power of their attraction. Then she said, "That was the stupidest thing you have ever done, Deacon Gunn."

"I won't be doing it again," he promised.

She came to him then, wrapping her arms around his waist and burying her face and Marie's in his chest. Deacon winced, but he didn't tell her to let go. Instead, he put his arms around her and Marie and held them tight.

The thought struck Aidan that his friend may have lost his birthright, but now he had something else of greater value.

He shifted his attention to Anne. She stood apart from everyone else. She watched the reunion misty-eyed but brave, always brave.

No woman was lovelier in his eyes. She alone held his heart—and suddenly Aidan realized he was a very rich man.

He held out his arms and she came running to him.

A day later, Colonel Witherspoon himself accompanied the party of men who came for Major Lambert's body. Aidan met them dressed in his customary shirtsleeves and black leather breeches, although he did add a starched neck cloth because Anne thought it attractive. He received the colonel in the great hall.

"I regret the actions of my officer," Colonel Witherspoon apologized sincerely but stiffly.

"His decisions are no reflection upon your command," Aidan answered with equal formality.

"Still, I appreciate your understanding, my lord." The officer chose his words carefully, "It is difficult up here. They don't like us." He referred to the highlanders.

"*We* don't trust *you*," Aidan corrected. "You are considered little more than henchmen when you support policies used unscrupulously. But that will change."

Colonel Witherspoon stretched his neck as if the collar of his uniform had grown tight. "What do you mean, my lord?"

"My wife and I are going to London."

He was visibly relieved by what he sensed was a change of topic. "To London? For what is left of the Season?"

"No, not for the Season. I've decided to take a more active role in politics. I'm going to fight the Clearances, Colonel. I'm going to abolish them."

His certainty took Colonel Witherspoon back. He shook his head, smiling apologetically. "I don't like them any more than you do. My men are soldiers. We take no pleasure in turning people out of their homes. However, the feudal system in Scotland is very strong, as you yourself know. In order to eradicate a practice like the Clearances, you would have to give up some of your own landowner rights, my lord. Are you ready to do so?"

"I abhor the practice, Colonel Witherspoon, and already refuse to exercise my rights in such a manner."

"Yes, my lord, but the world is made up of those who think differently than you. Your neighbors do not share your view. Please, don't mistake my meaning. I am a widow's son from a genteel but poor family. I understand what it is like to dependent upon the whims of my betters. I wish you luck with your battle."

"But you don't believe I will succeed?"

Colonel Witherspoon's smile turned rueful. "No, my lord. But I hope you do." With those words, he bowed smartly and left.

Aidan waited until the soldiers had passed through Kelwin's gates before he made his way to the servants' quarters. There Deacon and his brother Robbie shared a room, each healing from his injuries in his own bed.

He'd had Hugh go for Robbie the night before. The widow in Lybster had seen to Robbie's wounds and he was now on the mend.

Anne was lingering in the servants' hallway outside the Gunn brothers' door. "What is it?" he asked her.

"Deacon may be difficult but his brother is insufferable," she confided.

Aidan laughed. "Most revolutionaries are."

"But he speaks insanity," Anne said. "He plans to march to London and lop off the king's head. Cora sent Marie away because he was upsetting the child with his wild talk."

He sighed. "Let me put an end to it."

Her fingers laced with his. "Are you going to propose what we discussed last night?"

"Yes." He raised her hand to his lips and gave it a light kiss. "All will go well, Anne. Have faith."

She leaned against him and, for a moment, he savored the warmth of her body heat, the scent of her hair. She wore her blue dress, the one she'd been wearing the day he'd made her clean the stables. It was his favorite on her because he always chuckled over the memory of her spitting fire at him. Together they entered the sickroom.

"It's about time you made your way here," Robbie greeted him cheerfully. "What did our fine colonel have to say? Did he suspect two of the most notorious rebels in Scotland were under your roof?" He chuckled at the thought of outwitting the soldiers.

Deacon was quiet. Cora sat on the edge of his bed, holding his hand. His broken leg had been set but could not be moved.

"He didn't suspect anything," Aidan said lightly. He sat on the footboard of the rough-hewn bed and drew Anne to stand beside him, a possessive arm around her. "Robbie, I have something to tell you which you will not like."

"That you turned me over?" Robbie jested. He laughed at his own joke.

"That there is no gunpowder."

Robbie frowned, his mind working. "It's gone?" He looked to his brother. "Or are you teasing?"

"No, it's true." Deacon answered. He could not meet his brother's eyes.

"I destroyed it," Aidan said baldly.

His eyes bulging with surprise, Robbie repeated, "Destroyed it?"

"There will be no war in Scotland," Aidan said.

Robbie took a moment for Aidan's declaration to sink in. When he understood what they were saying, his infamous temper took hold. "You bloody traitor!" He lunged for Aidan, who had been prepared for such a possibility. Twice Robbie's size and with more strength, he blocked the man's assault and pushed him back onto the bed.

"I did what was right," Aidan told him.

"You did what protected you!" Robbie shot back.

"Yes," Aidan admitted. "And the people I love. There will be no more killing."

"You've fallen under the spell of an English temptress," Robbie flashed.

Aidan started to reach for Robbie's neck—but to his surprise, Anne laughed.

"I've never been called a temptress before," she said. "I thank you for the compliment, Robbie Gunn. But I'll advise you no one leads the Earl of Tiebauld around by his nose. Not his wife or his angry friends."

"I'll not stay under this roof," Robbie said malevolently. "I curse it and everyone in it."

"Brother—" Deacon started.

Robbie whipped around to him. "Let us go, Deacon. And when the time comes, Kelwin will be the first castle we burn!" So saying, he rose from the bed. "I'll get help to move you, brother."

He'd taken several steps toward the door when Deacon said, "I won't be going, Robbie."

"What?" He faced Deacon. "You won't be at my side? You'd choose to stay here over your own brother?" He glared at Cora and then Anne. "The women have made you both soft. They've sapped your lust for freedom."

"That's not true," Aidan said. "I've decided to take my seat in Parliament. I will take the Scottish question to them."

Robbie spit his opinion on the ground. "No one will listen."

"They will, if I am persistent enough," Aidan answered.

"It will take decades. Centuries even!" Robbie declared. "No man gives up power freely."

"Then I and my heirs will work for centuries," he vowed. "But I want no more of killing."

"What of Deacon and me, *Lord* Tiebauld? We are wanted men. Will you betray us? Will you turn us over to the English to save your precious peace?"

Aidan reached for Anne's hand. The time had

come to make the offer they had discussed the night before. "No, I have another proposition to offer you. One I hope you and Deacon both agree to. My family owns property in North America, purchased by my grandfather. Having lived with the aftermath of Culloden and being an English hostage for a time, he feared the family might someday be forced into exile. He wanted the place of exile to be of his own choosing."

Robbie had turned sullen, but Deacon was listening. "What place did he choose?"

"Canada. Along the St. Lawrence River," Aidan answered. "I'm told it's good land and I have the surveyors' reports as I had the land recently remeasured. I'm told the property could be developed profitably by the right men."

"For your own gain," Robbie shot back.

"No, for yours," Aidan answered. "I will deed the land over to the two of you. You can start fresh. When you are established, pay me what it is worth."

"I don't want to start *fresh*," Robbie mimicked. "I have lands, lands that were stolen from me."

"And will probably never be returned to you, either," Aidan shot back. He moved with Anne to the door. As they passed, Robbie childishly made a show of pretending not to want them to touch him. His actions disappointed Aidan. He'd hoped for better. "It's your decision," he said, opening the door. "I won't talk you into it. You can stay and fight—I can't stop you. Or you can try to build something new." He and Anne left the room.

Anne waited until they were out of earshot to ask, "Do you think they will accept your offer?"

"I don't know. Every man must make his own decision. I've made mine."

Norval was waiting for them in the great hall. "Everything is ready, my lord," he whispered conspiratorially.

"Every *what* thing is ready?" Anne asked.

"You'll see," Aidan answered cryptically, and led her to the front door.

She hung back. "My lord, I don't like surprises."

"Trust me, my lady."

"You ask for my trust quite often." She arched a suspicious eyebrow.

"Aye, and have you ever regretted it?"

Her expression softened. "No."

He grinned. "Then trust me now." He opened the door.

She hesitated a moment, and then went forward. Aidan and Norval followed, the manservant almost skipping, he was so excited to be a part of the surprise.

Outside, spring had truly arrived. The wind off the North Sea blew with as much force as always, but there was a difference in the air. Tender shoots of green grass peered around the cobbles of the courtyard, and the baaing of newborn lambs could be heard all the way from the sheep shed to the castle.

It was the time of year for a new life, for a new beginning, Aidan thought, as he piloted his wife in the direction of the chapel.

"What are we doing here?" she asked, curious. She frowned. "Aidan, I don't like surprises—"

He covered her lips with one finger, warning her to ask no more questions. "Close your eyes."

She didn't want to, but in the end curiosity got the better of her. She closed her eyes. Standing behind her, Aidan put his hands on her arms and guided her forward.

"There's a step here," he said in her ear, warning her of the rough-hewn slab of stone at the entrance of the chapel. "Over the threshold." Dutifully she lifted her foot higher.

"Open your eyes," he whispered in her ear.

Anne didn't know what to expect, but it wasn't what she saw. All of Kelwin was crowded into the chapel dressed in their very best, even Nachton McKay, the distiller, and his two other daughters. They held thin sticks with bright bands of multicolor ribbons tied to the top. The ribbons bounced and jiggled with the movement of the crowd.

Reverend Oliphant stood before the altar dressed in sacramental robes.

"What is this?" Anne asked.

Aidan took her hand. He glanced at their audience, drew a deep breath, and said, "Well, if you'll have me, I'd like to marry you. Only this time, it will be of my own choice . . . and I'll be present for the ceremony."

People chuckled at his words. They all knew the story. Anne's proxy marriage had already become the stuff of legend.

She looked around the room. There was Bonnie Mowat with all her boys. Fang stood proudly at the other end of the row, a head shorter than his oldest sons. Hugh Keith had placed himself at the very front of the church. He was flanked by his mother, Kathleen, on one side, and by his sweetheart, Fenella, and her mother on the other.

And there were others, so many others. People who were becoming the weave of the fabric of her life. The hopeful expressions on their faces and their total acceptance of her said louder than words that she was one of them.

"You can't refuse me," Aidan said bluntly. Did she detect a touch of desperation in his tone? She pretended to weigh her options, and people chuckled. "What of the banns?" she asked.

"The banns?" Aidan repeated. "Anne, it's too late for the banns. We've consummated the marriage."

His blunt words surprised and delighted everyone, including Reverend Oliphant. The clergyman pretended to cough, but Anne had caught sight of the sparkle in his eye.

Before she could answer, Aidan took her hand

and knelt on one knee. "Come, Anne. You already have my heart. Will you accept my name in front of my people?"

She thought she would melt right there on the spot. "Yes, my lord, I will marry you."

Everyone clapped and even cheered. It was Reverend Oliphant who brought matters to order. "Come, now. I'm anxious to see this business done so I can have another taste of that ale you are always bragging about, my lord. Let's get on with it."

Indeed, the ceremony itself was simple and speedy. Aidan didn't bother to don a jacket but married her in his white shirtsleeves. She smiled at the poetic justice of her wearing the periwinkle dress. And as he slid the wedding band on her finger, promising to love and honor her, she knew at last she had found her home.

Epilogue

1817

Being a politician's wife was not easy for someone who could be as shy as Anne, especially when her husband wholeheartedly threw himself into the role.

Aidan arrived in London with a mission. He had much to accomplish and a difficult road ahead. There were many late nights when Parliament took precedence over social and family life.

Society was intrigued by the "mad Lord Tiebauld" who so brashly declared the task he had set for himself. He was handsome and wealthy and claimed a colorful lineage.

England was entering an age of unprecedented world dominance, an age of the Politician. New ideas were being discussed, the middle class was growing and coming into its own. Many Britons wanted to use their world power judiciously. They'd had enough of war. The earl Tiebauld and his lady wife soon found themselves inundated with invitations.

Because Anne believed in his battle, she forced herself to overcome the shyness that had held her back during her Season on the Marriage Mart. She worked to become an accomplished hostess, one who made an extra effort to see *all* her guests were included at her social functions. Consequently she became a success.

Her sister-in-law, Alpina, saw to it they received vouchers for Almack's. Anne discovered the vaulted assembly rooms were a bore. She had missed nothing back in the days when they would not admit her. Of course, she'd changed much since then, too. Her values were different and not even the strong opinions of her Aunt Maeve and her beautiful cousins bothered her. In fact, once she relaxed and let down her guard a bit, they were actually decent people. Not thoughtful, but not the villains she had imagined them to be, either.

Alpina was not completely pleased her brother had returned to London only to plead the Scottish cause, but she delighted in pronouncing the marriage a success and in taking full credit. When within the first year of wedded bliss, Anne gave birth to Donner Burnett Black, no one was happier than Alpina.

"You knew it would be a boy," Anne reminded her one day when Alpina came to visit the nursery.

Alpina sat on the edge of her chair, holding baby Donner as if he were the most valuable treasure in the world. "Oh, Anne, I was grasping at straws. I feared Aidan had involved himself with a Jacobite rebellion and I prayed the responsibility of a wife would bring him to his senses." She smiled sheepishly. "Can you imagine such a thing?"

Anne hummed her answer, a combination of "no" and "maybe."

Her sister-in-law placed a benediction kiss on the baby's cheek and handed him back to Anne, saying, "Now, I can die in peace."

Her statement startled Anne. Alpina had not been well, but she had managed to live with her illness. Now, Anne realized her sister-in-law had merely been biding her time.

A week later, Alpina's condition took a tragic turn for the worse—but now, she didn't try to fight. As she'd told Anne, she was ready to die.

Anne was glad she and Aidan had been in Town to keep watch by his sister's bedside. Alpina had silently suffered so much pain, death came as a blessing. She left her estate to Anne, who used a portion of it to purchase rugs for the floors and hangings for the walls at Kelwin and the rest to start a school in Caithness. She named the school after Alpina, Lady Waldo.

Deacon accepted Aidan's offer to emigrate to British Canada. Two months after the gunpowder explosion, when he could walk on his own, albeit limping, he and Cora married. Aidan and Anne returned to Kelwin for the ceremony, and a great celebration it was, too. A week later, the couple left with Marie and many members of the clan Gunn to begin a new life.

Unfortunately, once he'd sided with Aidan, Deacon never heard from his brother again. Robbie Gunn refused to have anything to do with his younger brother, whom he considered a traitor. Robbie turned to highway robbery as a means to raise money for his rebellion. He was captured outside Glasgow in the fall of 1815 by English troops and hanged. It was Aidan's duty to write Deacon and inform him he was now laird of clan Gunn.

Deacon's response took several months to arrive. He thanked Aidan for performing such a "grim service." He finished by hoping Aidan was successful with his quest to fight for Scottish rights. "You are closer and dearer to me than my own brother," Deacon wrote, "but I tell you this, I and my children and my children's children will not set foot on Scottish soil until the English give back what was ours from the beginning: our right to self-government."

Hugh managed Kelwin in Aidan's absence. He turned out to be a good steward and the estate prospered.

Whenever they returned to the Highlands, Aidan and Hugh always took off hunting. They'd paint their faces blue, drink a toast to Deacon, and charge off on the trail after deer. Often, Fang's sons joined them. And once, Fang himself.

Anne, Fenella, and the other women shook their heads at such boyish nonsense, but what could they say? All men were really children at heart when it came to sport. If Aidan was happy tramping the hills dressed as an ancient Celt from time to time, well, Anne loved him enough to let him do it.

Several months after Donner was born, Hugh added a postscript to his letter reporting lamb counts that Fenella was expecting their first and Thomas Mowat had begun courting Fenella's cousin.

Sitting in his study, a book-lined room paneled in walnut, Aidan passed Hugh's letter to Anne. She nursed the baby in a chair beside his. Holding the letter in one hand, she read the postscript with delight.

"I can't wait to return to Kelwin," she said, shifting the baby to a more comfortable position. She could have hired a wet nurse, but had decided against the practice. Her father had once said it was natural and right for a mother to nurse her child and she had chosen to follow his advice. Aidan teased that she was being very "Republican."

If the truth be known, sometimes, when all was quiet and she was alone with Donner like this in the nursery, she could sense her parents' presence. She realized now they always hovered close because now she understood a parent's love.

"I can't believe you invited your Aunt Maeve and Uncle Robert up for a visit," Aidan said with a mock shiver. He was not impressed with her tight-fisted relatives. On the other hand, they adored him . . . or, at least, adored bragging about their connection to him.

Anne laughed. "You don't need to worry. I can invite them all I wish but they'll never make the trip. It's all form."

"Good."

Someone knocked on the study door. "My lord, Lady Tiebauld, your guests have arrived," the very correct butler said.

"They are here!" Anne said happily. They'd been waiting for the arrival of her old friends Tess and Leah and their husbands.

While she quickly made herself presentable, Aidan said through the closed door, "We'll be there in a moment, Baxter. Please make them comfortable in the blue salon."

"Yes, my lord," came the droning reply.

"I miss Norval," Anne said.

"I thought you wanted to pension him off." Aidan held out his hands to take Donner from her.

"I do. He's old and deserves to enjoy his remaining years in comfort. But he is one of the family. Baxter is so butlerish." She shivered.

Aidan laughed in agreement and opened the

door for her. Anne hurried ahead of him down the marble-tiled hallway to the blue salon.

She burst into the room and was rewarded with the welcoming cries of Tess and Leah. Her friends were more beautiful than she remembered them.

Tess and her husband, Brenn Owen, the earl of Merton, were expecting their second child. They had left their son Hal with his nanny, since he suffered a slight cold. Pregnancy only served to make Tess more radiant. Anne liked her husband immediately, especially when he took Donner from Aidan and dubbed him "a handsome baby."

Leah proudly showed off her son, Benjamin. He was over a year old and the happiest boy. Leah's husband, Devon Marshall, viscount Huxhold, absolutely doted on the child. Anne hadn't seen her for years and marveled over the sense of peace and maturity womanhood had brought to Leah.

Baxter interrupted the joyful reunion by announcing dinner. Donner's nanny took both the boys up to the nursery so the parents could enjoy their meal. Afterward, the women left their husbands to their brandy while they slipped back into the blue salon to enjoy tea and cozy confidences—as they had as debutantes.

"Can you believe how well our husbands are getting along with each other?" Leah asked, accepting a cup from Anne.

"Amazing, isn't it?" Tess agreed. "In fact, Brenn confided to me over dinner if Aidan is successful with his Scottish legislation, he will take a more active interest in his seat in the House of Lords and push for Welsh concerns."

Anne tilted her head thoughtfully toward Leah. "Now that you have met him, is the mad Lord Tiebauld such a terrible person?" At one time, Leah had been contracted to marry Aidan and had done everything in her power to avoid the liaison.

Leah laughed. "He is quite charming, but absolutely smitten by you. No, my dear Anne, I believe everything has worked out exactly as it was intended. You and Aidan are wonderful to each other."

Anne felt her eyes turn watery. She cried often now, but not out of sadness. Her life brimmed with happiness. Many times during the day, she would pause and reflect, scarcely believing her own good fortune. Now, she fussed with the creamer. "Yes, he has made my life worthwhile."

"I think he might say the same of you," Tess observed.

"I pray you are right," Anne said. "At least now his house is clean." She told them of the first time she'd seen the great hall at Kelwin. They laughed so hard, tears rolled down their cheeks.

Tess changed the subject. "Do you ever think back to the evening at Lady Ottley's musicale when we talked of sticks and pillows?"

Leah howled with laughter and covered her face

with her hands. "How could we have been so naïve?"

"But it all worked out fine," Anne said. "We did figure it out."

"Yes, but only after a few embarrassing moments," Tess confessed.

"I'm curious," Anne said. "If you had to sum up what you've learned about marriage—"

"And love?" Leah interjected, always the romantic.

"Yes, and love," Tess agreed softly.

"—What would you say to the young, impressionable girls we were back then?" Anne finished.

Her question made all of them pause to reflect. Tess sat back in her chair, her hand resting on her rounded belly. Leah stirred her tea. Both women considered the question carefully.

It was Leah who spoke first. "Well, I believe I have discovered—and I should say now that I don't want to be held to this opinion years from now, because I may change my mind—"

Both Tess and Anne laughed. "Well, truly," Leah defended herself. "I am the youngest, but I'd wager I know better than the two of you the twists and turns life takes. I've learned that sometimes what we see as misfortune is really destiny. Love is not always rational. It's almost as if God plays a hand." She smiled. "I've become philosophical. Still, who would have thought I would love so dearly a man who was my family's enemy . . . or have found so much happiness with him? Before him, I was lost. Now he is my life."

Tess reached for her hand. At one time, the two of them had been rivals. Now, they were friends. "I am glad you are happy."

"Thank you," Leah said quietly and then, on a stronger note asked, "Who is next?"

"I am," Tess said. She sat up, back straight, her hands slipping down to help support the weight of her pregnant belly, her spirit proud. "I have learned you can't really love someone unless you can come to them as a complete and whole person."

Anne frowned. "I'm not certain of your meaning."

Tess elaborated, "Before Brenn, I ran from marriage. I felt it was the same as a death sentence. It would be like being buried alive."

Leah made a distasteful sound.

"I now understand my feelings were because I didn't have a true purpose in life. I saw myself as an ornament for a man's arm and little else. My whole world revolved around the narrow focus of the *ton*."

"And now?" Anne asked.

"Brenn has shown me there is a whole world outside of London. I'm fascinated by the people I've met and by new ideas."

"Tess, you sound like a bluestocking," Leah said, referring to women who valued education over lighter pursuits.

"Maybe I am one," Tess answered resolutely. "I

was always too clever for silly painting lessons and endless musicales. I've discovered I want more. I've been writing."

"Writing?" Anne repeated in surprise.

"Yes, and I think I'm quite good. However, I've learned marriage is a new beginning, especially when you are with someone who lets you be the person you want to be."

"But you've always had strong opinions," Anne remarked.

"With you and Leah, but not with men . . . until Brenn. I hate to think of what sort of person I would be if I had stayed in London and continued my selfish, narrow-thinking ways. He has challenged me."

"And made you stronger," Leah added in agreement.

"Yes," Tess said. She turned to Anne. "Very well, what have *you* learned?"

Anne lifted her gaze to the gilded artwork on the ceiling and contemplated how much her life had changed.

"Well," she began, swinging her attention back to her friends. "I now understand the depth of love my parents had for each other . . . and also for me. When a parent dies, a child feels abandoned. Now that I am a mother myself, I understand a parent's love is always with you, even beyond death."

"But what of your husband?"

Anne smiled. "He's taught me that the best part of marriage is the laughter. I agree with you that fate intervenes and steers us toward people we would never have chosen for ourselves. I truly believe I was waiting for Aidan. He brings out the best in me, but I also bring out the best in him. Together, we make a whole. I could not imagine my life without him."

"That's how I feel about Brenn," Tess said.

"And I about Devon," Leah agreed.

For a moment the three friends sat in happy silence. Then Tess stood and spread out her arms, offering her hands. "Come on."

Leah and Anne both rose and clasped hands to make a circle.

"The Welsh believe in fairy rings," Tess told them. "They say there is powerful magic in their center. We've formed a ring of friendship and I think the magic here is more potent than any fairy could imagine. Don't you?"

"Yes," Anne and Leah said at the same time.

"Friends?" Tess asked.

"Always," Anne answered.

"Forever," Leah declared.

And so they were.

Afterword

"Family Vow Satisfied." The Caithness Crier, 21 June 1999, sec. C: 1

Very special Canadian friends Mr. and Mrs. Alexander Gunn and children will be joining the earl and countess Tiebauld for the opening ceremonies of the first Scottish Parliament. But this is more than an ordinary visit.

Almost two hundred years ago, Mr. Gunn's ancestor Deacon Gunn emigrated with members of his clan to Canada. They settled on land deeded to them by the then earl Tiebauld, where over the years the Gunn family fortunes have been very successful. However, no member of the Gunn family has set foot in Scotland since 1815.

Reached in his Toronto office last Thursday, Alexander Gunn told this reporter, "Deacon Gunn was driven from Scotland by the Clearances. He vowed neither he nor his descendants would set foot on Scottish soil until our right to govern ourselves was recognized. It has been a long time in coming, but no member of my family would miss the opening of the first Scottish Parliament convened in three hundred years. We are looking forward to the trip to Caithness."

During the Royal Opening Ceremony, the Queen will honor Lord Tiebauld for the role his family played in making this historic event a reality. Lord Tiebauld has promised to join the First Minister's aggressive legislative pro-gramme, including a bill to abolish the feudal system of land tenure. He is quoted as saying, "We must provide a better balance between public and private interests. I support the First Minister in his desire to find Scottish solutions to the problems we face as a country."

"I need to get away from it all!"

*H*ow many times have you cried out these words? The chance to change your life and maybe even be swept away by romance is so tempting . . . And as everyone knows, there's nothing like a good vacation . . .

*T*he Avon Romance Superleaders are your passports to passion. As you enter the world created in each book, you have the chance to experience passion you've only dreamed of. Each destination is different—you might be whisked into Regency London, or perhaps to a secluded mountain cabin. But at each stop along the way, an unforgettable hero awaits to take your hand and guide you on a journey into love.

Imagine long, lazy summers in the country—the sun caresses your skin by day as you bask in its warmth in your favorite hammock . . . and each evening you curl up by the fire as contented as a cat. But something—or someone—is missing . . .

Then a compelling stranger comes striding into your life. And suddenly, a fire of a different sort begins to keep your nights hot. He's all-male, he's all-trouble . . . and he's got you . . .

All Shook Up

COMING JANUARY 2001

by Susan Andersen

"Are you planning to stalk me around my office?" Dru asked. Then she lost it. "Who taught you your manners, anyway? It certainly couldn't have been Great-aunt Edwina."

A muscle ticked in his jaw. "No, the lesson I learned from Edwina was that talk is cheap, and in the end there's only one person I can depend on—myself."

"Indeed? You'll have to excuse me if I don't cry big, sloppy tears over how misused you were. Because it seems to me that Edwina's talk wasn't all that cheap—for here you are, aren't you? Half owner in our lodge."

He took another step closer. "And that bothers you, doesn't it, sweetheart?"

She deliberately chose to misunderstand. "That you're bad-mouthing the woman who made it possible?" She ignored her reaction to his proximity this time and thrust her chin up. "Yes, I can honestly say I find that rather tacky."

For a moment his eyes went hot with some emotion Dru couldn't pin down, and she felt a burst of triumph that she'd managed to push one of his buttons. It was only fair, considering he seemed to have a natural facility for pushing all of hers.

Then his eyes went cool and distant. "Well, see, that's the thing about us lowlife types," he growled, stepping forward again. "Tacky is mother's milk to us, and we live for the opportunity to get something for nothing." He ran a rough-skinned fingertip down her cheek, leaving a streak of heat in its wake.

Dru jerked her head back, but he just moved in closer. "And we don't particularly care who we have to step on to get it, either," he said in a low voice. "You might want to keep that in mind." His thumb rubbed her lower lip open, but he drew his hand back before she could slap it away. Giving her a slow once-over, he smiled insolently, and she saw that he didn't have bad teeth at all. They were maybe the slightest bit crooked—but very white and strong-looking.

The moment she dragged her gaze back to his eyes, he lifted an eyebrow. "The books?"

Blood thumping furiously in all her pulse points, Dru stalked over to the cabinet and pulled out the ledgers. A moment later she slapped them in his hands. "Here. These cover the past three years. Don't spill food on them and don't lose them."

"Guess that means I'd better not eat my peas with my knife again, huh?"

Embarrassed by her own snide rudeness, she resumed her seat, snatched up a pencil, and tapped it impatiently against the desktop, hoping to give the impression of a woman too busy for this nonsense. "Just be careful with them."

"Yes, ma'am." He gave her a bumptious salute and, with surprising grace for someone wearing several pounds of boot leather on each foot, strode out of the office.

Dru remained fuming at her desk long after he had gone. Things between her and J.D. were shaping up like Trouble with a capital *T*, but she had a bad, bad feeling that his being aggravating as all get-out was the *least* of her problems. She was more worried about the way she felt every time he was near.

Oh to be a Regency debutante . . . to wear beautiful gowns and to waltz (with permission, of course!) with a handsome nobleman, hoping he'll steal a kiss—and more—once the ball is over . . .

But what if your London season doesn't end in a spectacular match? Would you take the chance of traveling to the romantic Scottish Highlands and marrying a man you've never met? Who would want to be someone's poor relation anyway? After all, every woman needs a husband, and that's reason enough to sign . . .

The Marriage Contract

COMING FEBRUARY 2001

by Cathy Maxwell

"*T*hat is a wedding ring on your finger, isn't it?"

Anne had an unreasonable desire to hide her hand in the folds of her skirts. She clenched her fist. She wasn't ready for the confession, not ready at all.

He misinterpreted her fears, his gaze softened. "Your husband will be happy to know you are safe after such a bad accident."

"I hope he will," she managed to say. *Tell him,* her inner voice urged. *Now.*

Her husband looked down at the way he was dressed and laughed. He had a melodic, carefree laugh, for such a large man. Anne knew he would have a fine singing voice, too. And he didn't sound mad at all.

"It's a ritual I have," he explained with a touch of sheepishness over his peculiar dress. "Based on Celt customs. Well, actually, they are customs of my own. They make the sport more enjoyable. Adds to the game of the chase."

"Game?"

"Aye, a little danger is a healthy thing." He shrugged with a rueful grin, like a overgrown boy who couldn't help himself from pulling a prank.

Relief teetered inside her. Her husband didn't sound *raving* mad—just unconventional. He had a reason for being blue. Of course, she didn't know what to make of a man who considered it a game to fight a wildcat with his bare hands, a man who *enjoyed* danger—but then, this was Scotland.

And as long as he wasn't howling at the moon, her marriage might work.

Heat rose in her own cheeks. She attempted to make her interest a purely medical one. "Perhaps someone should put a salve on your scratches."

"They can wait." He abruptly changed the subject. "I'm sorry, I don't know your name."

She had to tell him before courage deserted her. This imposing man, clad only in a kilt, could overpower her merely by his presence. And they were alone together in the beautiful but desolate Highlands, where no one could protect her. Still, she had to tell him . . .

"My name is Anne. I've come from London, sent by your sister. And I am your wife."

Most women would do anything to get out of wearing a hideous bridesmaid dress. Of course, leaving town is one thing—but leaving this century is quite another! But that's just what Kelly Brennan does . . .

And she ends up in sultry, steamy New Orleans, landing in the arms of a dashing, wealthy, and tantalizing man, who woos her like a lady by day . . . and someone quite different by night. But is it too extreme to marry someone from another era, even if he proves that he loves you . . .

Time After Time

COMING MARCH 2001

by Constance O'Day-Flannery

"**M**r. Gilmore! Please."

Kelly heard him breathing heavily and, even through the darkness, she could see his shocked expression.

"Oh my god! I beg your pardon, Miss Brennan. I . . . I am mortified by my own actions."

Kelly pushed her hair back from her face. What could she say? She couldn't condone what had just happened, yet she was still reeling from the kiss, the first kiss in many years that felt as though it had awakened something in her she thought had died when she was twenty-three.

"I ... I saw you standing there in that nightgown, and for a moment I thought ... well, I thought you were someone else." He took a deep, steadying breath.

Kelly knew he meant his wife, his dead wife. This was becoming too uncanny, for in the darkness, he again reminded her of Michael. She couldn't help it. She giggled in nervousness. "You certainly surprised me, Mr. Gilmore."

"Please call me Daniel. And again, I implore your forgiveness. I most certainly am not the type of man who accosts his houseguests in the middle of the night."

"I didn't think you were." Now, why in the world did she want him to take her back into his strong arms? Craziness. Would it never end?

"I guess I shouldn't have been wandering around your home in the dark." She was rambling now, but who could blame her?

He'd kissed her! Just like that. *Kissed her and she'd liked it!*

"This is a most awkward situation, Miss Brennan."

"Call me Kelly," she whispered. "My husband died when I was much younger. I sympathize with your loss."

"You were married?"

"Yes. He died when I was twenty-three. Honestly, I don't know that I've ever really gotten over it."

"Was it the war?"

"The war ... No, it was an accident. Something that never should have happened. Well ... I guess I should say good night."

"Good night, Kelly."

He said her name . . . and she loved how it sounded coming from his lips. Lips that had felt so inviting, so impassioned . . . what was wrong with her?

"Good night," she whispered again and quickly opened the door to her bedroom.

Closing it behind her, Kelly leaned against it and sighed heavily. She looked around and sensed a familiarity she hadn't felt before. How could she possibly know this place . . . this house and, somehow, him?

If a proper young English lady finds herself having the ill fortune to be confined with a stranger in a public conveyance, she must take special care not to engage this person in any way—either by speaking or staring.

It is true that a carriage can be rather small, making it difficult to avoid speaking to a handsome stranger—even if he might not be a gentleman. But as everyone knows, conversation can lead to so much more. And a woman can be ruined if it's known she's committed . . .

The Indiscretion

COMING APRIL 2001

by Judith Ivory

She stared at his black hat tipped over most of his face. If he ever should play in a Wild West show, he'd be a stagecoach robber, she decided. Or a gunfighter with a "quick temper and a quicker trigger finger," which was a line out of one of her brother Clive's Buffalo Bill novels. She entertained this fantasy for a few minutes, smiling over it. Yes, something about him, a leanness, "a build as hard and dependable as a good rifle" (she, in fact, had pilfered one of Clive's contraband American novels just to see what they were about), not to mention something in his brooding attitude, spoke of a possibly harsh, very physical existence.

Her imagination put him in a big, tooled-leather saddle on a horse caparisoned in silver stars down its breast. To his black hat with silver beads she added silver guns in holsters at his hips and American spurs that jingled as he walked. She remembered what such spurs looked like and, more memorable, what they sounded like: a lot of metal to them, a silver band low on each heel, silver chains underneath, with jagged, spinning wheels at the back. Nothing like an English riding spur with its single, neat point affixed to an English gentleman's boot.

Something about his posture, his attentiveness, made her call over the road noise. "Are you awake?"

After a second, he pushed his hat brim up enough with a finger so that his eyes were visible, if shadowed. "Yes, ma'am."

He had a nice voice when polite, like a bow being pulled slowly over the lowest groaning strings of a bass. He took his time saying things, slow-talking his way over sliding consonants and drawn-out vowels. His diction was full of *ma'am*s, *thank-you*s, and *you're-welcome*s. A politeness that turned itself inside out when he used it to say surly things.

"Who's Gwyn?" she asked.

Sam sat there slouched, watching a lady he'd been sure wouldn't utter another word to him, while he chewed the inside of his cheek.

Why not tell her? he thought. "The woman I was supposed to marry this morning." He sighed, feeling blue again for simply saying it. Hell, what sort of fellow left the woman he'd courted for almost two years at the altar in front of all their friends and family? He expected a huffy admonishment from Miss Prissy Brit now—

"I'm so sorry," she said.

The coach turned sharply, and they both leaned to counter the force of the motion, him stretching his leg out to brace himself with the toe of his boot, her swinging from the hand grip.

Over the noise of their travel, she asked, "What happened?"

Sam frowned. Now where had this little lady been five hours ago? Because that was the one question he had been dying for someone to ask all day, though not a soul till now had thought to. Her concern and his needy longing for it from someone, anyone, shot a sense of gratitude through him so strong he could have reached out and kissed her.

He said, "I was on the way to the church, when out the window of my hackney, I saw the robbery I told you about. The fellow stopped the woman on a Plymouth street and grabbed at her purse. She fought him. He was puny but wiry and willing to wrestle her for it. It made me crazy when he dumped her over. I figured, with me being a foot taller and sixty or so pounds heavier, I could hop out, pin the punk to the ground, then be on my way with very little trouble. I wasn't prepared for his four friends." Sam sighed. "I spent the morning at the doctor's when I was supposed to be standing at the altar."

"But your bride—"

"My bride won't talk to me long enough to hear my explanation."

Their eyes met and held. Hers were sympathetic.

And light brown. A kind of gold. Pretty. Warm. He watched her shoulders jostle to and fro as she said, "Well, when she saw you like this, she must have—"

"She didn't see me. She only called me names through her front door. No one would let me in."

"How unreasonable."

"Exactly." What a relief to hear the word.

"You could send her a note to explain—"

"She returned it unopened."

"You could talk to someone, get a friend to tell her—"

"No one will speak to me. I had to bribe the stable-boy to get me to the coach station."

Her pretty eyes widened. "But people have to understand—"

Exactly what he wanted to hear, the very words he'd been telling himself all day. And now that he heard them, he realized how stupid they were. "Apparently not. 'Cause not a person I know does."

Bless her, her mouth tightened into a sweet, put-out line. "Well, how unreasonable," she said again. Oh, God bless her.

"Yes." But no. He looked down. "It is unreasonable. Until you realize that I left Gwyn at the altar once before, eight months ago."

She straightened herself slightly in her seat, re-adjusting her wrist in the leather strap. Aha! her look said. Maybe it just wasn't the right woman.

There's something about a man who works with his hands . . . His self-reliance and ruggedness—along with his lean, muscled body—make him oh, so appealing.

So if you're seeking a strong, silent type—a man of the land—you might want to check out Wyoming. Yes, this is someone who seems like he's only willing to speak when he's asking you out to a Saturday night dance—but once he takes you in his arms, you'll know he'll never let you down . . . and he'll probably keep you up all night long. Because this is the place you'll find . . .

The Last Good Man

COMING MAY 2001

by Kathleen Eagle

She heard the scratch of gravel, turned, and caught the shift of shadow, a moving shape separating itself from a stationary one. It was a horse.

"Where did you come from?" Savannah asked, approaching quietly, assuming it had wandered up there on its own, and she was all set to welcome the company. Then she got close enough to make out the saddle.

"The Lazy K."

The deep, dearly familiar voice seemed to issue from the mouth of the cave.

"Clay?" She jerked the hem of her skirt free from its mooring in her waistband and let it drop. Another shadow emerged, bootheels scraping with each step as though they were taken reluctantly. He looked bigger than she remembered. "Clay, is that you?"

"The real me." He touched the brim of the cowboy hat that was pulled low over his face. "Are you the real Savannah Stephens?"

She laughed a little. "I was hoping it wouldn't matter up here."

"It matters to me." He reached for her hand. "Welcome home."

He seemed to surround her entirely with a simple squeeze of the hand. She stepped into the shelter of him, her nose a scant inch below his square chin. She had yet to see his face clearly, to assess his life by counting lines, but it didn't matter. She knew Clay Keogh. Reflexively she lifted her free hand, her fingertips seeking something of him, finding a belt loop, a bit of smooth leather. All she wanted was a proper greeting, a quick embrace, but she heard the sharp intake of his breath, and she knew she had the upper hand. She'd turned the surprise on him. He was big-man sure of himself one minute, shaky inside the next, simply because she'd stepped a little closer than he'd expected.

A power surge shot through her.

She lifted her chin, remembering times gone by and aiming for a little humor with her old dare. "You can do better than that, Clay," she purred. Her own throaty tone surprised her. Having no humor in her, she couldn't help but miss the mark.

He touched his lips to hers, tentative only for an instant. His hunger was as unmistakable as hers. His arms closed around her slight shoulders, hers around his lean waist. He smelled of horsehide and leather, tasted of whiskey, felt as solid as the Rockies, and kissed like no man she'd ever known, including a younger Clay Keogh. She stood on tiptoe to kiss him back, trade him her breath for his, her tongue for his.

"Savannah . . ."

She couldn't understand why he was trying to pull away. There'd been a catch in his breath—she'd heard it distinctly—and it was that small sound that had set her insides aflutter. The surprise, the innocence, the wonder of it all. Good Lord in heaven, how long had it been since she'd been kissed?

"Shhh, Clay," she whispered against the corner of his mouth. "It's so good, finding you here."

"Glad to see—"

"But don't talk yet. Just hold me. It feels so good. You're not married or anything, are you?"

"I'm something." His deep chuckle sounded a little uneasy, which wasn't what she wanted. She wanted him easy. "But not married."

"Let me see you," she said, reaching for his hat. He started to duck away, but she flashed him a smile, and he stopped, looked at her for a moment, then bowed his head within her reach. "Girlfriend?" she asked as she claimed his hat and slid her fingers into the hair that tumbled over his forehead.

"No."

"Me neither."

"How about boyfriends?"

She laughed. "Completely unattached," she assured him, learning the new contours of his cheek with her hand.

"Well, I've never been to New York, but I hear there's a lot of variety there."

"There's variety everywhere, Clay. Don't tell me you've turned redneck on me. I won't have that."

"You won't, huh?" His smile glistened with moonlight. "Not much has changed here."

"That's what I was counting on."

It's one thing to get away from it all . . . and it might be another to visit the town of Gospel, Idaho. Still, even though it's not near very much, you can always have some eggs at the Cozy Corner Café and get your hair done at the Curl Up and Dye Hair Studio.

And there's the added attraction of Gospel's sheriff. He's easy on the eyes and not above breaking the laws of love to get what he wants. Before you know it, you'll have plenty to talk about in the way of . . .

True Confessions

COMING JUNE 2001

by Rachel Gibson

"*C*an you direct me to Number Two Timberlane?" she asked. "I just picked up the key from the realtor and that's the address he gave me."

"You sure you want Number *Two* Timberlane? That's the old Donnelly place," Lewis Plummer said. Lewis was a true gentleman and one of the few people in town who didn't outright lie to flatlanders.

"That's right. I leased it for the next six months."

Sheriff Dylan pulled his hat back down on his forehead. "No one's lived there for a while."

"Really? No one told me that. How long has it been empty?"

"A year or two." Lewis had also been born and raised in Gospel, Idaho, where prevarication was considered an art form.

"Oh, a year isn't too bad if the property's been maintained."

Maintained, hell. The last time Dylan had been in the Donnelly house, thick dust covered everything. Even the bloodstain on the living room floor.

"So, do I just follow this road?" She turned and pointed down Main Street.

"That's right," he answered. From behind his mirrored glasses, Dylan slid his gaze to the natural curve of her slim hips and thighs, down her long legs to her feet.

"Well, thanks for your help." She turned to leave, but Dylan's next question stopped her.

"You're welcome, Ms.—?"

"Spencer."

"Well now, Ms. Spencer, what are you planning out there on Timberlane Road?" Dylan figured everyone had a right to privacy, but he also figured he had a right to ask.

"Nothing."

"You lease a house for six months and you plan to do nothing?"

"That's right. Gospel seemed like a nice place to vacation."

Dylan had doubts about that statement. Women who drove fancy sports cars and wore designer jeans vacationed in nice places with room service and pool boys, not in the wilderness of Idaho. Hell, the closest thing Gospel had to a spa was the Petermans' hot tub.

Her brows scrunched together and she tapped an impatient hand three times on her thigh before she said, "Well, thank you, gentlemen, for your help." Then she turned on her fancy boots and marched back to her sports car.

"Do you believe her?" Lewis wanted to know.

"That she's here on vacation?" Dylan shrugged. He didn't care what she did as long as she stayed out of trouble.

"She doesn't look like a backpacker."

Dylan thought back to the vision of her backside in those tight jeans. "Nope."

"Makes you wonder why a woman like that leased that old house. I haven't seen anything like her in a long time. Maybe never."

Dylan slid behind the wheel of his Blazer. "Well, Lewis, you sure don't get out of Pearl County enough."